MONSTER'S PROOF

RICHARD LEWIS

SIMON & SCHUSTER BFYR

NEW YORK LONDON TORONTO SYDNEY

SIMON & SCHUSTER BFYR

An imprint of Simon & Schuster Children's Publishing Division
1230 Avenue of the Americas, New York, New York 10020

For information about special discounts for bulk purchases, please contact
Simon & Schuster Special Sales at 1-866-506-1949 or business@simonandschuster.com.
The Simon & Schuster Speakers Bureau can bring authors to your live event. For more information or to book an event, contact the Simon & Schuster Speakers Bureau at 1-866-248-3049 or visit our website at www.simonspeakers.com.
Also available in a SIMON & SCHUSTER BFYR hardcover edition.
Book design by Chloë Foglia
The text for this book is set in Bembo.
Manufactured in the United States of America
First SIMON & SCHUSTER BFYR paperback edition July 2010
10 9 8 7 6 5 4 3 2 1
The Library of Congress has cataloged the hardcover edition as follows:
Monster's proof / Richard Lewis.
Lewis, Richard, 1949– —1st ed.
p. cm.
Summary: As the only normal person in a family of math geniuses, sixteen-year-old Livey's life takes a turn for the extraordinary when her little brother's imaginary friend, Bob, turns out to be real and, as a creature of pure math, tries to rid the world of chaos and disorder.
ISBN 978-1-4169-3591-9 (hc)
[1. Mathematics—Fiction. 2. Supernatural—Fiction.] 1. Title.
PZ7.L5877 Bo 2009
[Fic]—22
2008011735
ISBN 978-1-4169-3592-6 (pbk)
ISBN 978-1-4169-9577-7 (eBook)

For Helen, Fran, Rob, and Jamey

ACKNOWLEDGMENTS

The pinnacle of my formal mathematical education was reached during my freshman year in college, when I intuitively understood the epsilon-delta definition of the calculus, which any math teacher will tell you is no mean achievement. In the years since, I've mostly read popular math books written for a general audience. For *Monster's Proof*, I have drawn on the myth, legends, and anecdotes of math and mathematicians in addition to creating my own.

Clifford A. Pickover provided me with the definition of vampire numbers as well as much Pythagorean lore in his terrific book *The Loom of God*. Gargoyle fractions and werewolf numbers are my own trivial definitions, but the proof of the nonexistence of boring numbers is due to Martin Gardner. I believe that it was great polymath John von Neumann who was the first to say (to a befuddled graduate student), "You don't have to understand it, you just have to get used to it." The joke about fields and cows is borrowed from math lore, as is Livey's complaint about her father's inability to count, and I first heard Darby's riddles for Aether from my son.

Dr. Mary Lynn Reed, a wonderful writer as well as professional mathematician, gave me pointers on the mathematics in this novel and saved me from a couple howlers. The errors that remain are my own.

Catherine DiCairano at the online writers' group Backspace introduced me to the world of cheerleading and to her cheerleader daughter, Amanda DiCairano, who patiently answered my questions about the sport. Amanda also provided me with anecdotes and photographs, including one of a locker filled with candy. My young daughter thoughtfully pondered this photograph and then reminded me her birthday was coming up. Many thanks to my colleagues at Backspace (bksp.org) and Zoetrope (zoetrope.com) who answered research questions and provided general help.

Thea Atkinson gave me a much needed boost of encouragement and some critical insights when doubt perched on my shoulder, whispering in my ear.

The manuscript also benefited from the keen eye of my editors, David Gale and Navah Wolfe, who spotted some pretty glaring weaknesses. The novel was greatly improved by their suggestions. Thanks also to my agent, Scott Miller, who zips things along and makes my life much easier.

PROLOGUE

THE GRAY METAL trunk arrived at 15 Beechwood Drive in River Oaks, Illinois, on a warm Thursday noon in July.

A delivery van pulled up to the curb, halting underneath a maple tree, its shade thick as fudge. Darby sat on the front steps of his house, playing with his Etch A Sketch. His mom had given it to him for his third birthday. Now, seven months later, he was an expert. His chubby fingers dialed the knobs, drawing conic sections. He especially liked hyperbolas. They made his teeth feel all zingy.

The deliveryman opened the van's back door. Using a hand trolley, he wheeled the trunk down the ramp, leaning back against the heavy weight. On the side of the trunk, stenciled in thick white letters, was the name DR. LUDAVICA ELL, and beneath that was a street address in Los Alamos, New Mexico. The latch was locked with a three-digit combination lock.

The deliveryman paused before the steps. "Hey, little boy, anybody home?"

Darby squinted against the bright sun. "Me."

The man waved his clipboard. "I mean somebody who can sign this."

"I can. I know how to write my name. In cursive, too."

"That so? Your mom home?"

"She's at work." Darby stood and yelled through the open door. "Dad! Somebody's here!"

Steps sounded, and a lanky man appeared in the doorway, a piece of chalk in his hand. The deliveryman glanced at his clipboard. "Dr. Jerry Ell?"

Jerry's gaze fell to the trunk. "Here already? That was quick."

"What is it?" Darby asked.

"Aunt Ludy's trunk." He said to the deliveryman as he signed, "The storage company had the gall to try to charge me for all the years they'd forgotten about it. Can you help me carry it up to the attic?"

"Ain't allowed. But listen, how about you write me a prescription for sleeping pills?"

"Sleeping pills?"

"Those damn Cubs. Get me all worked up and I can't fall asleep."

"Ah. I'm not a physician. I'm a professor. A mathematician."

"Hey. Wow. I've read about you guys, but I've never met a real live one before. How about ten bucks, then?"

Jerry agreed.

He and the deliveryman hoisted the heavy trunk by the side handles.

Darby followed them into the hall, still carrying his Etch A Sketch. "What's in it, Dad?"

"Books," his dad grunted.

Darby's great-aunt Ludy was in a private home, near the big state hospital in Elgin. The Ells visited her twice a year. A brilliant mathematician, she had worked for the government on the first hydrogen bomb project. Top secrets buzzed in that frizzy white-haired head of hers. She'd been in the South Pacific to see the bomb explode, and then a year later she had gone crazy. Now she wore an aluminum hat shaped like a star that she said kept alien numbers from reading her mind. Not only that, but she claimed government spies sometimes hid under her bed. She chased them out with her fractal sword, which was just a walking cane wrapped in gold foil.

Jerry tugged on the pull-down stairs, and the telescoping steps clattered open. The men hauled the trunk into the dim attic and stowed it in a corner by the old *National Geographics*. Through the dormer window Darby could see his nine-year-old sister Livey climbing a tree, with her best friend Chantelle giving her a hands-up.

After paying the man and closing the front door, Jerry returned to the attic.

Darby had just opened the combination lock. "Two five seven," he announced.

"How'd you guess?" Jerry said.

"Two, five, and seven are prime numbers and 257 is a prime number, too."

Jerry grinned. "That's my boy." He lifted the lid. Within the trunk were textbooks and math journals. He pulled out a thick tome and read the title. "Handbook of Mathematical Functions, Allen Fishbach, Editor." Sitting down on a short stack of *National Geographic* magazines, he idly flipped through the pages.

Darby wormed his way under his dad's arms. The pages were dense with formulae and equations.

"A bit advanced for you, son," Jerry said. "One day you'll understand them."

Darby pointed to some scribbling in the margins. "What's that?"

"Looks like something your great-aunt jotted down. Hmmm. She seems to be defining a Hilbert space of all Hilbert spaces—"

"What's a Hilbert space?"

"It's like our three-dimensional space but much more abstract. Let's see. She's applying an operator to this function…." Jerry's voice trailed off. He turned the page, where the scribbling continued. At the bottom, Ludavica Ell had written *Is this thingamabob for real? Needs proof.*

"Looks like she's conjectured some sort of mathematical object," Jerry said. He chuckled. "A thingamabob conjecture. I have a few of those myself."

Darby pointed out the window. "Livey just fell from the tree."

Jerry Ell tossed the book aside and rushed out to his daughter. She lay crumpled on the ground, her leg twisted under her. She was biting her lip hard, refusing to cry. Jerry sped her to the hospital's emergency room. From there, he called his wife at nearby Fermilab, where she worked as a theoretical physicist.

Maria Ell drove as fast as she could to the hospital. After comforting her daughter, who was rather proud of the cast being put on her leg, Maria turned to her husband. "Where's Darby?"

"Hunh?"

"Oh, for Pete's sake, you didn't leave him at the house all alone, did you?"

Jerry stared blankly at his wife.

Maria grabbed her handbag. "You stay here with Livey. I'll go home."

Jerry thought for a moment and then called out after her, "He's up in the attic."

When Maria got home, she found her son still in the attic, playing with his Etch A Sketch.

"Hi, Mom," he said. "I have a new friend."

She gathered him up in a relieved hug and pressed his nose. "Which friend is that?"

"Bob."

She frowned, thinking of the neighbors. Did any of them have a boy named Bob? "Where does he live?"

"In Hilbert space. He's funny. He looks like this." Darby showed his mom the Etch A Sketch, on which he'd drawn a tangle of triangles.

"That's wonderful," Maria said. She absently picked up a book and chucked it in the trunk, which she slammed shut with her elbow. Darby tossed the Etch A Sketch aside and squirmed out of her arms. "Can me and Bob watch *Scooby-Doo*?"

His mother watched him dash down to the living room, shaking her head. After descending to the hallway, she shut the stairs.

In the stuffy, shadowed warmth of the attic, a little brown spider began to build its web on Ludavica Ell's metal trunk.

1

BEEP-BEEP-BEEP. *Beep-beep-beep.*

Godeliva Elizabeth Ell, known to all as Livey, opened a bleary eye to squint at her alarm clock. "Shut up," she mumbled.

The rubberized alarm clock rolled off the lamp stand. It zigzagged around the room on its wheels, beeping louder and louder.

With a growl, Livey flung off her bedcovers and chased it down. She finally cornered the clock by her desk. "Shut up!" she yelled as she hurled it across the room. The clock bounced harmlessly off her dresser and fell silent to the carpet. Throwing it against something was the only way to turn it off.

Livey hated the thing with a passion, but she tolerated it because it did its job, which was to get a sixteen-year-old girl who was so not a morning person out of bed. One of her mother's inventor friends had given it to Livey three years ago, just before her parents' divorce.

After showering, she dressed in her blue-and-gold cheerleading uniform. It wasn't a game day, but the *River Oaks Record* wanted classroom photographs for an article on the River Oaks High cheerleaders. From her desk, she picked up an old red Etch A Sketch that she'd found in the attic yesterday when she was looking for things to donate to a cheerleaders' fund-raising drive. She went down the hall and opened the door to Darby's bedroom. Her ten-year-old brother was scrunched under the blanket, sound asleep with one of their dad's math texts open on the cover beside him. He hadn't taken off his glasses, which were skewed on his face.

Livey bent to shake him awake, but her attention was caught by the chapter title in the math book: "Mathematical Monsters and Pathological Math Functions."

A lot of kids read horror comics for their chills and thrills. Her brother, on the other hand, read scary math. "Rise and shine, genius," she said, shaking his shoulder. "Your Shedd Aquarium field trip's today."

He sat up, yawning. She showed him the Etch A Sketch. "Look what I found."

He stopped yawning and straightened his glasses. "Where'd you get that?"

"In the attic. I want to give it away for a charity drive."

"It's mine," he said, reaching for it.

"That's why I'm asking."

"You weren't asking. You were announcing." He studied the triangles drawn on the screen's silver coating. His brows dipped and his face twitched as though he were trying to remember something. Then his expression smoothed. "Bob," he said.

Bob? A distant memory came to Livey. "You mean your old imaginary friend? You were, like, four. You've outgrown him and you've outgrown that. Can I have it?"

He shook his head. "It's mine."

Livey left the room with an exasperated sigh. Darby didn't really

RICHARD LEWIS

want the toy, but he wouldn't let her have it either, just on principle. Younger brothers, she decided, should be starved for a week each month, but in the kitchen, she dutifully made him his lunch, as she did every school day. Two slices of white bread with a generous slab of Skippy Super Chunk peanut butter, topped with grape jelly. Any grape jelly would do, but the peanut butter had to be Skippy Super Chunk. Darby wouldn't eat anything else. As she munched on her breakfast, a raisin bagel, Livey got out the casserole from the freezer and put it in the fridge to defrost for dinner that evening. Their housekeeper, Mrs. Blink, came in three days a week to clean and make dinners, including extra ones that she froze for the days she didn't work.

Wiles limped to the bowl of dry cat kibble. As a kitten, he'd had an encounter with a garbage compactor that had mangled his right front leg. He sniffed the kibble with disdain and meowed at Livey.

She wasn't moved to pity. "You know how many starving cats in India would love to have that?"

Her father rushed out of his bedroom, the edge of his battered briefcase sticking out of his backpack. "Morning, Livey."

"Dad."

"Yes?"

"Look in the mirror."

He leaned back to look in the hallway mirror and blinked at the full coating of shaving cream still on his jowls. "Throw me a dish towel, will you?" He wiped off the cream. A big chin and long cheeks appeared. "Had this idea while I was lathering up. Wanted to write it down before I forgot."

Livey just shook her head. After the divorce, her dad had become obsessed with proving the Riemann Hypothesis, the world's greatest unsolved mathematical problem. Livey, who had trouble with basic algebra, knew more about the Riemann Hypothesis than she cared to. The Hypothesis was this incredibly exciting idea that all the zeros of something called the zeta function were on a straight line. *Well, excuse me,* she thought, *the* non-trivial *zeros.* Mathematicians were always making a fuss over what was trivial and what was not. The way her dad was fixated on the stupid hypothesis, working all hours of the night on it, he was becoming bones and shadow and now unshaved bristles.

He chucked the towel in the sink and gave her a quick peck on the cheek. "Go Falcons."

She gave him a look. "We're the Eagles, Dad."

But he was grinning. As he opened the hall door to the garage, he said, "How come you never hear of a team called the Buzzards?"

A moment later, she saw him riding down the street. Other dads drove cars. Some rode bicycles. Her father? He rode his unicycle. Like he was a circus performer. It was so embarrassing to see him on that thing. There were times when Livey had to pretend she didn't even know him.

Darby wandered out of his room, dressed in his blue school uniform, the collar of his jacket sticking up, his backpack slung over one shoulder, the Etch A Sketch in his hand. He paused in the hall for a moment to glance at the pull-down stairs to the attic.

In the kitchen, he shook the Etch A Sketch, erasing the triangles. "Didn't Mom give this to me as a birthday present?"

When their mom had left, Darby had thrown away every single thing she had ever given him. The Etch A Sketch had been a birthday gift. Livey even remembered the blue-and-white wrapping. "I don't know," she said.

Darby put the toy on the counter and plucked the meat cleaver from the knife rack. Using its dull edge, he smashed the glass.

"Darby!" Livey yelled.

"Don't worry, I'll throw it the garbage." He pried open his lunch sandwich to inspect the contents. "Did you use Super Chunk?"

"That was really stupid. You should have given it to me."

"Is this Super Chunk?"

The other week, she had tried to trick him with a different brand. The sandwich had come home untouched. He hadn't said anything, just whirred it into mush in the garbage disposal. "When have I ever not used it?" she asked, faking her offended tone.

With the tip of his finger, Darby pushed his glasses up the bridge of his nose, leaving a smear of peanut butter on the lens. "Last Wednesday."

Through the kitchen window, Livey watched him march out into the clear, cool September morning. The garbage cans were by the roadside for pickup. He tossed the ruined Etch A Sketch into one.

Her poor brother. During the summer, his best friend Charlie, who lived just a block away, had moved out of state. Then, two weeks after starting the school year at River Oaks Middle School, the teachers had thrown up their hands trying to teach a ten-year-old genius who read college-level math texts for fun and who had rewritten the U.S. Constitution for a history lesson. An anonymous donor had come up with a scholarship, and Darby had been transferred to the private and expensive Newton Academy for Gifted Children, way on the north side of town. He'd been attending for three weeks now and still hadn't spoken of a single person there.

"God, please let him make friends," Livey murmured.

A school bus halted at the corner where Darby waited, staring down at his shoes. He startled when the driver tapped on his horn. Squaring his shoulders, he climbed aboard.

THREE WEEKS AGO, Darby hadn't been staring down
at his shoes while waiting for the Newton school bus. He'd been
bouncing up and down on his toes. The elementary and middle
schools were within walking distance, so he'd never taken a bus
before. Not only that, but at Newton there would be others like
him. Maybe he could make a lot of new friends, maybe even a
new best friend, now that Charles had moved to Oregon. The bus had
turned the corner and stopped before him like a big rumbling promise. When he'd boarded, the seats were half-full with boys and girls
around his age, some younger, some older. Several were studying,
some listened to music players, others talked and laughed. Only a
few gave him disinterested glances.

The driver had consulted a clipboard. "Darby Ell, fifteen Beechwood
Drive?"

"Seventeen Beechwood," Darby corrected him. The Ells used to
live in 15, but when 17 came on the market, his father sold theirs

to move right next door. When Livey demanded to know why they should go through the hassle of moving into an exact same house, with the exact same leaky roof and exact same termite problem, their dad said, "But, honey, seventeen is a prime number." Livey dramatically lifted her gaze to the heavens. "Why," she exclaimed, "do I have to be the only normal person in this family?"

The driver corrected the list. "Darby Ell, *seventeen* Beechwood Drive."

Darby turned to take a seat and froze. The others were now staring at him. Dangling his backpack in front of him, he casually checked his zipper. Still up. As he shuffled to an empty seat at the back, they turned their heads to watch him pass. He could feel blood rushing to his lopsided ears, which, he knew from sad experience, made them more prominent yet.

The bus drove off. A tall girl got up from one of the middle rows, her blue skirt rumpled on her big frame, her square hands tagging the seat bars for balance as she walked toward Darby. She plopped down beside him with a smile. Darby couldn't tell if it was a friendly smile. He pressed his backpack to his chest.

"I'm Roz Arbito," she said, "and you're Darby Ell."

He nodded cautiously. "Nice meeting you, Roz."

"Is your IQ really over two hundred like everybody says?"

Darby glanced at the others, all looking back at him. "I guess."

"You guess? An IQ over two hundred and you have to guess?"

The others laughed.

Darby hugged his school bag tighter. His mom had once told him that his EQ was much more important than his IQ. She said that what mattered most to her was for him to be happy and well-adjusted. Then she'd run off to live with another man, which hadn't done a whole lot for Darby's emotional quotient.

"You'll have fun at Newton," Roz said, still smiling that unreadable smile, and returned to her seat.

On the north side of town, the houses were older and grander. The bus braked to another stop by a swanky garden. A boy with blue eyes stepped on board like an admiral onto his flagship, his school uniform looking custom tailored and freshly ironed. Another boy was behind him, carrying his schoolbag for him. The tall boy looked familiar to Darby, but before Darby could figure out why, he was standing in front of him.

"I'm afraid you're sitting in my seat," the boy said, a sharp edge to the polite tone.

Without a word Darby got up and moved to the next row up.

"Now you're sitting in Karim's seat," the boy said.

As Darby walked forward to the empty seat behind the driver, Roz leaned out and plucked the sleeve of his jacket. "That's Julian. He's the smartest student in the school." Her lips curled in a lazy grin. "That is, he *was* the smartest student."

Julian. Julian Bostick. No wonder he looked familiar. Darby had seen his photo in the local paper. Julian and some friends had gone exploring in the marsh and woods of the Oberlund Forest Reserve on the western fringe of River Oaks and stumbled across a skeleton. The police had finally determined the bones to be the disinterred remains of one of the original Oberlund clan who'd pioneered the area. The photo had shown Julian posing with a life-size plastic skull in one hand. In his other hand he held a vacuum bug collector, shaped like a pistol. Three of his friends stood in the background. There was also another photo of Julian in his ginormous bedroom, standing by a terrarium, with some creepy-crawlies creeping and crawling up his arm. Darby hated any bug bigger than an ant, and the thought of accidentally kicking a skull out of a tangle of roots made him shiver, but still, exploring in the Reserve seemed to him to be the height of adventure.

Julian's father was a federal judge, and Julian's mother was on the board of several foundations and charities and the county's orchid club, which sometimes met in her greenhouse. Julian himself had well-bred manners that charmed the teachers. He was polite to the girls, and when talking about them called them by their first names, instead of the mean nicknames some of the other popular boys gave them, like Toadbrains and Squidbutt. He was especially polite to Roz, whom he called by her full name, Rosalind. She sucked up to Julian big-time, laughed at his jokes, got him his lunchroom drinks. Julian called Darby by his full name too, Darby Ell, but with just enough singsong to make it sound like a girl's name. Darbielle. This wasn't very often, though. Mostly he just ignored Darby.

Nearly every recess, Darby would watch as Julian and Karim and six other boys strolled over to the soccer field bleachers and by the big sycamore tree, where they would disappear. Underneath the bleachers was an old plywood shack with a crooked door, its roof the bottom of the bleachers.

Early in his second week at Newton, Darby casually kicked a soccer ball at the tree and ran over to get it. With the ball under his arm, he put his eye to a gap in the plywood. The boys were inside sitting in a circle on a mat, laughing about something. Julian spotted Darby's eye and got up to crack open the door.

"Sorry, Darbielle," he said. "Members only. Move on."

Julian spoke politely, but Darby could have used that smile on his face to slice an apple.

"They don't have a name," Roz told Darby later, "but everybody calls it the Boys' Club."

"Do you think I could become a member?"

She laughed. "You? Are you kidding? Forget about it."

But Darby couldn't forget about it. In the library display was that newspaper article about Julian finding the skeleton. Darby read it again. Julian said his dream was to find a new species of insect. He would name it after his father. Or mother, if it was pretty. *My parents are my heroes,* Julian said. *My father helps me get the permit to go bug collecting in the Preserve. Remember, everybody, it's illegal to go collecting without a permit. But you don't need a permit to find a skeleton, you just have to report it.*

Darby wanted to be a member of the Boys' Club so badly that the other day at lunch he'd screwed up the courage to approach Julian and ask.

"See, Darbielle, that's the thing," Julian said in a kindly, almost regretful, manner. "If we let you join, then we'd have to let everybody join, even the girls."

Darby had slunk away, his ears burning, his eyes stinging.

Even today, as he boarded the bus, the embarrassment still lingered. He usually sat behind the driver, but this morning Roz waved him to her seat. He perched cautiously beside her, wondering what she wanted. Roz went out of her way to be snooty to him, as if she lived in a swank mansion on the town's north side instead of the run-down Evergreen apartment complex, where people kept stealing the playground equipment and weeds grew in the cracks of the basketball court.

"You have something on your glasses," she said.

Darby took them off and peered at the brown smudge on the right lens, and then sniffed it. Just peanut butter. He cleaned it off on the tail of his school jacket.

"Julian's mom was talking to my dad," Roz said. "Mrs. Bostick was very disappointed that Julian's essay wasn't chosen for the school's newsletter."

Darby put on his glasses. "Your parents know each other?" he asked dubiously.

Her face went a light shade of pink. "My dad's her gardener, okay? He takes care of her orchids. Judge Bostick helped me get into Newton."

"Sorry," Darby said. "I didn't mean anything. Somebody gave me a scholarship too, but we don't know who it was."

"Julian's mother didn't think your essay was good enough to be chosen. An essay on a math equation? One that you tossed off in, like, half a school period? Julian worked very hard on his."

Darby had written a few paragraphs about Euler's identity, the most beautiful and elegant equation in the whole world. $e^{i\pi} + 1 = 0$ connected five of math's most important constants through three of math's most important operations. "I didn't just toss it off," Darby protested.

"Julian's parents were very disappointed."

"It's just a newsletter, Roz."

"They expect Julian to be number one in everything. And Julian doesn't want to disappoint them. So today you'd better stay away from him. I'm just telling you, okay?"

"Sure. Okay. Thanks."

"Now get lost."

When Julian boarded the bus at his stop, he paused for a moment, putting on an exquisitely bored face for the others. "Another field trip to Shedd, how terribly exciting," he said. His gaze fell on Darby. His expression brightened. "But you never know, today something exciting *could* happen."

MOST MORNINGS, LIVEY got a ride to school with Chantelle and Chantelle's older brother Todd, who was a senior. He drove them in his old Toyota Corona that he was constantly pimping. If Chantelle was real nice to him, he would sometimes grumpily drive them to parties or to the mall.

Livey was getting tired of having to depend on others for rides. She had long ago decided that the highlight of her life wasn't going to be finding true love, or even becoming captain of the cheerleading squad. It was going to be getting her license, which was still one semester away. With a driver's license, she could get a part-time job, and with the job, she could start saving money for college.

This morning, as Todd turned into the high school's student lot, he pointed to an old Volkswagen Beetle rattling into a parking space. Gray patches of dent-filler spotted the car's original brown paint. "Why don't you guys ask him for rides?"

"That creep?" Chantelle said. "Are you kidding? He's a total emo, suicide without the glam."

River Oaks High had over a thousand students on its campus of sleek brick-and-glass buildings, but on the very first morning of the very first day of school, Livey had been instantly aware of the new senior, slouching along the halls in his own silent shadow.

"His name's Johnny Magnus," Livey said. "He's a senior, a transfer. Mr. Savard picked him to be his third-period assistant."

That was Livey's algebra class. Johnny was pretty good with math, she had to admit, but still, Mr. Savard could've chosen somebody who changed his clothes once in a while.

"*That* guy?" Chantelle said. "Well, aren't you lucky. Algebra with Mr. Savard plus the guy most likely to commit mass murder."

Johnny swung out of the Beetle, wearing the tattered jeans and thin black cotton shirt that he always wore. The shirt looked like something even Goodwill wouldn't want and had long sleeves that about covered his knuckles. His skin was so white it seemed to be lacquered with milk. A small silver cross dangled on his chest. His deep-set eyes brooded out of a sharply boned face, and his shaggy black hair looked as if he hacked at it himself, with long strands angling down in front of his ears. Silver duct tape was wrapped around the toe of one his scuffed boots. Livey wondered how he could afford the gas for his car. Johnny had the same early lunch period as she did, and sat at the loser's table, in the corner where the dirty trays were dumped. He always brought with him a margarine tub that he used as a lunch box. He would crack the lid just the littlest bit and pinch furtively at whatever was inside, as if ashamed to let anybody see what it was he was eating for lunch.

As he closed the Beetle's door, he caught Livey's eye for a moment and then quickly looked away. Slinging his backpack over his shoulder, he shuffled off.

Third period, Livey dawdled in the hall and then rushed into algebra class a second before the bell rang. She'd gotten pretty good at timing it.

Mr. Savard turned from the whiteboard and folded his arms across his chest. "Just because you are a cheerleader does not exempt you from the rules, Livey."

"But I'm not late, Mr. Savard."

"I want you in your seat *before* the bell rings. Next time, you get detention."

Livey was sure that Mr. Savard hated cheerleaders in principle and her in particular. Her inability to learn algebra was a personal insult to his teaching skills. He was dull, tidy man who wore dull, tidy brown suits and who shook the fizz out of his ginger ale before drinking it. Livey was positive that the neat square of brown hair on his head was a toupee.

She slid into her seat, the only sophomore in a class of ninth graders. Her freshman year, she'd taken Practical Math. But algebra was like death, or morning mouth after a garlicky dinner. You couldn't avoid it. Even the two Goths in the class who were part of the loser crowd did better in algebra than she did.

The classroom door opened again. Johnny Magnus slipped in. Why didn't Mr. Savard ever yell at his assistant for being late? After all, even though he was a senior, he was still a student. The rules applied to him, too, right? He took the chair in the corner by Mr. Savard's desk, and stared out the window.

As he sometimes did, Mr. Savard started class with a short talk on the history of mathematics. On the whiteboard he wrote a triangle of numbers:

$$1$$
$$2\ 3$$
$$4\ 5\ 6$$
$$7\ 8\ 9\ 10$$

"This is called a tetraktys," he said. "Now, Pythagoras, he of the Pythagorean theorem, was more than an ancient Greek mathematician.

He was also the founder of the Pythagorean cult. The Pythagoreans had some pretty strange beliefs. For example, whenever they heard thunder, they were to touch the ground to remember the universe's creation. They were also absolutely forbidden to eat beans."

Mr. Savard paused, and sure enough, one of the boys cracked a childish joke about bodily gas. Mr. Savard smiled tolerantly and continued. "But more interestingly to us in this class, numbers played a very important role in their religion. They believed that the numbers one through ten, which you see arranged here in the tetraktys, were living things that had created the cosmos. The tetraktys was more than just a symbol. It provided a gateway to mysterious and unknown forms of intelligent consciousness that exist in the cosmos." The way Mr. Savard said this, with glowing eyes, it was as if he expected a voice to start speaking from the whiteboard. "Now, as warm-up for today's lesson, I will show you another proof of the Pythagorean Theorem."

Halfway through the period, the *River Oaks Record* photographer came into the classroom to take photographs of Livey. She inwardly groaned. *Not this class, puh-leeze!* After taking a few shots of her at her desk, the photographer asked Mr. Savard if he could take a picture of Livey working a problem on the whiteboard.

Mr. Savard wrote down a problem and then with a little smile held out the marker pen to her. "Perhaps you could enlighten us with your wisdom?"

She reluctantly started in. The photographer snapped off shots from various angles. Soon she came to a halt, hopelessly tangled up.

In the back of the class, one of the loser Goths said, "What do you expect? She's a blonde."

"Oh, that's funny," Livey said. "You should be on YouTube, you're so hilarious."

"Quiet," Mr. Savard said. He sat on the corner of his desk, arms folded loosely across his chest. "Well, Livey? Where have you lost your way, do you think? Look at your third line. Minus x times minus x is positive x squared. A minus times a minus is always a plus. Bookkeeping, Livey. You must keep these things straight."

"I just don't get why a minus times a minus should be a plus. I never have. It doesn't make any sense. It's like saying an apple times an apple is an antelope."

Mr. Savard scooted off the desk. "How many times do I have to explain it? For example, the stop sign on President. You get a hundred-dollar fine if you run it. That's minus one hundred. But if you *don't* run the stop sign three times, a minus three, then minus three times minus one hundred equals the positive three hundred dollars you saved."

"That doesn't make sense either. I mean, if I obey the stop sign three times, the money doesn't appear in my pocket, right? How can I understand something that doesn't make sense?"

"You don't have to understand it, Miss Ell. You just have to get used to it."

She muttered under her breath, "Maybe the stupid tetra-whatever can give me the answer."

Mr. Savard's jaw tightened. "That's enough. You're wasting class time."

Before the end of class, Johnny passed out graded homework. When he got to Livey's desk he held hers back for a second. She looked up at him. His eyes were deep and clear, the black irises flecked with green spots. Funny, she'd never noticed that before.

"An apple times an apple is a unicorn," he murmured, and put her paper on her desk. Was he making fun of her? She couldn't tell, but there was no mistaking the red marks on her homework. Another D.

As the students filed out after the bell, Mr. Savard said, "Livey, a word with you, please."

Puffing out a sigh, she stepped to the side. Johnny had halted in the doorway, fiddling with his backpack.

Mr. Savard tapped his fingers on his desk, studying her as though she were a wrong answer to a simple problem. He finally sighed. "I fail to understand how the daughter of a professional mathematician and the sister of a certified genius can be flunking algebra."

What right did Mr. Savard have to be talking about her family? And with Johnny right there, eavesdropping? "I'm trying, Mr. Savard."

"I suggest you try harder. If you fail the next test, I'll have no choice but to put you on academic probation. You know what that means. You'll be dropped from the cheerleading squad."

DARBY HUNCHED ON the chair in the Shedd Aquarium's security office, feeling as doomed as a penguin on the world's last patch of melting icecap. He wished he hadn't eaten his sandwich. All that undigested peanut butter in his stomach was as heavy as mud.

Across the room the plainclothes security guard sprawled at her console. She kept clicking a pen as she studied the monitors. Every once in a while she'd aim the pen at Darby and give it a slow click. Like she was shooting him.

Darby's school jacket was draped on his lap. He picked up the sleeve and wiped sweat off his forehead. He was doomed, doomed, doomed. He needed somebody to rescue him, and fast.

Roly-poly Mr. Thomas waddled into the room. He was one of the field trip's escorting teachers, and his mustache presently bristled with all the friendliness of an irate walrus. "I finally got hold of your father," he told Darby. "He'll be here in an hour."

Mr. Thomas looked again at the objects lined up on top of the bookshelf by the monitor console. A rubber black-tipped reef shark about four inches long. One of those new TETRA KUIZ board games that Darby had started seeing around. A child's explorer set of plastic items: compass, binoculars, folding knife, flashlight, whistle. A Shedd Aquarium notebook.

All still in the gift shop's original packaging.

Mr. Thomas shook his head, his jowls quivering. "I can't believe it. Darby Ell? Un-unh, I would have said, not Darby."

"It's the sweet innocent goofy-looking kids you got to watch," the guard said.

Darby closed his lips tight over his gapped front teeth and straightened his glasses, which immediately slipped back to their usual tilt on his large, lopsided ears.

"He's not as goofy as he looks," Mr. Thomas said, coming grudgingly to Darby's defense. "He's certified genius, only ten, but does college-level math."

"I guess he isn't so smart after all, getting caught in front of all his friends like that."

Friends? Darby thought. *What friends?*

A while ago, after lunch break, the students had been allowed to roam the gift shop. Darby had been keeping his distance from Julian all morning. In the gift shop, he bought a notebook that had a stiff plastic cover with a hologram image of a shark that swam through the water when the notebook was tilted this way and that. He was once again admiring the notebook's cover when Julian sidled up to him. In one of Julian's hands was a souped-up version of a bug collector, shaped like a sleek automatic except the barrel sucked in instead of shooting out, trapping insects for view in a transparent oblong chamber. In his other hand was an explorer set.

"Which one should I get?" Julian asked.

"I don't know," Darby said cautiously.

"I think this," Julian said, holding up the bug collector. "It's more powerful than the one I have at home." He handed Darby the explorer set, and then plucked out of the racks the TETRA KUIZ and the shark. "Why don't you get these for me, Darby?"

Darby was pleased that Julian had actually called him by his first name, but he'd spent most of his money buying the notebook. "I only have about a dollar left," he said.

Julian winked a blue eye and smiled. Most astonishingly, it was a friendly smile. He put his arm around Darby's shoulder. "I don't mean buy them. Nobody's looking, so just slip them in your bag," he whispered. Darby was shocked into silence. The son of a federal judge, asking him to shoplift?

"If you get them," Julian added, "I'll let you join the Boys' Club."

The shock instantly faded. "You serious?"

"Absolutely. We'll have the ceremony tomorrow. You can sit in the back with me on the bus."

Join the Boys' Club! Sit with Julian on the bus! Have friends and go on adventures!

Well, he shouldn't have listened to Julian, shouldn't have let those blue eyes hypnotize him. When he walked out of the gift shop, a heavy hand had fallen on his shoulder.

And now he was sitting in the security office.

Dumb, dumb, dumb.

The guard clicked her pen and gave him a sharp smile.

Doom, doom, doom.

After Mr. Thomas galumphed out of the room, the guard leaned back, stretching her arms over her head. "You know what we do with shoplifters? We put them in with the Komodo dragons."

Darby wiped more sweat from his forehead. *I am abandoned. Oh, who will rescue me?*

He didn't pin much hope on his dad. Jerry Ell had once tried to rescue their crippled cat, Wiles, from a dog and had ended up in the same tree.

Darby's mom? No chance there. She now lived on the East Coast with her second husband.

Aunt Ludy? She was positively ancient and had lost all her teeth, and each year she got more and more ornery. Darby was her favorite person on earth. She would be willing to rescue Darby, no question, storming in with her star-shaped aluminum helmet and slashing about with her fractal sword. The trouble was, she was locked up in a place for crazy people.

There was his sister, Livey. Livey could rescue him. No doubt about that. Sixteen-year-old girls, especially a popular cheerleader like her, could do just about anything. It was Livey who'd rescued their dad and Wiles from that dog and got them down the tree. She could get Darby out of this situation, but she wouldn't, not right away. She would let him learn his lesson first.

So who did that leave? Nobody.

Well, wait.

There was Bob.

Funny how Livey had found that Etch A Sketch. Darby had forgotten all about it. Had forgotten about Bob, too, even though Bob had been awfully real to his young mind. He had disappeared from Darby's life after a Christmas visit to Aunt Ludy. Darby was playing in Aunt Ludy's Hilbert space machine, a cardboard box she'd covered with equations. He had mentioned Bob to her, and boy, she'd gone even more bananas than she already was. Whacked her fractal sword and snarled at Bob through her clacking dentures that if he didn't leave Darby alone, she would disprove him, make him go *poof!* Her temper tantrum had scared Darby so much, he hadn't dared think about Bob for days after, and then when he did, he'd lost interest in his make-believe friend.

"Help me now, O Great Bob," Darby muttered, and then snorted. Yeah, right. He wasn't a little kid anymore. This was serious, Adult-Type trouble.

"Something funny?" the guard said.

Darby shook his head. No, nothing was funny. Everything was *un*funny to the power of the doom squared. He blinked tears away and focused on the rubber black-tipped shark. An hour ago he'd been standing behind thick aquarium glass and studying the real creature as it glided incessantly with lazy sweeps of its tail. The guide said it swam 24/7, never stopping for a rest.

Darby frowned. Something was tickling the back of his mind, an old memory that had to do with the attic and Aunt Ludy's metal chest, the one with all those old books. Something he'd read many years ago, about a conjecture.

He thought, *Let us define a Hilbert space of all Hilbert spaces.* The black-tipped shark came back to mind. *Let us further define a certain function B for Bob and a simple linear operator that, like the tail of a black-tipped shark, always keeps the function moving in that space. . . .*

Hmmm. Interesting. He needed paper, though, to keep track of his calculations. Nodding at the gift-shop notebook on the shelf with the other items, he asked the guard, "Can I have that? I bought that one. I have a receipt for it."

"What for?"

"To write a confession."

She clicked her pen and then swiveled around to reach for the notebook. She tossed it to him, along with a spare pen on her desk.

Darby tore open the plastic package and began scribbling. The equations flowed. He lost track of time. His dismal circumstances faded away. What he was putting down was more than interesting, it was *beautiful*. The function was taking on a life of its own, as though it were alive and he was following along in its wake.

The guard pointed at one of the monitors. "Here come my boss and your dad," she said. "You're in for it now."

That jerked him back to the present. The scribbles on the notepad were suddenly nothing more than dead ink. Fear clamped his lungs. Sweat popped out on his forehead.

Help me, Bob.

The door began to open.

Darby felt the faintest of swishes. The back of his neck tingled.

And across the room, the plastic shark and the TETRA KUIZ and the explorer set vanished from the shelf top, one by one, as though an invisible creature was scooping them up in its mouth.

AS LIVEY WARMED UP for cheerleading practice with stretches on the gym's mat, she told Chantelle about her woes with Mr. Savard.

"It was like he was threatening to get me kicked off the squad," she complained.

"It's not a threat," Chantelle grunted as she bent over her long leg to touch her toes. "It's a rule."

"Can't you get your father or brother to help you with your algebra?" Ashlyn asked.

"Are you kidding? They explain math like lawyers. I get even more confused."

Chantelle switched legs. "You better study, girl. You *have* to stay on the squad."

Taylor was listening but didn't say anything. Livey suspected the brunette wouldn't mind at all if Livey got dropped from the squad. Taylor was the squad's alternate flyer.

The team ran a few laps around the gym. Coach Mazur clapped her hands and called them together. She wasn't much bigger than Livey, and had been a flyer herself on a national championship squad, but she could bellow like a foghorn. Coach introduced a new routine and stunt, which she demonstrated. As the biggest girls on the squad, Chantelle and Trish were the bases, and held Coach high above their shoulders in the Liberty stance. On her count, they threw her, and she expertly twisted into the cradle, the waiting arms of the other cheerleaders. "Easy as candy," she said.

After cheerleading practice, Livey left school with Chantelle. As they waited for the signal to cross busy President Avenue, Chantelle said, "I didn't want to say in practice, but Mandy told me to tell you that Derek Mankowski told her that he thinks you're cute."

Mandy was on the JV cheerleading squad, which cheered the soccer games, and Derek had scorned football to be the soccer team's top goal scorer.

"Cute," Livey said.

"You *are* cute."

"Uh-hunh. So are koala bears."

"You know Derek. That's how he talks. What he's really saying, he thinks you're hot. Hot and cute and—"

"Don't you dare say *bubbly*."

Chantelle grinned. "Like champagne."

"I thought he liked Taylor."

"I guess he's changed his mind."

"Too bad."

"God, Livey. This is Derek. He Who Drives a Porsche and is so hot he contributes to global warming. And he's asking you out."

"What, by saying I'm *cute*?"

"What you need, girl, is to fall in love."

"I've put that in my planner for after I get my driver's license."

With a mock scowl, Chantelle stabbed her finger into Livey's shoulder. "You know what's wrong with you? You're too Livey-like, that's what's wrong."

The light turned. They hurried across the four lanes. On the second row of stopped vehicles was a brown Beetle. Johnny's fingers played with an unlit cigarette. He was staring straight ahead at the Lexus in front of him. Probably wishing he could trade up.

As though he heard Livey's thoughts, he turned his head and looked right at her.

She glanced away.

At May's Market, Livey and Chantelle parted ways.

"And study your algebra!" Chantelle called back over her shoulder. "If you flunk that test, I'm gonna kill you!"

As Livey hurried home, she thought about summer cheerleading camp, and the boy from Ohio whom she'd met. They'd kissed under the stars. When camp ended and they had to say good-bye, she'd even cried. So it wasn't that she didn't know what a crush was like. But love, real love, scared her. It could do terrible things. When she was thirteen, her mom had gone to a mathematics and physics conference. There her coolheaded mother had fallen madly in love with a man who was as suave and sophisticated as Jerry Ell was not. Dr. Silas Djurek wore Armani suits and drank fine wine and no doubt disposed of his used dental floss in the proper manner instead of absently leaving the yucky strings on the bathroom counter. Livey's mom had abandoned her children to follow the Slimy Jerk to Washington. Had left them, just like that, and paid for a housekeeper.

Over the last year, Livey and her mom had started to repair their relationship with e-mails and phone calls, but it was still fragile. A few months ago, her mom came to Chicago to give a lecture at the University. Livey visited her in her hotel room. Her mother was wearing a new perfume. Gone was the familiar Chanel that Livey had grown up with, the comforting smell of her mother. The Slimy Jerk had gotten her mom to change her perfume to this awful stinky stuff! This had upset Livey so much that she'd gotten angry all over again. She dumped the bottle of perfume over the carpet and furniture and curtains and got it all over herself, too.

Livey was still thinking about that perfume and how she could smell it on somebody a mile off when she turned the corner and came to her house. The door to the garage was open and the car was gone. A little girl of five was sitting on the front steps.

The girl stood. "Where's Darby?" she asked accusingly.

It was the same girl who waited every afternoon for Darby's school bus. She would play with Darby for a while at the Lincoln Park playground. The dark blue of her crushed velvet shorts had partly faded into white lines, and the sequined words on her pale blue T-shirt were missing a letter to state that OD IS LOVE. Dark freckles sprayed across her sharp little face. Her short black hair stuck up everywhere, sprinkled with playground sand.

"He went on a field trip. Shedd Aquarium. I guess he's not back." Livey glanced at her watch. Four thirty. "You were waiting the whole time at the park? By yourself?"

"He promised to tell me about vampire numbers."

Vampire numbers? Livey instinctively brushed the sand off the girl's hair. The girl flinched away at her touch. "You were waiting a long time. Do your parents know where you are?"

"No."

"Don't you think you should tell them?"

"No." The girl sat back down on the steps.

Livey reached over the girl and unlocked the front door. "Why don't you wait inside?"

The girl turned around and peered into the foyer. "Are there monsters in there?"

"Only my algebra," Livey said lightly.

Livey's dad kept a whiteboard in the living room to jot down math in case he got inspired. He also had whiteboards in the garage and in his bedroom and in the master bathroom. The bathroom one got filled up the fastest.

On the living room board was a note in her dad's precise handwriting. "Livey—gone to Chicago to pick up Darby."

Why would he have to pick up Darby? Wasn't Darby supposed to come back with the rest of the kids? Livey sighed—some questions about her father and brother were simply unanswerable. The family car, an old Montero Sport, was leaking oil. She hoped her dad made it. He wasn't very mechanically minded. One time they were on their way to visit Aunt Ludy and the engine had started steaming. "Too much water in the radiator," he had said.

The girl sat down on the living room couch. She wouldn't give her name. She wouldn't give her home phone number. "You're a stranger," she said to Livey in that same accusing tone. She didn't want a drink and didn't want a cookie and didn't want to watch TV. She just perched there on the edge, swinging her feet and humming under her breath.

Livey tried to get her dad on his cell, but it was turned off. Her dad hated cell phones. He didn't like his cell phone ringing and breaking his concentration whenever he was in deep thought. When he was back in shallow thought, he forgot to turn it on.

Livey preheated the oven and got out the chicken casserole from the fridge before setting the table. Her father and brother didn't really care what or where they ate—canned spaghetti on paper plates on the living room floor would have been just fine with them—but a proper sit-down dinner was one of Livey's lines of defense against the general weirdness of her family. Even Livey's mother, a theoretical physicist who could herself get rather lost in her thoughts, had insisted on sit-down dinners. Friday nights she would use the crystal and open a good bottle of wine. After the divorce, the only thing she had taken was the crystal.

Livey perched on a kitchen counter stool to keep an eye on the girl and opened her algebra textbook. Propping her cheeks on her hands, she started studying.

Soon she was imagining the square roots of x sinking their fangs into her neck. It was so totally unfair that staying on the cheerleading squad depended on getting a C in algebra. One was love and fun and a Starbucks latte with the squad after a game, and the other was the work of the devil. Satan was x and Osama bin Laden was y and the quadratic equation was part of their wicked plot to take over the world.

"Tell me, Wiles," she muttered to the cat napping on top of the fridge, "why is a minus times a minus a plus? Hunh? Whoever decided that? Did they have an election or something?"

Wiles snoozed in a most ungraceful, uncatlike manner. He lay on his back with his rear feet propped up in the basket of silk flowers. He yawned and flopped over. After a long stretch, he hopped down onto the counter. He studied the casserole, contemplating a way to remove the heavy glass cover. In this family, even the cat was a genius.

"Scram," Livey said. "If you're hungry, there's still that kibble in your bowl."

He jumped onto the floor and with imperious indignation hobbled over to the couch. The girl frowned down at him. He sniffed her ankle and then tossed himself up beside her, his tail on her lap, his head dangling over the edge of the sofa. She started humming and swinging her legs again.

Through the kitchen window, Livey saw the Montero nosing up Beechwood, trailing smoke. It sputtered up onto the driveway. Her dad got out and opened the hood, while Darby ran to the front door.

The girl stood as he entered. "Hi, Darby."

He pushed his glasses back on his nose and blinked at her. "Oh, hi."

"You promised you'd tell me about vampire numbers."

Darby slung his backpack onto the couch, startling Wiles. "Right. Take two numbers and multiply them together. If their product has the same digits as the original two numbers, without any zeros at the end, then the product is a vampire number. For example, 27 times 81 is 2187. So 2187 is a vampire number."

The girl sucked her cheek in thought. "Cool." She sat back down. "I'm going to think of another one."

Livey whispered to her brother, "Who is she?"

Darby shrugged an *I-don't-know*.

"Well, what's her name?"

Another shrug. He got a chair from the dining-room table.

"So how was the field trip?"

"Okay." He put the chair in the hallway and stood on it to pull down the spring-loaded steps to the attic.

"You mean it sucked," Livey said. She suspected he was being bullied, but he refused to talk about it. "Don't worry. You'll make your own friends soon enough."

Darby was climbing the steps. "Who cares about the stupid Boys' Club?" he said. He vanished into the gloom. A moment later the weak attic light came on.

"What are you doing up there?" Livey called.

He didn't reply. There was a scrape of something being moved. Then he shrieked. "Livey!"

She bolted up the steps. Darby had backed up against a dusty tower of newspapers and old magazines, pointing in fright to a tiny brown spider smaller than her pinkie nail. A part of its web floated free from a metal trunk he had tugged from the corner. "Oh, for Pete's sake," Livey said. "This cute little thing?"

"That's what you see. I see a creature with compound eyes and fangs."

Livey rolled up an old newspaper and gently scooped up the spider, which she puffed into the opposite corner. "There you go, Darbs. Safe from compound eyes."

Darby knelt down before the trunk. Stenciled on its side in white paint was the name DR. LUDAVICA ELL. The trunk had been in the Ells' attic for ages, first at 15 Beechwood and then this house. "Just old books and math journals," her dad told her, but still, she'd become curious enough about it that she had eventually hacksawed the combination lock. Her dad was right. Nothing but books and journals.

"Who cut this?" Darby said, inspecting the combination lock.

"What are you doing?"

"You shouldn't have cut it. The combo's easy. Two five seven. Each digit is a prime and—"

"Zero zero zero is easier. What are you doing?"

He tugged on the latch, which was stuck. "Do you ever remember Aunt Ludy saying anything about the Thingamabob Conjecture?"

Loopy old Aunt Ludavica, convinced that alien numbers and government spies were trying to listen to her brain waves. "Honestly, Darby, what *are* you doing? You're not starting to believe the crazy stuff she says, are you?"

Darby tugged harder. The latch snapped open, catching his fingers. "Ow," he said.

From behind them came a quiet voice. "I wouldn't open that if I was you."

It was the girl, standing on the steps, her head poking into the attic space.

"There's monsters in there," the girl added, in that same serious voice.

Darby snatched his hands from the trunk.

"Oh, for Pete's sake," Livey said. She flipped the top open. "See? Nothing but old books."

◧ ◨ ◧

The strange, nameless girl scampered out of the house without a thanks or good-bye after Darby promised to tell her about gargoyle fractions.

He retreated into his bedroom with a thick book he'd taken out of the trunk. Dust bunnies clung to his clothes and hair. "Take a bath!" Livey told him. "You're filthy!"

Jerry Ell came in the house, wiping his hands on a rag. "Going to have to call the garage tomorrow."

"Why don't we just get a new car?" When Livey finally got her driver's license, a ten-year-old Montero Sport was not going to fit the occasion.

Her dad spotted the algebra textbook before her and grinned. "Wow. We're going to make a number theorist out of you yet."

"I don't mind numbers, it's xs and ys I can't stand. Why did you have to go pick up Darby?"

"Some silly mistake. They said he was shoplifting at the gift shop."

Livey nearly fell off her stool. "What? Darby?"

"I couldn't believe it either. They had him in the security office, but the items they said he took weren't there. Nowhere to be found. And there was nothing on the security tape, either. The security guard went into hysterics. She was ranting and raving, tearing the office apart." Her dad snorted. "The people they hire these days. A whole afternoon wasted."

AFTER DOING THE DISHES as quickly as he could, Darby raced for his bedroom.

His bossy sister had gotten her dad to remove the bedroom door's lock, saying it was a safety measure against a house fire. Yeah, well, how come she didn't remove *her* bedroom door lock? He pushed his dresser across the door and then flung himself onto the carpeted floor. Reaching underneath his mattress, he pulled out his new Aquarium notebook and Aunt Ludy's math book. For the umpteenth time, he studied Aunt Ludy's scribbling in the margins. He didn't understand her notations and symbols, much less the mathematics they represented.

Then he turned to the simpler equations he'd written in the security office.

What on earth had happened back there?

Flopping onto his back, he stared absently at the poster on the wall opposite the bed. The poster was a copy of Leonardo da Vinci's famous Vitruvian drawing, the one of the naked man with four legs and four arms standing in a circle. Livey had insisted Darby cover the man's naked bits, which Darby had done with a real maple leaf, long turned brown. The shaggy-haired fellow returned Darby's gaze with a somber one of his one.

"You wouldn't believe it if I told you," Darby murmured.

He saw again those gift shop items disappearing, one by one. Something had swum out of Hilbert space and swallowed up the evidence of his shoplifting.

Something he had summoned.

He took a deep, quavering breath. "Bob?" he said. He waited, his heart thudding, his gaze darting from one end of the room to the other. Nothing. Sitting up on the edge of the bed, he whispered again, "Bob? Are you there?"

Still nothing.

Maybe it was just as well. Maybe it was a bad idea to summon something that could gobble things up.

But still, whatever it was, it had helped him. And how could a mathematical creature be dangerous? Math was good, and good math was beautiful.

Maybe he had to be in danger before he could summon Bob. "You know, Julian's going to ask me for that stuff. He won't care I got busted."

That didn't work either.

After a moment's thought, Darby knelt by his bed, closed his eyes, and clasped his palms together. "Dear Bob, thank you for helping me. Amen." He waited a second, and then peeked with one eye. Nope.

Somebody pushed on the bedroom door. It was Livey. "Darby? *MythBusters* is on."

He shoved the book and notebook back under the bed and took a seat at his desk. "I'm busy."

"Too busy to watch your favorite show?" Livey pushed the door open a few feet, shoving against the dresser's weight. "I wish you'd stop dragging that dresser around. It ruins the carpet."

"Next time, knock, like you to tell me to do."

"What's going on?"

"I'm working on something. You wouldn't understand."

"Ooooh, you're hurting my feelings. What happened at the aquarium?"

Unlike their dad, Livey had the suspicious mind of a detective. "I already told you. They made a mistake."

"Un-hunh. Your clothes are in the washer. You can put them in the dryer yourself." As she left, Wiles limped in through the door's gap and jumped up onto Darby's bed to sprawl on his pillow.

"You wouldn't believe it either," Darby said to the cat as he shoved the dresser back across the door. Sitting back down at his desk, he turned on his computer and called up his powerful, all-purpose mathematics program.

As Wiles dozed, Darby entered his equations into the program's graphing component. There appeared on his monitor a single pixel dot that expanded into a small equilateral triangle, which slowly grew bigger. Then the triangle rotated and began to move left to right, other triangles following it like a body following a head. The triangles shimmered in rainbow colors, weaving in and out of each other but maintaining a sleek, graceful shape. The object swam lazily across the screen before diving back down into the screen and vanishing into a dot.

Then, without warning, the instant-messaging icon pinged. "Bob has just signed in."

A message appeared. ***Hello, Darby.***

"Holy cow." Darby gasped. His fingers trembled as he typed a reply. ***Is that u, Bob?***

I prefer the name Alpha Omega Function, my dear boy, but Bob will do. It is a pleasant palindrome. There is no need to pray to me.

I am not so presumptuous as to think I am divine.

"Holy smokes," Darby said. *So u r real?*

What is this mutant language? Your dictionary function does not have these words. Please speak to me properly.

Darby typed more slowly. *Sorry. Who are you?*

I am part of another universe. You could say I am a mathematical object, but I assure you I am not a lifeless object.

Holy smoking cow. *How did you get here?*

Ah. Allow me to show you. There appeared on the monitor a photograph of an idyllic tropical island. *This is an island in the Enewetak Atoll in the South Pacific.* Another photograph flashed onto the screen, showing an ugly building of pipes and cylinders and metal sheeting that squatted among the palms like an enormous toad. *This is Mike. The first thermonuclear hydrogen bomb.* A third picture displayed men wearing dark goggles lining the rails of a ship. *7:14 a.m., November 1, 1952. The control ship, thirty miles away. What I cannot show you is that in a hot storage room belowdecks a group of people, including your great-aunt, had gathered to pray before a tetraktys—*

Darby interrupted, his fingers flying.

A what?

The sacred symbol of the Pythagorean Brotherhood.

Those guys? There extinct.

Watch your spelling, my dear boy.

They're extinct.

Not at all. Never have been. Your great-aunt had just been initiated into a Circle. Her mentor was a senior scientist. They were praying because they worried the bomb would ignite the atmosphere. They did not realize the greater danger.

There followed a video of the bomb exploding, the building vaporizing in a ball of fire brighter than the rising sun. The fireball roiled, spinning its terrible beauty.

When the bomb exploded, a random quantum fluctuation of density and pressure created a black hole. In normal circumstances it should have consumed the earth.

Whoa.

No response for a moment. *I am not a horse. Do not whoa me.*

Sorry, just a figure of speech. I mean, wow.

From this black hole there at once blossomed a baby universe, which included me as the Alpha Omega Function. I was newly born, and with a newborn's curiosity, I slipped through the black hole into your universe. With my newly created but supremely adaptable intelligence, I instantly realized the danger the black hole presented to your earth, and therefore I kicked it away before it could start to destroy the planet. It was a consummate act of self-sacrifice, for that meant, of course, I could not find my way home again.

In Darby's mind, a memory twanged. *We have a movie like that. An alien got stuck on earth and phoned home.*

Another pause. *I am not an alien. I am the Alpha Omega Function.* If words could be typed frostily, then these dripped icicles. *And there is no way to communicate. The black hole spun into space at the speed of light. It is now somewhere beyond a radius of 50 light years. That is a tremendous volume in which to lose something the size—how large is your eyeball?*

About one inch.

2.54 centimeters. Thinking I would find someone to help me, I inspected the minds in the prayer Circle. Dull and graceless. Your great-aunt's mind, however, was elegant.

Darby loved his great-aunt, but as he now muttered, "Not any longer."

Yet, in this universe, I had neither substance nor form to ask for help. As a first step, I encouraged her to conjecture my existence, which she did, but subsequently she would not prove the conjecture.

That's probably because she went crazy.

Yes, I know. Most unfortunate. But now that you have proven my existence, I therefore do exist. Thank you. But Darby . . .

Yes?

Proving that I exist is not the same thing as a full proof of who I am. You shall have to complete the full proof of the conjecture before I am completely free and realized. Then I can find my way home.

Darby thought of Aunt Ludy's complicated math. *I'll try, but it won't be easy.*

I will help.

By the way, what happened to that stuff you swallowed up?

Safe in Hilbert space. Once you prove me, I will be able to return the items. In person.

A movement caught Darby's eye. It was Wiles, standing on the bed with his back arched and his tail fluffed. The cat was staring intently at the computer. Darby frowned, recalling Aunt Ludy's temper tantrum, the way she'd swung her fractal sword. He typed, *Bob? You're not dangerous, are you?*

Dangerous? I love truth and beauty and elegance. You have a beautiful mind, Darby.

With that, the messaging box closed.

Flushed with pleasure at the compliment, Darby sat on the bed and stroked the cat. "It's okay, Wiles," he said. "It's all right."

Livey didn't sleep well that night. She kept waking, thinking she'd heard something, but the only sounds were the house's normal rhythms: the ticking of her clock, a soft gurgling of pipes, her dad's snoring coming softly through the thin bedroom walls.

Finally she got up to check on Darby. His bedside lamp was on. He was asleep on top of his blanket, a new Shedd Aquarium notebook open beside him, mathematical equations scribbled on the pages. She put the notebook on the dresser, spread the bedcover over him, and turned off the light.

As she closed the door to the darkened room, the screen saver image on Darby's computer caught her attention. A beautiful geometric shark swam lazily across the monitor and then dived into the deep.

7

DARBY COPIED AUNT Ludy's Thingamabob Conjecture into his new Shedd Aquarium notebook. Seated on the school bus behind the driver, he studied the equations, lost in their world. He startled when somebody plopped down beside him.

Julian leaned closed, peering over Darby's shoulder. "What do you have there, Darbielle?"

Darby closed the notebook and shoved it into his bag.

"That's from the aquarium, isn't it? Don't you have something for me?"

"They caught me. You knew they would catch me. You were setting me up."

"Set you up? It was an initiation for the Boys' Club. You want to be a member, don't you?"

"Not anymore. You were just jealous about the essay. Nobody can be number one all the time. Your mom and dad should realize that."

Julian's blue eyes tightened into shards. "Who are you to talk about my parents? Your mother ran away with another man. Oh, yeah, I know all about that. It was the scandal of the century, my mother said." He spun on the seat, his school bag swinging and catching Darby on the face.

Darby was sure that had been deliberate, but it was Julian's words that stung more. Darby forced them out of his mind by thinking about Bob. During classes, Darby went through the motions of schoolwork and lessons, but mentally he was working on his great-aunt's conjecture. He could almost sense Bob's presence, helping him. Every once in a while, when he thought nobody was looking, he'd jot down in the notebook an idea or derive another equation.

At lunch, he snuck out of the lunch room and squirreled himself away in the alley behind the school's boiler plant.

After eating his sandwich, he leaned against the brick wall with the notebook on his knees and teased out several more equations. A shadow fell across the mouth of the alley, and big Roz turned the corner. He shoved the notebook behind his back.

"Hi," she said.

"Hi," Darby replied warily.

She sat down beside him and took out a pack of Juicy Fruit from her skirt pocket. "Want one?" she asked.

Roz was offering him gum? What was going on? He took a stick. "Thanks."

She wadded a piece into her mouth. "So what happened at the aquarium?" she asked as she chomped. "After you got caught?"

"They let me go."

"Phew, I'm glad."

Darby glanced at her out of the corner of his eyes. She was?

"I heard Julian ordering you to take that stuff. That was really mean. He's stuck-up, too. I've decided I don't like him."

She did? "I thought you wanted to be a member of the Boys' Club."

"Who wants to be a member of a club where they don't allow girls? That's so sexist." She nudged him with her elbow. "We should start our own club. We could call it the No One Else Allowed Club."

After a moment, he relaxed and returned her grin. "The Absolutely No One Else Allowed Club."

"What's that you're working on all secretlike in your notebook?"

"Just some math."

"Math? Hello. BORing."

If you only knew, Darby thought.

She fidgeted with her gum wrapper foil. "Listen, Darby, I'm sorry I've been so stuck-up and everything. I'd like to be friends."

He tensed up again, mostly out of disbelief. Roz wanted to be friends?

"I know," she said. "I don't deserve to be your friend, but I'd like to be." Her neck had reddened. Her voice quivered.

Holy cow. She did want to be friends.

"Well, sure," he said, with growing wonder.

Her grin was wide and relieved. She knocked her knuckles against his. "Cool," she said and jumped to her feet. With a wave, she ran off to the playground.

What do you know, Darby thought. He stroked the cover of his notebook. Now that Bob had come into his life, things were starting to look up.

Every day when Darby got off the school bus, the little girl who loved numbers was there to meet him. She always insisted he follow her to the kids' playground at Lincoln Park and tell her about numbers.

When he got off the bus today, she was squatting by the statue of President Lincoln. Town legend said that Lincoln had once fished at the park's pond, an event commemorated by a life-size bronze statue of the gaunt President in his top hat.

"He's got ants," the girl said, pointing to his feet.

"I don't think he cares," Darby said.

"I wouldn't want ants crawling all over on me."

As usual, she wanted to play first on the swing in the sand pit, with him pushing her. This was the only time she let him touch her, on her back. The park was popular with the neighborhood stay-at-home moms and their toddlers. They often looked at Darby and the girl and then smiled at each other. How cute, friends playing together.

The truth was, Darby hardly knew a thing about her. He didn't know her name or where she lived or even how old she was. She didn't say and he didn't ask. It was like they'd made a deal. For him to ask would somehow wreck the fun of it, for him and for her. Once she was satisfied with what he told her about the day's special numbers, she would run in her awkward, knock-kneed way over the pond's wooden bridge and vanish.

"You promised to tell me about gargoyle fractions," she said as she swung.

"Divide 3 by 5."

She dragged her feet on the ground to stop swinging, and squinted fiercely in thought. "It's 1.66666666 . . ." She only stopped saying the sixes when she finally ran out of breath.

"That's right. And you know what 666 is, don't you? Gargoyle fractions have the Mark of the Beast. Be careful when you run into 20 divided by 3!"

She snorted. "I wouldn't be scared. Tell me another number."

"How about perfect numbers? A perfect number is one that is the sum of the numbers that divide it. 6 is a perfect number because it is divided by 1 and 2 and 3, and 1 + 2 + 3 equals 6. The next perfect number is 28, because 1 + 2 + 4 + 7 + 14 equals 28."

She thought about that. "Perfect numbers are boring."

"There is no boring number. The first boring number you come to is interesting precisely because it's the first boring number. And perfect numbers are very rare. The ancient Greeks discovered the first four, 6, 28, 496, and 8128, and even today, with supercomputers, we've only found around 30 of them. Nobody knows if there is an infinite number. And nobody knows if a single odd perfect number even exists. It's like a unicorn. Nobody's ever seen one."

The girl pushed off on the swing again. "I have. It's got this curly horn like a gold licorice stick. Unicorns are very shy, you know."

Darby agreed with equal gravity. "I bet they are."

"Tell me about werewolf numbers."

He laughed. "You sure like your monsters, don't you?"

"I have to keep track of them. It's my job."

"Let's see. A werewolf number would be 4 divided by pi. Because it turns into a long, shaggy, continuous fraction." With a twig, he scratched it out into the dirt by the girl's feet.

$$\frac{4}{\pi} = 1 + \cfrac{1^2}{2 + \cfrac{3^2}{2 + \cfrac{5^2}{2 + \cfrac{7^2}{\ddots}}}}$$

"So," Darby continued, "on full moons stay away from 4 over pi."

"Full moon, hunh," the girl said thoughtfully. The way she said it, Darby could imagine her on the next full moon creeping out into the Preserve to look for a werewolf number. "Okay, so what else?"

"How about alien numbers? I'm working on finding one." He told her about Aunt Ludy's Thingamabob Conjecture, not for her sake but for his, to work out the main steps of the arguments again.

She obviously didn't understand any of it, and maybe she wasn't even listening as she swung, but then she said, "You be careful. You could find a number monster that eats you up."

"Not this one. This number likes truth and beauty and elegance."

A brown-and-white butterfly flitted over a nearby bush, catching the girl's attention. "Is that butterfly causing a storm?"

Darby was confused. "What?"

"My brother told me butterflies can cause storms."

"Oh, he means chaos theory," Darby said, but thinking *brother*? This was the first time she'd mentioned any family.

She pumped the swing harder and higher, going as high as she could, and then at the very top of the arc jumped off the seat. Before Darby could react, she tumbled heavily to the ground.

Darby bent over her in concern. "Are you all right?"

She sat up, brushing sand from her face. "Drats," she said. "I was sure that time I was gonna fly."

The Conjecture was hard going. Darby's dad often spoke of the mathematical landscape, but because of the Shedd Aquarium and the black-tipped shark that had started Darby on the Conjecture, Darby thought of it in terms of underwater reefs. It was like he had to swim out a mile just to get to the offshore reef where Bob lived. Darby had to learn all he could about the various notations and symbols that Aunt Ludy had used and the mathematics they represented. He did this by going online as Guru Lasees. The name was an anagram for Euler and Gauss, two of the greatest mathematicians the world had ever known. As Guru Lasees, Darby searched websites and math archives and sent off e-mails to math experts he thought could explain things to him. He didn't tell his father. He wasn't so sure his dad would approve of what he was doing.

Every once in a while Bob would pop up in an instant message to encourage him and give him suggestions. Aunt Ludy's math was soon much clearer to Darby. He was finally out to the reef and looking through a mask at the colorful corals and the deeper crevasses. Bob—the full, real Bob—was down there somewhere.

Bob was curious about many things besides his proof. It was like he couldn't stay still. One evening he showed Darby an online article about scientists measuring the humor of knock-knock jokes.

Is a knock-knock joke a greeting ritual? he asked in the IM box.

No, jokes are jokes. You know, funny.

I do not know. You shall explain, please.

Let's try one. I say knock-knock—

Why?

Pretend I'm at your door, okay. I say knock-knock, like I'm knocking, and you say who's there. Ready? Knock-knock.

Enter.

No. You say, "Who's there?" Knock-knock.

Who is there?

Yul.

Enter, Yul.

No, you say, Yul who?

I see. Yul who?

Yul never know.

A pause. *I do not understand.*

Yul. You will. Get it? You will never know.

A longer pause. *Then why would you knock on my door?*

It's just a joke, a play on words. It's funny.

An even longer pause. *Ah. I see. Yes, it is funny.*

Other times Bob would flash pictures on the computer screen. The Great Wall of China, for example. He wondered why it wasn't a straight line. The Washington Monument he approved, for it had symmetrical elegance. A picture of a child deformed by chemical poisoning bothered him greatly, and he wondered why nobody was doing anything about it.

One evening he put on the screen a photo of Darby's mother working in her rose garden. She was kneeling and looked up at the camera with a smile, her blond hair wrapped in a scarf. It was a picture Darby had taken. He thought he had erased it, along with all the others of his mom, but Bob must have resurrected it from the hard-drive data.

Who is this? Bob asked.

My mother.

Ah. Doctor Maria Ell?

Not anymore. She's remarried.

And her friends call her Mare for short?

Darby frowned. *You aren't eavesdropping on her e-mails and stuff, are you?*

I have read her papers in the archives. She too has an elegant mind.

I don't want to talk about her.

Why not?

She left us.

Why would she leave you?

Bob. Really. I don't want to talk about her.

Bob showed another picture, this one of Livey in front of last year's Christmas tree. *Who is this?*

Livey. My sister.

Does she have a beautiful mind?

Darby snorted. *Ha,* he typed. *The only numbers she cares about are on the sales tags at the mall.*

NEARLY A THOUSAND miles away, in a big black building at Fort Meade, Maryland, a man stared out the window of his corner office at the sprawling parking lot and the well-guarded gates. A duty officer was reading him a report, her voice soft as the carpet underfoot. As he listened, he was also thinking about the dinner reservation with his wife that evening, as well as idly noting a pattern in the colors of the parked cars. This did not mean he wasn't paying attention. He could juggle a dozen different things in his head and still have a lot of brain left over.

"Guru Lasees," the man abruptly said, interrupting the duty officer. "Does that ring a bell?"

"No, sir. This is the first time that user name has come up on the intercepts."

"It's an anagram for Gauss and Euler. Where is this fellow?"

"Illinois." She paused. "He's a ten-year-old boy."

"We're keeping an eye on a ten-year-old boy?"

"His searches triggered all the flags, sir. He's sniffing around the material in a systematic pattern."

The director of Z Ops of the National Security Agency was still studying the cars in the lot. "The spacing of all the yellow cars approximate Euler's series," he said.

The duty officer smiled tentatively. She was in awe of her boss, and wasn't sure how to handle his famous digressions. Although he was only in his early fifties (and handsome as a movie star), he was a legend in the NSA. He didn't just break codes, he busted them wide open. On the wall was a photo of the president awarding him the Medal of Freedom in a secret ceremony for code-breaking work that the public would never know about.

He turned around and took the folder from her. Within were several short papers, the longest only six pages. The words were typed on an old typewriter with uneven lettering, and the equations were penned in ink that had turned brown. The first paper was titled THE THINGAMA-BOB CONJECTURE, and it had been written in 1952 by Ludavica Ell of the hydrogen bomb project. She had subsequently gone mad. Federal agents had confiscated all her work. Because she knew too many secrets, the government had her committed to a private institution that was actually a covert government facility.

The paper had long been infamous within the top levels of the NSA. Many believed the Conjecture to be a useless fringe product of a lunatic mind. But others, like the director, who was himself a world-class mathematician, saw something there. The Conjecture hinted at the existence of a mathematical object with astounding properties. If the Conjecture could be proven and the object more rigorously defined, then it might allow backdoor attacks on the most secure of enemy codes.

Teams of NSA mathematicians had failed to prove the Conjecture. The director resisted a constant temptation to try himself. He did not want to waste years of effort on something that would probably defeat him. But more than that—considerably more than that—the director was afraid of what could happen should he in fact succeed in proving the Conjecture. Theoretical mathematics was traditionally the purest and most abstract of the intellectual arts with no real-life applications, but no longer. The very existence of Z Ops was proof of that. Top secret mathematics to fight the nation's enemies—a mere hundred years ago, theoretical mathematicians would have chuckled at the thought.

Who knew what genie would be uncorked if the Conjecture was proven? Even the friendliest genie could bite, and bite hard.

Still, the director could not deny the powerful allure of the Conjecture, as if something was whispering in his ear, *prove me, and the world shall be yours.*

The various mathematical ideas that Ludavica's paper contained were in the public domain—it was the unique way they had been woven together that held the key. The director had put the paper and its ideas behind a security moat. If the NSA eavesdropping computers caught anyone sniffing around these particular ideas in any systematic manner, he was to be informed.

"What else do you know?" he asked the duty officer.

"The boy's name is Darby Ell. He's apparently some sort of genius. He's also Ludavica Ell's great-nephew. She's still alive, a resident at the Silverwood Home for Mental Health."

The director remained silent for much longer than usual, a silence the duty officer found unnerving.

"That's one of our black budget facilities," she added, just to say something.

"I know what it is," he snapped.

The duty officer pressed her lips together and glanced down at her shoes.

The director sighed. "Sorry. That was uncalled for. And by the way, congratulations on Brandon winning that photo contest. It's a terrific photo. I've always appreciated strong black-and-white compositions. Perhaps because there's already too much gray in the world."

She was startled he would know about her son winning the prize, and pleased. "Thank you, sir."

After she left, the director looked out again at the parking lot. White was the overall most popular color for cars, but in this lot, it seemed to be dark blues.

He turned to his desk and called for all of Ludavica Ell's files. He scanned through years of psychiatrists' reports, filled with the usual psycho-jargon of schizophrenia. But there was one early report that he lingered over. In this doctor's opinion, Ludavica Ell was mad as a hatter, no doubt about it, but her mental illness was not organic. He concluded she had willed it on herself, as though she were using her madness in order to hide from something.

Or to hide something in her madness.

Among the items in the files were standard security reports and surveillance video disks. There were also several home videos. The director popped one of the latter into a machine.

The video had been taped during one of the Ells' family visits to Silverwood. Ludavica was playing with her great-nephew, Darby Ell, who was five at the time. The boy's mother was doing the filming. Ludavica and the boy pretended to space-travel through a cardboard box. The crazy old woman was wearing an aluminum hat to prevent spies and aliens from reading her mind. In the box, she whispered something to Darby, but the boy was too interested in the back of the box to pay attention to her.

Ludavica's whisper was inaudible. The director summoned one of the NSA tech wizards, a young man who looked like he should be playing video games at a mall arcade, not working on state secrets. The director told him what he wanted, to tease out the audio on the video and find out what the woman was saying. The kid nonchalantly tossed the video in the air as he left the room.

The director flipped through Ludavica's other papers. All were attempts to disprove the Conjecture.

It was almost as though she had not wanted her Conjecture and its potential to fall into government hands.

A traitorous act, one could say.

And some people would indeed say it, but there was much gray and uncertainty in the world.

Later that day, the director attended a meeting chaired by the national security advisor. Even though it was not on the agenda, the advisor brought up the subject of Guru Lasees.

"I normally wouldn't micromanage this," she said, "but I am curious. How did this boy get hold of the Conjecture?"

One of the other men fiddled with the end of his red bow tie. He had short gingery hair and black eyes that looked as if a cigar had burned two holes in his skull. "Isn't he Ludavica Ell's great-nephew? Perhaps she put a bug in his ear."

The director of Z Ops disagreed. "That would be the last thing she would want."

The man with the red bow tie chewed his lip in thought. "I think you're right. I think she went nuts so she doesn't have to cooperate with anybody on this. She's getting old. I think somebody should pump her full of chemicals and get her head straightened out enough that she spills whatever beans she's got left about this Conjecture before she kicks the bucket."

There was a silence.

"Hey," the man said with a shrug. "You know me. I say the things that everybody thinks about but doesn't dare mention."

"We've had the best and brightest minds look long and hard at this

Conjecture," the advisor said. "What's a boy going to do?"

"Perhaps that is what's needed," a woman said. "Child geniuses often have a fresh and unique way of looking at things. I don't know how he's stumbled on to this, but I wouldn't discount his efforts."

The advisor idly tapped her pen on her folder. "As highly unlikely as it is, if he does prove the Conjecture, then he'll be in possession of a vital state secret. Which we would dearly love to have, but there is no guarantee that he would be able to keep it as a secret. What if he were kidnapped, for example?"

The man with the bow tie said, "We could bring him in ourselves. For safekeeping."

There was another long silence. The director thought of black-and-white photographs, and of shades of gray, and of treacherous paths along the corridors of power, powers both known and unknown. He straightened the cuffs of his suit jacket. "I don't think such a drastic course of action is necessary at the moment. Let me see what I can find out. I'll use the personal touch."

LIVEY KEPT SEEING Johnny Magnus around the school at odd places and times. One study hall, she was assigned to run notes from the admin office. Taking an invoice to the chemistry lab, she ran into him sitting on the second-floor landing, right under the sign that said NO SITTING ON STAIRS. He was staring out to space, idly fingering the cross on his necklace. It wasn't any of her business, and she didn't care, honest, but since she had to go around him, she asked, "Shouldn't you be in class?"

"Who are you, the hall monitor?" he replied.

She rushed up the stairs. Just before she turned the corner, she glanced back down. All she saw was the tail end of Johnny's shadow slipping away from the landing.

Another day, she got a library pass from her earth science class to do research for a paper on earthquakes. Her teacher required at least one citation from a real book, and not just the Internet, and the book she wanted was shelved on the very top shelf in the back of the library.

She couldn't quite reach it, and there weren't any step stools in the aisle. Poking her head around the stack, she saw Johnny leaning against the window, staring out at the Quad.

"Hey, could you help me here?" she said.

He slowly turned around.

She pointed to the book. "I can't reach it."

The light from the window highlighted his sharp bones and the sparse stubble on his pale chin. He wordlessly fetched a stool from another aisle, which he placed in front of Livey. She stood on the chair. This close, he smelled like warm engine oil. There were smudges on his hands, but at least his fingernails were reasonably clean, as was his black hair. Genuine black too, not dyed.

Livey grabbed the book and stepped off the stool. Chantelle would have told her not to bother with the losers, but that wasn't Livey's way. She gave Johnny her brightest, most bubbly cheerleading smile. "Thanks. So are you going to the game on Friday?"

He looked down at her. "How tall are you?"

The question threw her. "Five two," she said, exaggerating by half an inch.

"Next time get the stool yourself."

Livey never ever blushed, but a warm flush flooded up her neck. She tried to think of something sassy to snap back at him, but her mind was a total blank as she watched him saunter away.

Julian's parents, Judge and Mrs. Bostick, came to a Newton school assembly. Mrs. Bostick had brought one of her orchids to talk about. It was flowering, a big blossom in green and gold, the school colors. The flower was beautiful. So was Mrs. Bostick. Smart, too. The way Julian was looking at her, he seemed to be saying to everybody, *That's* my *mother*.

At the end of her talk, Judge Bostick rose to the lectern. He was a

lot older than his wife, and looked as stiff and rigid as a dictionary. His
handsome chin stuck out like a page marker. Expecting to be bored,
Darby spread the Conjecture out on his brain to start thinking about
the next step. But the judge wasn't boring. He told funny stories about
being a judge that had everybody laughing. Judge Bostick then grew
serious and talked about what obeying the law really meant, that you
should obey the law not because you didn't want to get punished, but
because you wanted to help build a just and prosperous society. Darby
saw Julian looking around the auditorium, as if to make sure that
everybody was paying attention to his wonderful father. His glance
caught Darby's, and the proud smile on his face sank away, leaving a
flat expression.

After assembly, Darby was heading across the foyer when Principal
Mikkelsen called out his name. With the principal were Julian and the
assembly's honored speakers.

"Julian's parents would like to meet you," the principal said.

Judge Bostick smiled genially upon Darby. Mrs. Bostick's smile was
as sharp and bright as her green eyes. Julian looked as if he wanted the
ground to split open underneath Darby's feet and swallow Darby up.

The judge's handshake was hearty enough to pump blood to
Darby's ears. "We've heard much about you, young man."

"That was a remarkable essay you wrote for the school newsletter,"
Mrs. Bostick said. "I must admit I had a hard time following it, but I'm
sure that a few folks with specialized knowledge found it absolutely
delightful."

"Thank you," Darby muttered.

"You scored one hundredth percentile on that math test," the judge
said. "Are the universities sending you letters yet?"

"We've been getting a few. But my dad says it's too early to be
thinking of that."

"We expect similar letters for Julian. However, he only obtained a ninety-sixth percentile on that test. I keep telling him he really should apply himself more to his studies and less to his insects."

"He'd do well to follow your example, I'm sure," Mrs. Bostick said, anointing her son with her smile. Julian's lips twitched in response. When the judge and Mrs. Bostick turned their attention back to the principal, Julian shot Darby a sizzling look of pure hatred.

One of Darby's classes at Newton Academy was art. Darby had never liked art classes, and this class he especially didn't like. The teacher, Mrs. Ojinaka, floated about in billowy dresses, her towering hair wrapped in a bright turban. She had a thing about drawing the human hand. Forget color and composition and basic technique. It was hands they had to draw. According to Mrs. Ojinaka, if you could draw a hand, you could draw anything. So Darby drew hand after hand on his sketch pad. They looked terrible. They were ugly sausagelike hands.

Julian, though, drew hands that looked alive. He was so good he could deliberately draw badly, mimicking Darby's lousy efforts.

One class, Darby had to go the bathroom. When he returned, Mrs. Ojinaka was standing by his table, her hands on her hips, a thunderous look on her face.

"What's this?" she hissed, pointing at Darby's sketch pad.

On the top sheet was one of Darby's sausage hands. The middle finger was extended at a stick figure in a flowing dress and turban.

"I didn't draw that," Darby protested.

Mrs. Ojinaka sent him to the principal's office.

When he was seated before Principal Mikkelsen, Darby found out that he was in trouble for more than just the drawing. In fact, the drawing trouble was minor compared to this other trouble. Principal Mikkelson had the newsletter with Darby's essay and also another sheet of a paper, a printout from the Internet.

"Somebody has brought this very serious matter to my attention," he said, and handed both to Darby. "Compare." He sat back with arms folded across his chest. His expression, normally a bit squinty, as if he found life slightly puzzling, was now as stern as stone.

Darby scanned both sheets. He noted that the Internet printout had a "Bostick Orchids" computer ID.

"Well?" the principal said.

"The articles are mostly the same."

"So you admit you plagiarized? This is a very serious matter, Darby, one that can get you expelled."

"You can't plagiarize yourself," Darby said. He tapped the Internet printout. "I wrote this, too. This comes from the college's math department blog, where I posted it. This writer, Guru Lasees, that's me. An anagram for Gauss and Euler. You can check the archives for IP addresses and all that, and besides, I have the original document on my home computer if you don't believe me."

That took all of the granite out of Principal Mikkelsen's stony face. He let his arms drop and reexamined the sheets. He was so embarrassed that he let Darby off with a halfhearted warning about the drawing.

When Darby rejoined the art class, he gave Julian a hard-eyed stare. After class, Julian pushed Darby into the corner of the hallway by the stairs. "Do you have a problem, Darbielle?"

Darby had taken the Internet printout with him. He folded it and put it into the pocket of Julian's school jacket, like an elegant pocket square, and patted it. "You can tell your mom her little trick to get me into trouble didn't work either."

Julian snatched the printout and crumpled it into a ball. "At least I have a mother. Yours ran away. Didn't want anything to do with you. A smart woman, your mother." Julian flicked the ball into Darby's face and marched off.

Darby watched him go. *You just wait, Julian, you just wait until I prove Bob.*

◢ ◣ ◢

At lunch, Roz joined him in the alley with her own sandwich. "I heard Julian pulled a prank on you," she said. "He was bragging about it."

"I'll get even," Darby said darkly.

"How?"

Darby was so upset he didn't hesitate. And besides, Roz was a friend. "When I was little, I had an imaginary friend I called Bob. But guess what. Bob isn't imaginary. He's real." Darby pulled out his notebook. He briefly explained about Bob, turning the pages that were quickly filling up with parts of his proof.

Roz's confused expression turned into one of delight. "Really? Wow. That's so totally awesome."

"He instant messages me on my computer to talk to me."

Roz laughed. Still grinning, she turned her head and called out, "Hey, guys! I got it."

Julian sauntered around the corner, with two others of the Boys' Club, Andy and Karim, a step behind him.

"So what did you find out?" Julian asked.

"Darby has an invisible friend," Roz said, getting to her feet. She pointed at the notebook. "He lives in there and talks to Darby by instant messaging him. That's what Darby's been doing."

Julian smiled. "Is that so? Must run in the family. I hear he's got an aunt locked up in a psych ward."

Roz tilted her head and studied Darby. "Look at those ears. They can sure turn red, can't they?"

Darby was stunned. He couldn't think, and all he could feel were his burning ears.

As Roz walked away with Julian and the others, she said, "So can I join now?"

Julian put his arm around her shoulders. "Absolutely. You can be our spymaster."

10

DR. SZABO, DIRECTOR of the Silverwood Home for Mental Health, greeted her visitor at the main entrance and whisked him through the security check.

"How was your flight?" she asked.

"On time," the director of Z Ops said.

"Miracles do happen."

The director did not enlighten her that he had used one of the NSA jets, which was waiting to whisk him back home.

"She's quite lucid today," Dr. Szabo told the director. "A word of advice. She's as harmless as a lamb, but don't say you're from Washington. She has a thing about government spies."

Before the director had boarded the jet, he'd gotten the audio technician's report. The only distinguishable words the tech could tease out of the home video were Ludavica's repeated insistence that her great-nephew "burn the book." What book, the director had no idea, and this was one of the things he wanted to ask her.

In the visitor's lounge, the director pressed a linen handkerchief to his nose, anticipating a sour air, but was pleasantly surprised at the subtle pine scent. The carpet was thick underfoot, and designer ornaments decorated the space. *Rather plush,* he thought to himself, although the patients he saw were much as he thought they'd be. A man turned a page of a book he held upside down, nodding sagely to himself. A woman stood over a potted plant, shaking her finger in argument with it.

The doctor led the director to a second floor residence hall. Inside a well-appointed bedroom, an old woman wrote equations on a blackboard. Already small, she was further hunchbacked with age. On her white hair rested an aluminum hat, its brim shaped like a many-sided star.

"Good morning, dear," the doctor said. "You have a visitor."

The woman turned around with a mild look of surprise, her fingers clenched around the chalk.

"Good morning, Lud—," the director said.

"Shut up," she snapped. "Don't mention my name. They're looking for me. The president has issued a secret order for my capture."

Dr. Szabo said, "This gentleman is also a mathematician."

The old woman snorted. "Let me see your socks."

The director lifted the cuffs of his trousers. She bent low and looked.

"There are two kinds of mathematicians," she pronounced. "Those who wear silk socks and those who wear different colored socks and those who don't wear socks at all."

"That's three kinds."

"You can count. It appears that you are indeed a mathematician." She squinted at him as if burrowing into his mind. "Do you eat beans?"

"As a matter of fact, no. I'm allergic to them."

She slowly nodded. "Leave us," she imperiously ordered Dr. Szabo.

The director gave a discreet nod at the doctor, who withdrew. After she left, Ludavica wrote on the blackboard the digits 1 through 10, arranged in a triangle, and gave the director another sharp squint.

"The tetraktys," he said.

"A dangerous thing," she said. "Me, *I* eat beans. I eat all the beans I want."

"I would think you do." The director stepped over to the dresser and looked more closely at the framed photograph. A father, his pretty blond teenage daughter, and a boy. "That's your great-nephew, isn't it?"

"Darby."

The director held her gaze. There was an intelligence peeking out of her eyes. He decided to come straight to the point. "He's working on your Thingamabob Conjecture. Trying to prove it."

She gasped and splayed skinny fingers against her sunken chest. "You must stop him."

"How would he know of it?"

She turned to the dresser and put a hand on the photograph, her expression troubled. "I don't know."

"Could you have written it down in a book somewhere? Some notes on a margin, perhaps?"

She whirled on him. The quick motion toppled the hat off her head. "Yes! The handbook! The Fishbach!"

The director bent down to pick up the hat. After he handed it back to her, he straightened the cuffs on his shirt. "And where is this book?"

Her gaze had sharpened on his cuff links. She backed away and put a hand to a plastic tube by the dresser. "Who are you?" she hissed.

He at once realized his mistake. Out of habit he'd worn a pair of special NSA cufflinks, a discreet sign that told others, to whom these things were important, of his own elite status.

From the tube she whipped a walking cane, covered in gold foil. "Who are you? You're a spy. You want the proof, don't you?

You want Darby to succeed. You stay away from him!"

She lunged, the tip of the cane gouging his cheek. Dr. Szabo, who had remained hovering at the door, yelled for a nurse. The man rushed in with a needle and injected the old woman. Within seconds she'd fallen limp into the nurse's arms.

The director pressed his handkerchief to his face and examined the large splotch of blood. "Harmless as a lamb, is she?"

When the director finally got home that night, his wife was awake in bed, a physics journal in her hands.

He kissed her. "A little bit of light reading?"

"What happened to your cheek?"

"Wounded in battle," he said lightly. "Sorry to miss dinner. I'll make it up."

"You'd better. But it wasn't a lost evening. I had a nice long chat with Livey. I was thinking, darling, it might be time to try to break the ice, invite her and Darby to spend a week with us during Christmas vacation."

"Are you sure? The way your children feel about me, you'd need a nuclear-powered ship to break the ice."

"I do think it's time to at least try."

"I think you're right." Silas Djurek flopped down on the bed, still in his suit and wearing his shoes. He put his hands behind his head and said, "You know, I was thinking about their great-aunt."

"Ludavica? Why on earth are you thinking about her?"

"I was looking through some of your old home videos. There's one where she's playing in a cardboard box with Darby."

Maria smiled. "I remember that. Her Hilbert space machine. She's as nutty as a loon, but I've always liked her. She and Darby played together like great pals." Her smile sank away, her eyes seemed to fracture, and she murmured, "Darby."

"She mentioned a book on math functions she owned. Fishbach."

Maria took a deep breath, blinking heavily. "We had a trunk of hers in the attic. Probably still there. Jerry's always been a pack rat. Why are you asking?"

Silas touched the bandage on his cheek and winced. "Stings," he said. "You know how things go in cycles? There's new interest in her work."

"General interest or your specialized kind of interest?"

"It's a shame what happened to her."

"You're sidestepping."

"Darling, you know that there are some things I'm simply not permitted to talk about. But those aren't important anyway. Let's discuss Christmas and your children."

She straightened up against the headboard. She was eager with plans. Silas took her hand and kissed it, listening to her with part of his mind, but also thinking of something that had nothing to do with Christmas, something much more important and almost certainly dangerous.

Did he have the strength to see it through?

He was afraid he had no choice.

11

LIVEY HURRIED HOME from cheerleading practice, wishing she'd worn her warmer pair of sweats. Gray clouds swirled low, and soon it began to drizzle. At the Lincoln Park's playground, Darby and that strange little girl were seated in the plastic castle. Darby had that notebook open, and they were both looking at the pages. Darby was wearing his school uniform jacket, but all the girl had on was her dirt-stained T-shirt that said OD IS LOVE.

"For Pete's sake," Livey scolded, "don't you two have enough sense to get home before it starts to rain?"

The girl looked at her and then stuck her head out the castle to look up at the sky, squinting her freckled face against the drops.

"Get home before you catch a cold," Livey told her.

"Is she always this bossy?" the girl asked Darby.

"She's an older sister," Darby said, as if that explained things.

Livey waved a hand. "Go home."

The girl stuck out her tongue at her and ran off.

"What a brat," Livey said.

Darby put away the notebook.

"What's that math you're always working on?"

"Just something," he said. He was quiet for a moment and then added under his breath, "That Roz is going to be sorry too."

The Ells' housekeeper, Mrs. Blink, was as round and red as a Russian beet. When Livey got home, she pulled her aside into the kitchen, filled with the aroma of an apple pie in the oven. "I was cleaning Darby's room and there is something there."

"What?"

"I don't know what it is, but it make my hair stand on end."

Livey stifled a smile. Mrs. Blink had always been superstitious. She wouldn't go up in the attic, for example, claiming that her "not-funny" bone hurt whenever she set foot on the pull-down stairs.

"Maybe it's termites."

"I don't know," Mrs. Blink said doubtfully. "Wiles, he doesn't go anymore into Darby's room."

Livey frowned. Come to think of it, Mrs. Blink was right. Wiles was staying clear of Darby's room.

Mrs. Blink wiped her hands on a towel. "Is Darby doing something he shouldn't?"

"All he's been doing is math. Like Dad."

"Maybe you better check."

Livey waited until Darby went into the bathroom for his shower, and then sneaked into his bedroom. His notebook was on the desk. She flipped through the pages. Just equations. Pretty complicated ones, but nothing to worry about. Darby had done some doodling, too, turning half of page number 17 into a pretty bad drawing of their house on 17 Beechwood, giving it a halo of triangles as if their home was blessed by mathematics. She was about to close the notebook when one of the formulas underneath the picture caught her eye. What do you know, all this complicated math, and here was some basic freshman algebra, a minus x times a minus x. . . .

Darby's computer chimed, startling her. It was instant messaging service. Somebody named Bob had signed in. *Darby, are you there?*

Livey put down the notebook and stared at the screen. Darby hardly ever used IM. Who was this guy? Some online predator? Was this what Mrs. Blink had sensed?

She quickly typed: *Who r u?*

A moment. Then: *And you are?*

Darby's big older brother. Who r u?

His math tutor.

Whats yr name n where do u live?

Apologies, but I don't give out personal information on the Internet.

How do I know u r his math tutor?

Do you know what the Mandelbrot set is?

Livey wasn't a mathematician's daughter for nothing. She would play along. *It's that bubbly-looking thing.*

Elegantly put.

Livey sensed amusement. Annoyed, she typed, *U tell me then.*

The Mandelbrot set can be defined as the set of complex c-values for which the orbit of 0 under iteration of the complex quadratic polynomial $x^2 + c$ remains bounded.

That still doesn't prove anything.

Prove? That is more ironic than you know. Can you prove to me you are his big older brother?

Again Livey sensed amusement, but he signed off before she could reply. Her irritation lingered, and she wasn't pleased when her dad brought home one of his students to have dinner with them. The guy was an international student, and had the scrawniest neck and biggest

Adam's apple that Livey had ever seen. When they passed around the meat loaf, he asked, "Does this have pork in it?"

"Just beef," Livey said.

The guy lifted a forkful to his mouth. "You know one of the best things I like about America?" he asked as he chewed. "Bacon. I never ate bacon before. It's so delicious that even if it comes from pig, it is not pork."

"Next time we'll have BLTs," Jerry said.

Darby had divided his helping of meat loaf into two squares, and the peas he arranged into circles. That's how he ate his dinners, by geometry.

The student began talking to Jerry about entropy, a topic he was working on. To be polite and include Livey in the conversation, he asked her, "Do you know what entropy is?"

"A disease?" Livey hoped the frivolous answer would disqualify her from further participation.

Darby made a face. "You ought to dye your hair black so nobody can mistake you for a du—"

Livey pointed her fork at him. "Don't you dare say it." Of course she knew what entropy was. It was a measure of disorder. Her mother had taught this to her early. *Livey, could you please decrease the entropy in your bedroom?* "And by the way, who is this Bob guy you chat with online?"

Darby lowered his fork. "Were you snooping?"

"Yup."

"Dad! Can you tell Livey not to be such a snoop? I don't snoop on her."

"You aren't giving out any personal information, are you, Darby?"

Livey was surprised. For once her dad was being practical-minded. He even sounded stern.

"Of course not," Darby said indignantly.

"Then who is he?" Livey demanded.

"He helps me with math."

Jerry's brows perked up. "A mathematician?"

"You'd like him."

"What are you working on?"

Darby hesitated, glancing at the international student, who was busy scooping up a second helping of meat loaf. "A proof of something. I'll show you when I'm done."

Jerry grinned. "Like Andrew Wiles, hunh, working for years in secret on Fermat and then springing his proof on the world."

"But he got it wrong and had to fix it." Darby squared his shoulders. "Not me. I won't get mine wrong. It'll be perfect the first time."

After dinner, Darby flopped down on his bedroom's carpet, still dotted here and there with Pringle crumbs that had been yesterday's snack. Why hadn't Mrs. Blink vacuumed today? He brushed some of the crumbs to the side and then worked on the proof while waiting for Bob to come online.

The math that Aunt Ludy had been using was half a century old. Darby was applying a more modern technique that he had researched online to help him navigate the Hilbert spaces he needed. He was becoming more familiar with the abstract coral gardens of the offshore reef where Bob lived. It was like he was a scuba diver glimpsing parts of a beautiful creature without being able to see the whole of it.

The computer chimed. Darby quickly took his seat.

Your sister was asking about me, Bob said.

She's a snoop. Don't worry about her.

That is not logical. If she is a snoop, should I not worry about her?

No. She won't be able to figure you out.

Your mother could.

Why do you keep talking about her?

Why are you so hostile?

A mom doesn't just leave you. She didn't even fight my dad for custody. She said you keep Darby, like I was the sofa or something.

She writes you letters she does not send.

Darby stiffened. His fingers mistyped, and he had to backspace. *She does? Well, I don't care. I won't read them, I won't ever forgive her. And I'm not going to talk about her, so stop.*

A pause. *As you wish. Darby, may I ask, what is this?*

On the monitor flashed a picture. Relieved that they were no longer talking about his mother, Darby relaxed and typed, *That's the Leaning Tower of Pisa.*

Shouldn't it be straight?

The Straight Tower of Pisa wouldn't be so famous.

It is rather inelegant. Where is it?

In Italy.

Ah, yes. Italy. Perhaps soon I will be able to visit.

Um, Bob, when I prove you, could you take care of Julian and Roz for me? They're bullies at school. And Julian says bad things about my mom.

As you do.

Darby frowned. *I do not.*

Do not lie, Darby.

Well, yeah, okay, but I'm allowed to, she's my mom. Julian should keep his big fat mouth shut about her. Can you help me?

Not to worry, my dear boy. You are very close to finishing the proof. Keep up the good work!

After Bob signed off, Darby allowed himself a minute of pleasurable daydreaming, about Julian and Roz being scared out of their pants. Maybe even literally. He chuckled at the thought of them running around the lunchroom like chickens wearing only their underwear.

Thus inspired, he returned with renewed energy to his notebook and the proof of Bob.

12

HIGH CLOUDS OBSCURED the stars. The path through the woods was soggy from the day's drizzle. A group of people in olive-colored robes with simple hoods filed down the dark trail, carrying oil lamps.

They came to a clearing of wet grass and weed surrounded by trees, their leafy tops a jagged silhouette against the clouded night. The Elder was already waiting. The flat trunk of a deadfall provided a platform that was lit by oil lamps. On the platform was a wooden board with ten metal studs arranged in a triangle. The lamplight reflected smooth as oil off the bronze studs.

Before the board was an open brazier filled with glowing coals.

The twenty or so people lined up in two semicircles, facing the platform. One was a garbageman, another a banker. One of the women was a lawyer, another a housemaid. In the Secret Order of the Pythagorean Brotherhood there was no rank based on wealth or distinction. There was only a reverence for the all-encompassing Spirit of Number, from which all was created.

The Elder chanted, "O holy tetraktys, root of all wisdom and cre-ation, we come to you in humble adoration. Come to us, o divine Spirit of Number, and grant us knowledge. Reveal thyself, o blessed number!"

The Elder threw a handful of powder onto the brazier. The embers hissed, and a light haze of smoke wisped into the air. The smoke eddied and whirled and then formed into triangles, much more distinct than the last time. The voice that whispered to the Elder was much clearer.

Patience. The boy's mind is beautiful. Soon he will open the way for me to come in beauty and in truth, and you shall lead my disciples.

The Elder bowed in adoration.

13

IN THE CAFETERIA, Livey sat at her usual corner table with the other cheerleaders.

Taylor leaned across the table to sweetly ask, "How'd you do on the algebra test? We sure don't want you to get dropped from the squad before the big game."

As if it would break her heart, Livey thought. But she smiled just as sweetly. "I did fine."

Johnny had passed out the test for Mr. Savard. When he got to her, he whispered "Good luck." Had he said that sarcastically? Even now, thinking back on it, she couldn't tell. But despite all her studying, she had also needed all the luck she could get. She'd left three problems blank.

At the table, they started talking about Friday's postgame party. Trish, the squad captain, was going out with Stewart Ricci, and the party was going to be at his house. Ashlyn asked Chantelle if Todd was going to be giving rides and if there was room for her.

"I'm going with Derek in his Porsche," Taylor announced. "Too bad there's only room for me."

Chantelle said, "Oh, I don't know, you can squeeze two in the passenger seat, especially if you're as small as Livey."

Livey kicked her under the table. Taylor was a drama queen. Why get her all stirred up?

Ashlyn complained that her parents wanted her home by one. "I wish I had your dad, Livey. He never cares what time you get home."

"Livey's a *good* girl," Taylor said. "She's always home before midnight."

"It's so totally annoying," Livey said lightly. "If I stay out past midnight, my clothes turn into Wal-Mart discounts."

In the cafeteria, several hundred students joked and laughed. The weather had changed again, with a bright blue sky beyond the windows. The green lawn stretched away to the stadium. Tomorrow night, those big lights would blaze, and Livey would be aglow underneath them, chanting and cheering and dancing with the rest of the squad. They would give the Eagles that little bit of extra spirit to win the game—

She felt somebody watching her. She glanced to the cafeteria's back corner, where the dirty trays were dumped. The general all-around losers' corner. Johnny sat where he always sat, his back to the wall. On the table in front of him was his margarine tub. He hadn't even opened it.

The way he was getting skinnier by the day, Livey suspected there wasn't anything in there to eat. Poor students got a lunch subsidy, but maybe he was too proud. Maybe he would rather bring a pretend lunch.

Livey usually ate one of the cafeteria's salads. But at home this morning she had made a sandwich of leftover meat loaf, complemented by an apple from the fruit bowl, because otherwise the meat loaf wouldn't get eaten. She didn't like wasting food. She looked at Johnny's lunchbox and then impulsively grabbed her bag and threaded her way through the tables to sit down across from him. The others at the table fell silent and stared at her in confusion. She wasn't just breaking an unwritten social rule—it was as if she was doing something impossible, like floating in midair.

Johnny looked at her without expression. He fiddled with his lunch box. The cuffs of his cotton shirt were threadbare. One of the cuffs was caught up on his wrist. She could see the black edges of a tattoo.

"How did I do on the test?" she asked.

"I'm not grading them. Mr. Savard will give them back on Monday."

"I've been wanting to ask you something. When you said an apple times an apple is a unicorn, what did you mean?"

For a moment she thought he wasn't going to answer. Then he threaded his long white fingers together and put his elbows on the table. "If you have an infinite universe," he said, "then anything that *could* happen *must* happen, and anything that *could* exist *must* exist."

"So somewhere Harry Potter lives, hunh?" She smiled, putting all her warmth and charm into it. She was determined to get him to like her. He didn't smile back. She leaned forward, while trying to see if there was any food in the margarine tub. "Where are you from?"

He nodded over to the cheerleading table. "Your friends are wondering what you're doing here."

She glanced over her shoulder. Chantelle and the others were staring at her.

Opening the brown bag, she took out her meat loaf sandwich. "I don't know why I brought this. I'm not really hungry. You want it before I toss it?"

He lifted the tub's lid. Inside was a chunk of bread that looked like the out-of-date stuff the supermarkets threw out. Livey could imagine him picking through the Dumpsters for his food. "Brought my own."

"How about the apple?" she said jokingly, holding it up in her palm.

"The very first time a girl gave a guy an apple it didn't turn out so good." He looked at her again, but this time it was like a stab, his eyes cold and hard. "I don't need your charity. I don't need to be your friend. All right?"

14

BECAUSE OF HER petite size, Livey was one of the cheerleading squad's flyers, doing the high stunts and the throws. She was practicing the new Liberty and twist that Coach had shown them, with her bases, Chantelle and Trish, holding her up and then tossing her on the count, but she was having a hard time. She blew the stunt yet again, this time falling awkwardly and missing her teammates' hands, waiting to cradle her. She landed with a heavy thud on the mat. Trish bent over her. "My God, Livey, are you okay?"

Chantelle put her hands on her hips. "Your knees went limp on the throw," she said. "Remember to stay tight."

Livey puffed air up her sweaty face and glared at her best friend. "How about some sympathy first before the critique," she said, rubbing her thigh.

Livey was having trouble concentrating. It wasn't just her worry about the algebra test. It was Johnny Magnus, and the way he'd humiliated her in the cafeteria. God, how stupid she'd been. She should have learned her lesson that first time, in the library. At least then she'd been humiliated in private.

Across the gym, Coach Mazur stepped out of the office, where she had been called to the phone. "Let's pack it in, guys. Livey, can I see you for a second?"

Wondering what this was about, Livey limped over and took a seat in the cluttered office.

"You okay?" Coach asked as she poured a cup of water from the dispenser. "That was a nasty fall."

"I'm fine," Livey said, although her leg was hurting.

"You're anticipating the throw and leaning out. Study Taylor, how she does it."

Livey's heart lurched. Was this a subtle hint that Taylor was going to be picked, even though she was heavier and harder to cradle and had the cheerleading charm of a squid?

Coach Mazur handed Livey the cup. "Thanks," Livey said, taking a gulp.

"I just spoke with Mr. Savard. I asked him to grade your algebra test, just in case we have to figure out what to do. You flunked."

Livey burst out coughing. "But I couldn't have failed!" She wheezed. She was stunned. If she were dropped from the squad, then she would totally and utterly die, and maybe even perish for real. Tears threatened, but she told herself she wasn't going to cry. Not her, not Godeliva Elizabeth Ell. "I studied hard, Coach, I really did. I was sure I got a C minus at least. I studied for, like, *hours*."

"I worked out a deal. Mr. Savard will give you extra-credit homework to do by Monday. If you get ninety percent on that, he'll bump your grade up to a pass. See him before you go home."

Relief flooded through Livey, part of it expelled in a deep quavering sigh. "Thanks, Coach."

"But Livey. This is your first and last chance."

◪ ◪ ◪

In his classroom, Mr. Savard handed Livey two sheets from a yellow legal pad. On every second line he'd written down a problem.

"So many?" Livey asked in dismay.

"Miss Ell," he said, "I would be grateful if I were you. I have never before given a student a second chance like this."

"Oh, I am. Thank you *so* much, Mr. Savard."

As Livey left the room, she was wondering why he would give her, his least favorite student ever, a second chance. Maybe he wasn't so awful, after all.

Because she had to stay, Livey had missed her promised ride home. Now she had a long walk on an aching, bruised leg. After she hobbled a block down President, a brown Beetle rattled up beside her.

Johnny leaned across the front seat and stuck his head out the passenger window. "Want a ride?"

"That's okay."

"You're limping."

She hugged her schoolbag to her chest and said as coolly as she could, "I don't accept charity."

"That makes two of us," he said.

She was still wearing her workout clothes, and she was suddenly aware that her Soffe shorts, doubled up on the waistband, were riding awfully high on her legs. He leaned across and opened the passenger side door.

"Get in," he said.

It was an order. That he expected her to obey was infuriating. She would walk away, she *should* walk away, but instead she found herself stepping off the curb while casually straightening her waistband and tugging at the hems of the shorts. She got in and closed the door. A small cross like the one Johnny wore dangled from the rearview mirror. The gearshift knob had been replaced by a plastic skull. She snapped the seat belt in place and rested her schoolbag on her thighs. Dialing Chantelle on her cell, she got a busy signal but said anyway, "Chantelle? It's okay, I got a ride with Johnny Magnus." A pause. "Don't worry. I know how to take care of myself."

Out of the corner of her eyes she saw Johnny smile. It was a new kind of smile she hadn't seen on him before. If she were writing a story for English, she would have called it *sardonically amused*.

Johnny stuck an unlit cigarette in his mouth and stepped on the accelerator. The engine spluttered and threatened to die. He slammed the dashboard with the palm of his hand and the engine steadied. The gas gauge was below empty. Maybe it was broken. He smelled like dirt. Not in a bad way, though, but like good loam. Like the soil Livey's mom used to turn over with her spade when she was working on her rose garden.

Livey had loved helping her mom in the garden. When her mom hadn't returned after a month, her dad had ripped out all the bushes. Darby had helped.

What a strange thing to be thinking about, while in a strange car with a strange guy.

The Beetle came to the stop sign on Lincoln. Johnny slowed and looked both ways but didn't stop, rolling through the sign. "That's minus one hundred dollars," he said, talking around his cigarette, still unlit in the corner of his mouth.

"You trying to quit?" she said.

"Excuse me?"

"Smoking."

Again that smile. "Haven't really started." He took the cigarette out of his mouth and crushed it into the ash tray. It was crammed full of broken cigarettes, none of them smoked.

Without glancing in his rearview, he cut across the traffic on President, weaving around the cars. The Beetle's engine was more powerful than she would have thought. He was a terrible driver, stepping on the gas, and then hitting the brakes. At the next intersection, he turned onto South Farm Square, again doing a slow roll through a stop sign.

"Cops in this town are pretty strict," Livey said. "We're not talking about an algebra problem when you don't stop at the stop signs."

"Never knew a town that didn't have strict cops," he said.

Which, of course, raised the question, how many had he lived in? *Or,* Livey thought, *had run from?*

In the South Farm Square shopping center, a woman was backing out from a parking spot in front of the post office. Johnny had to brake hard. At that moment, the door to the adjacent Christian Book Store swung open, and Pastor Jimmy barged out, his black leather jacket flopping open. He was the youth pastor at the River Oaks Community Church, where the teens had their own special service. Livey scooted as low as she could, but too late. He saw her and stepped to the side of the Beetle. "How's it going, Livey? Haven't seen you in church for a while."

"There was summer cheer camp and then it's been real busy at school. You know."

"Maybe Johnny here can take you this Sunday."

Johnny lifted two fingers off the steering wheel in a casual greeting. "Hey, Pastor." The car in front moved. Pastor Jimmy tapped the top of the Beetle as though in blessing, and Johnny drove on.

Livey stared at him. "You go to church?"

"You sound surprised."

He probably goes just for the doughnuts, Livey thought. The youth church offered Krispy Kremes, a sure way to tempt anybody into attendance. "So where are you from? I mean, before here?"

"You already asked me that."

See? Livey told herself, hearing that coldness back in his voice, seeing that clench of his pale jaw.

Then he took a deep breath, as though forcing himself to relax. "Have you ever seen a moonbow?"

"What's that?"

"A rainbow, except it's at night, and caused by moonlight. There's this place . . . moonbows, they're magic."

Wherever he's from, he misses it, she thought. "Do you like it here in River Oaks?"

He drove in silence for a while. "I hate it," he finally said. "But there are some things you just can't avoid." He swerved around a UPS truck, barely missing an oncoming car, which angrily honked its horn. Cutting across two lanes, he spun onto South Beechwood. Half a block ahead was a railroad spur for the freight trains. The signal began to clang and flash, and the gate jerked to life, starting to lower. Johnny floored the accelerator.

"Johnny!" Livey yelped.

The Beetle flashed underneath the lowering gate and bounced across the track as the locomotive barreled around the curve, blaring its whistle.

"You can stop and let me out," Livey said angrily.

"Here?" He sounded genuinely surprised.

"I don't care what you do with your life, but you don't take risks with *mine!*" She was practically yelling.

His lips twitched, as though he were secretly amused and trying not to laugh. "I wouldn't take risks with your life, believe me." Even as he said that, he barely slowed for a third stop sign.

A siren sliced through the quiet of the residential streets, and a patrol car's lights flashed behind them. Johnny groaned and pulled over to the curb, opposite the duck pond at Lincoln Park.

"Told you," Livey said. She could have gotten out then, but she wanted to see this. The patrolman walked up to Johnny's window and brusquely asked for his license and registration. Johnny dug his

RICHARD LEWIS

license out of a grimy leather wallet and handed it over. The patrolman inspected it through his sunglasses and then said, "You ran that
stop sign."

Johnny was looking up at him, facing away from Livey. "That's
right. I did."

The patrolman's sunglasses sat like a shield on his face. He flicked
the corner of the license with his thumbnail and then abruptly handed
it back. "A lot of kids play here. Drive carefully." He walked away.

Astonished, Livey turned around and watched him get back in his
cruiser. "I can't believe it. He didn't even give you a warning."

Johnny was putting away his license. He looked at her. The blackness of his eyes was as dark and cold as a clear winter night, their green
flecks like sparks of fire.

They were the kind of eyes that made people do things.

She realized then that they were only a block from her house. She
had never told him where she lived.

She shoved open her door. "Thanks for the ride. I'll walk the rest of
the way." She shut the door without looking back and limped as fast as
she could into the park. As she crossed the arced bridge over the pond,
the little girl who played with Darby rushed by her. The sound of little
tennis shoes slapping on the wooden bridge suddenly stopped.

"Hey, you! Bossy sister!"

Livey gritted her teeth and turned around. "Yes?"

The girl was staring at her aching left thigh. "Your leg hurts."

"Doh."

"It will get better soon. Bye." And then she dashed off again.

15

MR. SAVARD SELECTED a fat white mouse from the cage. Stroking its head to calm it, he took it across the room to a large terrarium. Opening a hinged section on top, he released the mouse, which fell to the leafy floor. It squealed and bolted around the terrarium before perching on a branch. There it quivered in silent fright as a snake began to move among the leaves.

Flicking its tongue, the rattlesnake inched closer and struck.

Within seconds, the mouse was dead. The rattlesnake stretched its jaws and swallowed the mouse headfirst. The little pink tail disappeared almost as an afterthought.

Mr. Savard did not watch. There was no joy in the death of innocent creatures. Yet he had to feed his snakes so that he could continue to extract their venom, which he sent to a laboratory. Antivenin saved lives around the world, and Mr. Savard did his part to help. His father and grandfather, who had lived in the high Arizona desert, had also done the same. Family traditions were important.

When Mr. Savard was a boy, his grandfather had taken him to meetings of the Secret Order of the Pythagorean Brotherhood. Circles, they were called. The young Mr. Savard, who had loved numbers ever since he could count, was intrigued that one could worship the Spirit of Number.

Now he was an Elder of the local Circle. An enlightened Elder, who thought that many of the ancient rules were unnecessary. To be sure, sometimes he did touch the ground after a thunderclap, and he did avoid eating beans, but that was unimportant. What was important was the Spirit of Number, which, Mr. Savard had long been certain, could save the world from lurching even further into disaster.

He was not so naive as to believe that math by itself could solve the world's problems. No, it was the process of math, the logic, the calm reason, the unbiased thinking, the objective certainty of what was true and what was wrong. In math, what was right was clearly right, and what was wrong was clearly wrong. If people, from the homeless to world leaders, applied the spirit of math to their problems and disputes, then the world would be a far more peaceful and orderly place.

As the snake began to digest its meal, Mr. Savard returned to his office. He shook the fizz out of a can of ginger ale, and sipped a glass as he contemplated an old, handwritten paper on the desk before him. His grandfather had been a Los Alamos scientist and leader of the Circle in which Ludavica Ell had been initiated. The paper was one of her early drafts of the Thingamabob Conjecture, which she had privately written up for her Elder.

Mr. Savard's grandfather had made attempts to prove the Conjecture. He had attached pages of his efforts. At the bottom of the last page, he had broken off in mid-equation and written in capital letters: "DANGEROUS KNOWLEDGE! ESTERICI LEVEL ONLY!"

Mr. Savard sighed and shook his head. The exalted Estericis who led the brotherhood were hidebound traditionalists with glue for brains. There was no question that they knew about the Conjecture, but they had swept such knowledge into the vaults and pretended not to know a thing about it. It was fortunate in the extreme that Mr. Savard had found this copy of the paper among his grandfather's voluminous documents. He had become intrigued by the Conjecture, and began to puzzle his way through his grandfather's math.

Up to that point in his life, the Spirit of Number was simply a Higher Concept. Then, during prayers before the tetraktys, the Spirit of Number had spoken to him out of the wind, out of the fire. Falling prostrate to the floor, he whispered, *Who am I to be chosen as your prophet? I am just an ordinary high school algebra teacher.* Apart from a secret desire to be voted Teacher of the Year, he was not an ambitious man. But chosen he was, to prepare the way and renew the Secret Order of the Pythagorean Brotherhood, to make the Brotherhood a pure vessel for the Spirit of Number, who would guide the world back to sanity, to genuine peace and true justice for all.

Mr. Savard still trembled at the awesome task he had been assigned.

In his kitchen, he fussed together a salad with lightly grilled fish. After he ate, he strolled through the warehouse extending below his converted loft. He lived in the old industrial section of town, by the freight tracks. A select night crew of immigrants was busy boxing and packing TETRA KUIZ games.

"Are we keeping to schedule?" he asked Manny, his foreman.

"To the dot," Manny said. The foreman was a barrel-chested fellow whom Mr. Savard had pulled out of the gutter in front of the Blue Light, the notorious bar near the Evergreen apartments. This had been on a Sunday afternoon, when Mr. Savard had gone looking for somebody to save. To worship and make plans was fine and necessary, but he had felt a need to go out and actually do something concrete. The Spirit had led him to Manny. Mr. Savard was now tutoring Manny every Saturday in basic algebra, and Manny was an eager, if sometimes befuddled, student. More importantly, he was now a responsible, hard-working, clean-living father and husband.

The idea for the TETRA KUIZ game had come to Mr. Savard during a prayer, and its success had come as a surprise. He kept scrupulous accounts of the money, and paid the IRS their share without complaint. Mr. Savard had no desire to be rich—he owned only three brown suits and two brown toupees, for who needed more? But to spread the message, and to reorganize the brotherhood, would require money. The TETRA KUIZ game was loading up the coffers.

Mr. Savard had spent some of the money on an anonymous scholarship for young Mr. Darby Ell to attend Newton Academy. It was the Spirit who had told him to do this. The boy, the Spirit said, would finish the proof, and then the Spirit could finally be revealed in all its Truth and Beauty, with Mr. Savard as its chief disciple.

Contemplating a loaded pallet of TETRA KUIZ games ready to be shipped to California, Mr. Savard thought again of the sister. He wondered once more how it was possible that dull Miss Godeliva Ell could be the sister of brilliant Mr. Darby Ell. He sincerely wished that Livey would one day find the joy of algebra, and prayed to the Spirit to touch her, but she was one of those rebels who hardened her heart.

The boy, on the other hand, was making progress on the proof. Mr. Savard didn't wish for the equilibrium of his home environment to be disturbed. And if Miss Ell were dropped from the cheerleading squad, she would no doubt give way to much wailing and gnashing of teeth.

This was why he had for the first time given a student a second chance.

THE BRIGHT BLUE weather continued and promised a gorgeous night for Friday's home game. Livey bounced through her classes.
Even algebra couldn't dampen her spirits. Johnny Magnus didn't show,
and she didn't see him elsewhere in the halls, either. It wasn't that she
was looking for him, she honestly wasn't, but after all these days of him
popping unexpectedly into view, his absence was odd. Instead, it was
Derek Mankowski who seemed to be crossing her path more often
than usual, giving her secret smiles.

"You know, I haven't seen Johnny today," she said to Chantelle.
They had finished lunch and were sitting on a bench in the Quad.
Chantelle had her face up to the bright sun, her eyes closed.

"Johnny who?"

"Johnny Magnus."

Chantelle opened her left eye and squinted at Livey. "You're thinking about *him*?"

"He gave me a ride home after practice."

Chantelle's other eye popped open. "You got a ride with *that* guy?"

"I was hurting pretty bad from that fall," Livey said defensively. "He saw me limping."

"You weren't limping last night."

That was true, Livey thought. When she'd gone back to the school in the evening to decorate the football players' lockers, the ache in her thigh was completely gone. Just like that little girl said it would be.

"Well, I was hurting, and it was just a ride," Livey said.

Chantelle pointed her finger. "I got this feeling he's bad news all the way around. You best stay away from him, is what I have to say."

And that, of course, made Livey feel even worse that she hadn't confided in Chantelle about the ride, his weird nonsmoking smoking habit, the way he drove, and especially that look in his eyes. . . .

Chantelle chattered about Alain O'Brian, her latest crush. Alain wasn't into sports. He played drums for a garage band. Chantelle didn't say a word about Derek, which should have aroused Livey's suspicions.

Last period, as the cheerleaders gathered in the gym before the students streamed in for the pep rally, Taylor cornered Livey by the stands. "Did you put the candy in Derek's locker last night?"

Confused, Livey said, "What?"

"Derek's locker. The candy in it. Was that you?"

"I didn't even touch his locker."

"It was all lined inside with candy."

"It wasn't me, I swear. I don't know his combination. I don't even know where his locker is, exactly."

"There was a big chocolate *L* in there. And lots of Hershey's Kisses."

Ah, that explained Derek's smiles. But the way Taylor was getting all steamed up, Livey knew she had better defuse this quick. "*L* stands for *love*, too, you know. Let him think it was you, because it sure wasn't me. Honest, Taylor." She flicked a glare at Chantelle, who was standing nearby and eavesdropping with a way too innocent look.

Livey waited a minute and then sauntered over to Chantelle's side. "It was you, wasn't it?"

"What was?"

"Don't give me that innocent look. I don't need a matchmaker."

"Yes, you do."

"God, Chantelle."

Chantelle draped a big arm around her. "Well, He sure isn't helping you, so it's up to me." She squeezed and let go. "Now it's up to you to help yourself."

The students began to pour into the gym.

Livey casually looked around the packed bleachers. No Johnny Magnus anywhere.

Probably sick, Livey thought. *And why am I thinking about him?*

She redid her hair scrunchy and resolutely put him out of her mind.

17

FROM BEHIND THE jungle gym, Darby watched Julian, Roz, and the rest of the Boys' Club stroll across the soccer field. They disappeared around the back of the bleachers into their clubhouse. After waiting another minute, he scooted along the side of the field to the big sycamore tree and climbed the bleachers to sit in its shade. He pretended to read a book as he spied on the Club through a crack in the wooden tread between his shoes.

The Boys' Club had gathered in a circle around a TETRA KUIZ board.

"O holy tetraktys," Julian chanted, "root of all wisdom and creation, we come to you in humble adoration. And come to us, o divine Spirit of Number, and grant us knowledge. Reveal thyself, o blessed Number!"

Even sitting out in the open, Darby could feel the expectant silence, as if a spirit was going to materialize from the board. *This is silly,* he told himself, but if it was so silly, then why was he holding his breath, wondering what was going to happen?

Then one of the boys broke wind, a magnificent orchestral fart.

Roz pinched her nose. "Gross!"

The circle burst into howls of laughter, and fell apart.

But Darby wasn't smiling. All of a sudden, the final steps of the proof plopped down into his brain. Just like that.

That afternoon, as he rushed off the bus, he told the little girl that he was really busy and couldn't play. Her face fell.

"You *have* to play," she said.

"I'll give you a puzzle to think about until tomorrow. Why don't Eskimos ever eat penguins?"

"Duh. Penguins only live at the South Pole."

"How about this one, then. Imagine you dive off a sinking ship and are surrounded by sharks. How do you survive?"

"Do I have to swim, or can I walk on the water?"

"Duh back. You swim, like everybody else."

"I don't know. How?"

"Think about it. I'll tell you tomorrow."

She ran happily to the playground swing.

In his bedroom, Darby shucked off his school jacket and threw himself down on the carpet with the open notebook. The late-afternoon sun spilled through the window like a blessing. He feverishly wrote out the last few pages, an exultant, dizzying sprint. He saw more and more of Bob. Mathematically speaking, Bob was as simple as the triangular number 10, yet one that was ceaselessly on the move, one point moving to another with the same breathtaking elegance and beauty of an imaginary black-tipped shark.

Imaginary, because Bob was unlike any other mathematical object that Darby had ever encountered.

Well, of course. He was from another universe.

Darby finished the last equation and then wrote, with emphatic strokes of his pen, *Q.E.D. Quod erat demonstratum*, the traditional fancy

Latin way of saying that the proof was complete and without flaw.

It was so beautiful, so simple, so elegant that tears pricked Darby's eyes.

"At last. Well done, my boy." The soft voice came from everywhere in the room. The air quivered. Shimmering triangles appeared from all four corners and then came together, weaving in and out of one another, curving through space, their motion made visible by the faint sheen of colors trailing behind them.

Darby backed up against his bed, both awed and frightened out of his wits.

The triangles streamed toward the poster of da Vinci's *Vitruvian Man*. Everything seemed to hold its breath.

And then the Vitruvian man stepped out of his circle, expanding to life size as he did so. A real man, the size of Darby's father, except he had four arms and four legs and was wearing only a maple leaf. His brown eyes were clear and deep. He smiled at Darby, a kind and friendly and even mischievous smile that raised a dimple on his cheek.

Darby's fear evaporated. "Whoa," he breathed. "You can do that?"

"It is probably best if I manifest as one of your kind, Darby." Bob's low, rich voice sounded like stained glass.

"Um, not exactly. You have four arms and four legs."

Bob studied his four hands. "I rather like the symmetry. But as you wish." Two of his arms and two of his legs vanished. He looked down at himself. He removed the maple leaf. Darby looked away.

"What's this?"

"Um, it's a penis. You pee through it. Urinate."

"Rather unsightly, do you not think? I shall remove it as well."

Darby quickly peeked. What the maple leaf had covered was now smooth flesh, like a doll's. "Maybe I better get you one of my dad's old suits."

"No need." Bob shimmered away, like water draining through a filter. A moment later he reappeared, dressed in chinos, an open-necked shirt, and a tweed jacket. With his mane of brown hair parted in the middle, he looked like a cross between a rock star and a mathematician. In his hand was a Shedd Aquarium shopping bag, which he handed to Darby. "I believe these are yours."

Darby stuck his hand in the bag, and yowled as something bit his finger. A tiny black-tipped shark wriggled on the end of his thumb. He shook it off. "Better put that back in the ocean," he said.

Bob picked up the shark and thrust his hand into a fold of Hilbert space. "Indian Ocean or Pacific?"

"Or, wait, the Shedd Aquarium."

"Elegant idea," Bob said with a wink. Darby thought he heard a plop. Bob withdrew his empty hand and nodded at the bag. "Look again."

Darby cautiously peeked. Within were the TETRA KUIZ board game and the Shedd Aquarium explorer set. The explorer items, however, were no longer plastic toys. Like the shark, they were real—a real metal knife, flashlight with batteries, powerful binoculars, a shiny brass compass with a wrist strap, a solid silver whistle. "G-geez Louise," he stuttered.

"I thought you would be pleased," Bob said, sounding pleased himself. "The originals were unsightly. Unsymmetrical, poorly formed. Truth, beauty, and elegance, Darby: Let these three guide your life."

"But how do you do it, make things real?"

"A trivial exercise. Everything material in your world has an idealized mathematical proof of existence that can be manipulated. The material elements fall out like the remainders do in long division. Your universe is rather messy and simplistic."

"Nice! Can you divide me out an iPhone?"

There was a rapid double knock on the door, with Livey saying at the same time, "Knock-knock."

"Quick, hide!" Darby hissed at Bob as he shoved the explorer set under the bed.

Bob didn't move. "Who is there?" he called out, with another wink at Darby.

"Bob, this isn't a knock-knock joke!"

"Who's that with you?" Livey demanded, pushing open the door. She stopped and stood there, damp from a shower, with only a towel wrapped around her. Darby winced, anticipating one of her blood-curdling cheerleader-trained screams, but she just stared silently at Bob.

He smiled pleasantly. "Hello, big older brother."

She emitted a sharp little *eek* and beat a quick retreat but was back in a second, her bathrobe belted tightly around her. "Who are you? And why are you in my brother's room?"

Darby pushed his glasses up on his nose. Oh boy, how to handle this? "This is Bob. Bob Alpha. You know, my math tutor. Bob, this is my sister Livey."

"We have met, I do believe," Bob said. "Although not in person."

"I didn't know you were going to, like, actually *visit*." She turned to Darby while keeping her gaze on Bob. "You should have told me."

"Sorry. I forgot."

"Where are you from, Bob?"

"Italy," Darby said. "His real name's Roberto, but he likes palindromes. You know, same spelling either way. He's visiting. A conference."

Bob spread his arms. "The truth is that I prefer to think of myself as having no particular nationality. Mathematicians are a universal brotherhood, no?"

Darby could tell that his suspicious sister was weighing this. Over the years, many mathematicians from around the world had stayed with them. So Bob's presence wasn't too far out of the ordinary. Still, Darby added the one thing that was sure to tip the balance in Bob's favor. "It's okay, Livey. Bob knows Mom."

She perked up at that. "You know my mother?"

"Maria? Our Mares? A delightful woman. She has an elegant mind."

Darby could see that striking home, reassuring his sister. "Darby, why don't you show Bob to the living room and get him something to drink? I'll go change."

In the kitchen, Wiles was sleeping upside down in the empty fruit bowl. He woke with a stretch and then froze when he spotted Bob. After a second, he bolted, losing traction on the bowl's smooth surface before tumbling out and sprinting with crippled stride to hide underneath the couch.

"That's Wiles," Darby said. "Our cat."

"Ah, yes. *Felis sylvestris catus*. Others prefer to call the species *felix domesticus*. The debate rages. But what is wrong with him? He is unsymmetrical."

"His leg got caught in a garbage compactor."

"Is that so? Why do you keep him?"

"Hunh? Because he's our cat." Darby opened the fridge. "What do you want to drink?"

Bob inspected the contents. "Rather messy," he said.

"It is?" Darby said in surprise. What Mrs. Blink kept neat, Livey tidied up into super neat.

Bob did his shimmer thing into the fridge, obscuring the contents with a crystalline mist. When he remerged as Bob, the shelves of the fridge had been rearranged by geometry. All the round things were on the top—the head of lettuce that should have been in the crisper, the eggs that should have been in the egg rack, the round chocolates that should have been in the gold box. The square chocolates were in the middle rack with the individual squares of leftover lasagna, along with the rectangular jug of milk.

"There," Bob said in satisfaction. "Much more elegant, do you not think?"

Darby sort of agreed, but he quickly said, "Holy cow, Bob, put everything back the way it was."

"Holy cow?" Bob said, perplexed. "Do you worship cattle?"

"Just a saying. Put everything back, quick!"

"Why?"

"Because Livey will think *I* did it. And please, you'd better not do that vanishing trick if anybody's around. It would be hard to explain."

Bob did as Darby asked and then pointed to the milk. "I shall try some of that." Darby poured him a glass.

Bob took a sip and nodded appreciatively. "Excellent vintage."

"Um, Bob? You use the word vintage when it's about wine. For milk, it's like whole milk, low fat, chocolate. What you're drinking is low fat. Livey won't let Mrs. Blink buy anything else. And the Cokes in those cans? They all have to be diet, because if we have regular, she might take one by mistake, or so she says."

"Low fat," Bob repeated. He wandered out to the living room with the glass, which he sipped as he studied the scribbled equations on the white board.

"My dad's working on the Riemann Hypothesis," Darby explained. He suddenly thought of something. His brows shot up, his ears shifted, and his glasses slipped down his nose. "You wouldn't be able to help him prove it, would you?" he asked, shoving his glasses snug to his face again.

"That is certainly possible," Bob said, and finished the milk. He handed the glass back to Darby. "May I try something else?"

Darby got him one of the Diet Cokes and a napkin to wipe his milk mustache.

Livey rushed into the living room dressed in her cheerleading outfit.

"Holy cow," Bob said. "That is a most interesting costume. Are you attending a ball?"

Livey looked nonplussed. Darby quickly said, "That's a cheer-leading uniform. She's a cheerleader. There's a football game tonight." To Livey he added, "Guess what? Bob says he can help Dad with the Riemann Hypothesis."

"Gosh, you're not another one of those Riemann addicts, are you? You guys get together and it's like, hello, what planet did you all come from?"

"Planet?" Bob said absently, studying the can of Coke. He held it up to his ear and shook it.

Darby realized that Bob didn't know how to open the pop tab. He thought that this was it, Livey was going to bust Bob right on the spot and order him out of the house.

Instead, Livey sighed and said, "You mathematicians. Don't open that, it'll spray everywhere now. I'll get you another." She did, popping the tab for him.

"Thank you, Livey," he said. He did something with his smile, added some sort of oomph to it that made her neck go pink. Darby stared in fascination. He had never seen his sister blush before. Bob was still smiling at her as he raised the can and took a sip.

His eyes widened. The sip spurted out his mouth. Livey squealed and jumped back. Bob fell into a coughing fit, Darby slapping him on the back so he could whisper in his ear, "It's not like milk; pop drinks are carbonated."

The hallway door to the garage opened, and Jerry Ell stepped into the hall, home from his afternoon classes at the college. He caught sight of Bob and said a pleasant but puzzled hello. Darby quickly introduced Bob as an Italian mathematician. He was worried that his dad would ask questions about where Bob had studied and which professor he'd studied with, questions that mathematicians always asked each other, but Bob mentioned the title of one of Jerry Ell's papers that was float-ing around the Internet. "I do not understand the lemma you used."

Jerry's face lit up with delight and he whisked Bob to the white-board to explain.

Outside, a car honked its horn. Livey said, "That's me, got to go. Bye."

Bob glanced away from the whiteboard. "It was wonderful meeting you."

She caught Darby's eye and nodded at the Diet Coke can on the counter. "Make sure that goes into the recycle bin."

Jerry discussed his ideas on the Riemann Hypothesis with Bob as twilight faded into night.

Darby finally broke in. "Dad, I'm hungry, and I bet Bob is too."

Jerry glanced at his watch. "Listen, want to go to the football game? We can grab a hot dog there to eat."

"I would be pleased to go to the football game, but I would rather not eat any dogs of any temperature."

Jerry chuckled. "Darby, you want to come?"

Jerry made an effort to attend Livey's home games, while Darby usually stayed at home and watched TV. But he figured that he'd better go along and keep an eye on Bob.

As his dad changed his clothes, Darby explained to Bob that a hot dog wasn't a real dog. It was a sausage made out of beef or pork.

"Even so, I am a vegetarian," Bob announced.

Darby made both of them a quick peanut butter and jelly sand-wich. Bob took a bite and nodded in appreciation. "Delicious."

"It's the Skippy Super Chunk peanut butter. It's the best. My sister once tried to trick me with Jif."

"I see," Bob said, although Darby wasn't sure so sure he did. Darby had to keep reminding himself that as human as Bob seemed, he was actually as alien as you could get—an intelligent, conscious, math-ematical function from another universe.

Bob finished the rest of his Coke and contemplated the empty can. "What is a recycle bin?"

"It's a garbage can for things you can recycle, like paper and metal. It's out the back. I'll throw that away later for you."

"Your sister likes to be tidy, does she?"

"The hangers in her closet? They're half an inch apart. It's like she measures with a ruler."

"That is good. She possesses a wonderful symmetry." Bob opened his mouth wide, wider than any human mouth could possibly go, and his even, white teeth turned sharp and triangular. He popped the Coke can into his mouth and swallowed it. "There," he said. "All gone, neat and tidy."

18

MR. SAVARD WAS feeding the mice, which he would later feed to the rattlesnakes, when music suddenly began to play, coming from everywhere. Triangles appeared in the corners of the room, not just ordinary triangles, but the most beautiful triangles that Mr. Savard had ever seen in all their sine and cosine glory. He fell to his knees. His soul trembled to the music, not just ordinary music, but the music of the spheres.

A voice spoke—whether Mr. Savard was actually using his ears to hear, he could not say.

Do not be alarmed. Go to the football game. There look for a guest accompanying Darby Ell and his father. For unto you the Spirit of Number has been proved.

The triangles melted away, the music faded.

Mr. Savard grabbed his coat and rushed out of the house.

OVER THE YEARS, Livey had met many of her parents' weird mathematician friends. Some had spent a night or two in the guest room off the garage. One gnomelike man from Australia would get up at four in the morning and bang pots in the kitchen in order to wake her dad so they could start talking math before the sun rose. After a couple days, her mom checked the man into the Holiday Inn.

Then there was the woman mathematician from Columbia University in New York City. She had never seen cows. Even though River Oaks was a Chicago suburb, it was within short driving distance of working farms. No way did Livey think of herself as a country girl, that's for sure—not when her favorite place on earth was downtown's Michigan Avenue—but never having seen a cow? Unbelievable. Livey's dad piled them all into the car and drove the woman out to the nearest farm, where a farmer kept a small herd of Angus cattle. As they drove down the graveled road by the fenced pasture, they spotted one of the cows. Little Darby piped up helpfully, "Angus cows are all black."

The woman studied the cow and then said, "There exists a field, containing at least one cow, of which at least one side is black."

That was how mathematicians thought.

This guy, Bob, wasn't any different. Shaking and listening to a Coke can! Was he working out the mathematics for sloshing liquids? But he sure was cute. He reminded her of somebody, but she couldn't say who. Brad Pitt? Not exactly, but close.

At the high school stadium, the crowd streamed in, students and families and River Oaks fans all wanting revenge for last year's conference championship defeat against the Wildcats.

Livey spotted her dad taking a seat on the home side bleachers. With him was Bob. Darby, too.

Somebody else pushed through the line toward them, and pushing rudely, too, causing one of the town's matrons to stumble.

"Oh my God," Livey said to Chantelle. "It's Mr. Savard. He's actually come to a game." Mr. Savard briefly greeted her father and brother but positively slobbered all over Bob. The way he fawned, practically bowing to Bob in awe and adoration, you'd think Bob was some sort of superstar to boring algebra teachers.

Livey scanned the bleachers, checking out everybody else who'd come.

But no Johnny Magnus.

Not that she was really looking for him.

The game started. Livey kept an eye on her family as she cheered. Her dad leaned close to Bob to talk over the noise of the crowd and the announcers and the band. He pointed at the lines and goals, explaining the rules of the game. Bob seemed interested not only in the game but also in the cheerleaders and their cheers and time-out routines. A couple times he caught Livey's eye and smiled at her. She smiled back and shook her blue-and-gold pom-poms.

Despite the crowd's spirited enthusiasm, by halftime the Eagles had lost a few feathers and were down by sixteen points. The Wildcats were too big and fast. *But you never give up,* Livey thought as the cheerleaders gathered on the field for their halftime dance. To her disappointment, Bob wasn't in his seat to watch.

The routine led up to the new stunt they'd practiced all week. Standing in the one-legged Liberty stance way above the ground, Livey felt herself losing her balance as her bases were getting ready to throw her. Oh God, she was going to blow it, right in front of everybody. As if anticipating her humiliation, the music became a jangle of noise, and the glare of the lights blinded her.

Out of nowhere, one of those blazing squares of light seemed to wrap around her and stabilize her. Livey nailed the twist, tight and fast. It was almost as if something was helping her spin. It was kind of dizzying, as a matter of fact, but when she bounced out of her teammates' cradling arms to her feet, exhilaration swooshed through her. She felt like she could will the Eagles to an upset victory.

During the second half, the Wildcat quarterback began throwing incompletes and interceptions. One pass into the end zone, the ball was dropping into the receiver's outstretched hands when it spurted out of his reach and bounced off the grass. The Wildcats' coach threw his clipboard down to the ground.

For the Eagles, the ball couldn't do anything wrong. An Eagle pass got swatted by a Wildcat lineman, then bounced off another defender's helmet into a loopy zigzag and fell right into the hands of a startled Eagle who ran it in for a touchdown.

The Wildcats' coach threw his clipboard to the ground.

With ten seconds left in the game, the Eagles were down by one and attempting a thirty-yard field goal. The kicker kicked. The ball arced high and began to fade short and wide. Then it seemed to straighten up and nicked the inside of the goalpost. The ref thrust his arms upright in the air, signaling the three points.

The Wildcats' coach threw his clipboard to the ground. He stormed onto the field, with his team following him, demanding that the football be checked.

In the uproar that followed, Livey noticed that Bob was back in his place and on his feet, shaking his fist and booing at the Wildcats' coach with everyone else. He seemed to be hugely enjoying himself. He caught her eye again and winked at her, as though they were sharing a secret. Flustered, she looked away. That was when she spotted Johnny Magnus, leaning against the side railing halfway up the stands. She couldn't be sure, the way the crowd was bouncing around all over the place, but it looked like the only thing Johnny was paying attention to was Bob.

The referees finally got the teams settled down for the last few seconds of the game. The Eagles' kickoff was run out of bounds for the final play. The crowd whooped, the band burst into the Eagles' fighting song, Livey and the other cheerleaders danced.

Next time she looked, Johnny was gone.

GOING HOME AFTER the game, Darby sat in the back of the car with Livey, who was going to shower and change before heading out to a party. Bob was in the front seat, marveling at the strange behavior of football coaches.

Bob had pretty much behaved himself for the first half of the game, sipping a regular, not diet, Coke. The high school teacher who sat with them had shown Bob how to shake the fizz out first. He was Livey's algebra teacher, of all people. Mr. Savard had fussed over Bob like Bob was royalty or something. As Bob watched the game, he said he found football rather delightful and the cheerleaders, he said, were rather quaintly charming. Darby wasn't so sure that Livey would like to be described as *quaint*.

When the teams went to their locker rooms at halftime, Bob commented on the numbers on the scoreboard. "Three and nineteen. Prime numbers."

"Unfortunately, they're the wrong way around," Jerry said. "We're losing."

"This is not a good thing?"

"Of course, it's only a game, but Livey's going to be disappointed."

"Ah. And we do not wish for her to be disappointed, do we?" Bob excused himself to get another Coke and didn't return until the final kickoff of the game. Mr. Savard had been beside himself with worry.

But Darby knew what had happened.

Boy, he sure hoped Livey would never find out that Bob had cheated for the Eagles. She'd freak. And not quaintly, either.

In the car, Jerry said, "Hey, Bob, we have a spare guest room. You're more than welcome to stay with us."

Darby heard Livey muttering under her breath, "Oh, God."

"That would be delightful," Bob said.

"Terrific. We'll swing by and get your stuff. Where are you staying?"

"Where am I staying?" Bob repeated in a bemused tone.

"The Holiday Inn off Roosevelt," Darby said.

"That's practically on our way home. A minor elliptic detour."

Next to the hotel was a Baskin-Robbins, doing a brisk Friday night business. "I'll go help Bob," Darby said as they swung into the hotel's parking lot. "Dad, why don't you and Livey get an ice cream? Vanilla cones for me and Bob."

"Well, look who's being bossy now," Livey said.

"Butter pecan, Liv. How can you resist?"

Mention butter pecan in the vicinity of an ice-cream parlor, and Livey turned into a zombie. Darby smiled as she marched off.

In the lobby, he told Bob, "You're going to have to make yourself a suitcase." He pointed to a loaded trolley. "Like one of those. And some clothes to put in it. We'd better find someplace private so you can do that thing you do."

Darby waited for an empty elevator and went up with Bob. "Quick, now," he said.

Bob's arm vanished up to its elbow in Hilbert space. He withdrew a battered plastic suitcase, which had a name tag.

"You didn't take this from some room, did you?" Darby asked.

"Why not? It already has clothes in it that will fit me."

"You can't do that. It's called stealing. Put that back and make a new one."

"Your lovely, symmetrical sister is right. You *are* bossy." But Bob did as he was told. He returned the first suitcase and withdrew another, a shiny aluminum one. The name tag said *Bob Alpha Omega*. "Are you satisfied?"

"I'm cool."

"Truly? I am rather warm myself."

As they strode across the lobby, a security officer cut across and intercepted them. "Excuse me, sir," he said to Bob. "Are you a guest here?"

"We were going to be," Darby said. "But there's this lady smoking in the stairwell on the third floor. We'll be finding a better hotel."

That sent the officer scurrying for the stairs.

"You lie very well," Bob said.

"You better learn how yourself."

Bob looked horrified. "Not I. I cannot lie. I am truth."

"Then you're going to have to learn how to fudge it."

His dad and sister were back with the ice cream. Jerry popped the trunk and tucked Bob's suitcase away. Bob studied his vanilla cone with interest.

"What, they don't have ice cream in Italy?" Livey said in a teasing tone.

"An interesting conical shape."

Darby stood in front of Bob and licked his cone, giving him the eye signal, *You eat it like this; you don't pop the whole thing in your mouth like you did the Coke can.*

Bob followed Darby's example. His brows rose. "Delicious."

Halfway home, Bob began to wince and twitch. As they got out of the car, he whispered to Darby that he needed to see him at once and in private. Darby took him into his bedroom. Bob's face was pinched with distress, and his knees were jittery. "Something is wrong," he said through clenched teeth. "I feel very uncomfortable. As though something inside me is going to burst."

Darby instantly understood. "It's what you drank. Your bladder's full and you have to go pee. Um, you're going to need your, you know, penis."

"Ah. I see."

"The bathroom is down the hall. Better use it quick before Livey does."

Bob rushed off before Darby could explain to him certain rules. Livey swept into the bathroom after Bob had emerged and then marched right on out again. She ordered Darby to her bedroom.

"I don't care if he's from Italy," she said, "but this is America, and in America we lift the toilet seat."

Darby sat Bob down on his bed and explained that rule and others. "Always put everything back where you got it from," he said. "And no noise on Saturday and Sunday mornings when she's sleeping in. And wet towels go back on the racks, and don't you ever *ever* use her toothbrush if you can't find yours."

Bob plunged his hand into Hilbert space and retrieved a SpongeBob Squarepants toothbrush. "This item?"

"That's a kid's brush."

"Truthfully, Darby, my teeth do not require brushing." Bob opened his mouth and again his teeth became sharp and triangular and shimmered through black space for a moment before reappearing as normal-looking teeth. It was a good reminder to Darby that as charmingly human as Bob might appear to be, he was still an alien.

Boy, he *really* hoped Livey wouldn't find out. She barely understood ninth-grade algebra. How was she going to be able to understand a math function from another universe?

The front doorbell chimed.

Livey called out, "Darby! Your little friend is here!"

Bob stared at the bedroom door. "What little friend is that?"

"Just this weird girl—"

Even before Darby finished speaking, Bob vanished in a silvery swish of air.

Darby went out to the foyer. His sister blocked the front door, her arms folded across the blouse and jacket she'd put on, giving the girl the stern Livey eye.

The girl was saying, "But he promised to tell me the answer to the riddle."

"Do you know what time it is? It's ten o'clock!"

"No, it's not. It is nine fifty-three."

"I want to know your name and where you live."

She scrunched up her nose. "I'm not going to tell you."

"Oh, for Pete's sake," Livey said.

Out on the street, a car with several of Livey's cheerleading friends pulled up to the curb and honked. Her best friend, Chantelle, the one who always played the stereo too loud when she came over to visit, leaned out to yell, "Come on, Livey, we're already late."

Livey got her bag and told Darby, "You make sure she gets home."

The girl firmly shut the door and turned to Darby. "Where is he?"

"Who?"

"Bob. He's dangerous."

"He's not dangerous. He loves truth and beauty. And how did you know he was here?"

The girl didn't answer. She marched past Darby down the hall and into his bedroom. Standing by Darby's bed, she squinted fiercely around the room. "Come out," she demanded. Nothing happened. She picked up Darby's notebook from the desk and opened it to the last page of the proof. She traced the final letters with her fingers. "Q.E.D.," she intoned.

There was a quivering of air. Rainbow triangles appeared, restlessly moving about. Bob's soft voice sounded from everywhere. "My dear Aether. What do you wish?"

"You know what."

Bob remained silent, the triangles darting even more restlessly.

"What's going on?" Darby said.

"He promised he'd go back to where he belonged." The girl put her hands on her hips. "You did. You promised. *I have to be proved first and then I will go.* That's what you said."

"I find this world rather fascinating, in a morbid way," Bob said.

Aether looked at Darby. "I told you he was dangerous."

Darby held up his hands. "Whoa, stop. What did Bob call you? Your name?"

"Now I bet he doesn't want to go."

"Either? That's your name?"

"Aether. A-E-T-H-E-R."

Darby pushed his glasses up on his nose. "And you are who, exactly?"

The triangles melded together and Bob appeared, still holding the SpongeBob toothbrush. "She is a minor epsilon of a transcendental variety. An angel, you might say."

Darby felt for his desk chair and slowly sat down. "Holy cow. Really?" But to his surprise, he really wasn't as surprised as he should have been. Bob himself was incredible, so what was an angel?

Aether scowled. "I'm not an angel. I'm a sentinel seraph."

"Not a very good one," Bob said. "A careless pipsqueak."

She stomped over and kicked his shin. "You tricked your way past me."

"I most certainly did not! You were being derelict in your duty. Playing hyperdimensional hide-and-seek with your cherub friends. If you had only taken the time to point me back in the right direction, I would not be here."

"And now you're proved. Time for you to go. Or else."

"Aether, my little seraph, let us be rational with each other. I am on your side, the side of truth and beauty and elegance. Who would not want to go home? This world is full of misery and asymmetry. Yet how do I get home? Permit me several days to locate the proper space-time coordinates."

Aether thought for a moment. "Two days."

"Three. I wish to assist Darby's father with the Riemann Hypothesis."

"That's right," Darby said quickly. "If my dad proves it, he'll be famous and get a better job." Also, Darby thought, he still needed Bob to go to school with him on Monday and get Julian to dance the funky chicken. In his underwear. In front of everybody.

"Okay. Three days. Promise?"

Bob lifted an eyebrow. "I am offended. You wish for me to make a promise? A promise is not required. Three days it is."

Aether still seemed doubtful, so Darby added, "You can trust him. He can't lie."

"Three days, then." She headed for the door, then stopped. "Oh. Darby. The riddle about the sharks. What's the answer?"

Bob perked up. "What riddle is this?"

Darby said, "Imagine you dive off a sinking ship and are surrounded by sharks. How do you survive?"

"Trivial," Bob said at once. "You stop imagining."

Aether frowned. "That's it?"

Darby nodded.

"That's stupid."

"It is an excellent solution," Bob said, offended.

"Yeah, for you. You don't have any imagination." She turned around and then stopped again. "Oh, Darby. Don't tell your sister about me."

"I won't."

"Promise?"

"Promise."

Bob chuckled. "I am not sure you can trust Darby. He lies most elegantly."

21

THE RICCIS LIVED on the north side of town, in a grand old Victorian house that had been renovated into a grand new Victorian house, with a Jacuzzi and heated pool replacing the old garden gazebo.

Livey and Chantelle squeezed by the people packed in the foyer. In the game room, boys hooted over the pool table. Music blared on the back patio. The only spot of quiet came from a mezzanine lounge overlooking the living room. Ashlyn and several others knelt around a coffee table, playing a game. Then they burst into laughter.

Mr. Ricci had silver hair and one of those faces that looked like it should have been carved on the side of a mountain. He certainly wasn't shy. He stood tall and straight in the center of the living room. Whenever the River Oaks Record quoted him on something, they always referred to him as "a respected pillar of the community and a deacon at River Oaks Community Church." He was letting everybody at the party know that he wasn't going to tolerate any sinning on the premises.

How dumb. Nobody was going to play beer pong in this place, but already Livey spotted a couple boys in the pool room sharing a water bottle that wasn't water.

"Soft drinks and snacks on the patio," Mr. Ricci told Livey and Chantelle.

It was a cool night, but not cold. Thin wisps of cloud floated high, catching moonlight. So far, only a few people were dancing to the music, not yet cranked up to full volume. More people were soaking in the large Jacuzzi or diving into the pool.

Chantelle grinned. "Bring your swimsuit?" Livey loved a good summer tan but she hated swimming. All she could manage was the undignified dog paddle.

Chantelle went off in search of Alain, while Livey went off in search of food. She was starving. A splash of water from the pool caught her across the face. Derek's wet head popped up by the edge of the pool. "Hey, Livey."

Taylor surged across the pool, sleek as an otter, giving Livey a warning look before grabbing Derek playfully from behind and pushing his head back under water.

Livey wiped her face dry with a napkin, wondering why she'd bothered coming. She would much rather be home, curled up in bed with a purring Wiles and a cream-cheese bagel.

Not to mention all that algebra makeup she still had to do.

As she debated whether to call her dad for a pickup, Ashlyn rushed up to her.

"You gotta play this game!" she raved.

Curious, Livey followed her to the mezzanine lounge. On the coffee table was a square of polished wood the size of a backgammon board. Pegged into the wood were ten metal studs, arranged in a triangular pattern. Below the last row of five studs the name TETRA KUIZ was elegantly inlaid with mother-of-pearl. The studs were silver colored, their rounded ends the size of a pinkie nail and so polished Livey could see her contorted face as she knelt by the coffee table. Four others, including Ashlyn, joined her.

"Put your thumbs on any two of those metal thingies," Ashlyn told them. "Now, one of you asks a *who is* question about you guys at the table, but the question has to have a number in it. Like *who is going to marry before they are twenty?* The board will hear you and it will give a little electric buzz to the two thumbs of the person who is the answer. Nobody knows who that person is, right, so you have to guess from one another's reactions."

Livey folded her hands in her lap. "I'm not going to get shocked."

"It's just a little buzz, it doesn't hurt."

"That's it?" Cole said. He was the team's punter, and his head had the unfortunate shape of the ball he kicked. "That's so retarded."

Ashlyn shook her head. "Just wait until you play it."

Her eyes were glowing. Livey wondered if she'd taken something.

"How does it know whose thumbs are whose?" Cole persisted. "It might buzz two different people's thumbs."

"But see, that's the cool thing. It picks out just one person. How, I don't know."

Cole picked up the board and turned it over.

"Solid wood," Ashlyn said. "It says in the instructions that it channels energy from the spirit of a magic number, so that's why it only activates if the question has a number in it. And the spirit can't lie, it always tells the truth. Cole, you ask a question. Remember, it has to have a number."

Livey decided to play along for a couple rounds to keep Ashlyn happy, and put her thumbs on two studs.

Cole asked, "I go to River Oaks High. Who goes to River Oaks High too?"

Ashlyn gave him a look. "The board's not stupid. It knows when you say a *real* number."

He shrugged. "All right. So who's going to have a—who's going to have one baby before graduation?"

Mandy Kovacs, the chubby freshman JV cheerleader kneeling across from Livey, stiffened. Her face bloomed red. "This game's stupid," she said, getting to her feet. She pushed through the crowd that was oozing its way up the stairs to spill into the lounge. Livey and the other players stared after her, glee rising in Ashlyn's face.

"God," Cole said in a whisper that cut right through the party's growing clamor. He raised his voice. "Hey, Nate, come over here, you gotta play this!"

Kitty Cabriola, a junior on the golf team, shifted her stance, an uncomfortable pinch to her face. "Maybe we shouldn't ask, like, personal questions."

"But that's the fun of it!" Ashlyn exclaimed. Nate wandered over and took Mandy's place. Livey could smell the beer on his breath. Cole excitedly explained the rules to him. Livey began to feel uncomfortably warm.

"My turn," Ashlyn said. "Who's going to die before they are—"

Livey snatched her hands away.

Ashlyn snapped, "Livey, you broke the connection."

"Even if it's just a game, nobody needs to know anything like that." She squeezed down the stairs and made her way to the back patio to tell Chantelle she was leaving. Fog misted the tops of the trees. The music had been cranked up, setting a packed crowd to dancing. She edged around the fringe of dancers pulsing by the side of the pool. Just as she spotted Chantelle shimmying with Alain, Derek twisted out of the pack, still wearing damp swim shorts and an unbuttoned shirt that showed off his lean body.

"Finally!" he shouted at Livey over the music.

Taylor stormed up out of nowhere. Livey turned to face her, lifting her hands in a gesture of innocence. Without warning, Taylor put her hands on Livey's chest and shoved her into the pool. It happened so quickly and unexpectedly that Livey didn't have time to catch a breath before she splashed into the water. She went straight down, the blaring music instantly replaced by the sound of bubbles, and kicked her way back to the surface, where she clutched at the side, too stunned to say anything.

"I told you!" Taylor screamed. "I told you to stay away from him!"

The crowd near them stopped dancing to watch the drama. Chantelle herded Taylor to the side, calming her, before bending down to help Livey out of the pool. Livey was soaked to the skin. Her shock turned to anger, which she controlled with great effort. Everybody was watching her, wondering what she was going to do. She was *not* going to lose her cool and add to the already inevitable gossip. She grabbed a towel embroidered with a fancy *R*, draped it around her shoulders, and stalked back through the house and out the front door. On the sidewalk she took out her cell from her bag to call her dad, but water had gotten into its innards and it didn't work.

No way she was going back inside. Four blocks away was a shopping arcade with a 24-hour coffee shop. She would use their pay phone. Hugging the towel, she started down the street, cursing Taylor under her breath, and then startled when somebody said, "What happened to you?"

It was Johnny, leaning against the side of his Beetle, an unlit cigarette in his mouth.

"If you're going to crash the party, go ahead," Livey said.

He eyed her wet hair and the towel. "Did you have fun?"

Livey hesitated. He was going to hear about it soon enough anyway, so she said, "Taylor pushed me into the pool."

He chuckled. "Derek?"

"She owes me a new Nokia."

"I'll give you a ride home."

"Not the way you drive. I'll call my dad from the arcade—wait, do you have a cell phone I could borrow?"

"Sorry. I'll walk you."

"What, like I'm a dog on a leash?"

"You're prettier."

He fell into step beside her. They walked in silence. The fog had lowered and thickened, adding to her chill. The street lamps cast haloes. The duct tape on Johnny's left boot flashed in and out of her view. All he had on were those ratty jeans and that thin black cotton shirt, but he looked as loose and relaxed as if this were a warm summer night.

He suddenly spoke. "Your teeth are chattering. I should have driven you."

"The coffee shop's right up there." They were now on Oak Boulevard, the main strip through the north part of town. Johnny sucked on the cigarette and then plucked it out again. "The football game. Who was that man with your father and brother?"

"Bob?" she said, recalling the way Johnny had been watching him.

"Is that what you call him?"

"And how do you know who my brother and father are? You've never met them."

"It's not that big a town. I've seen them around. But not Bob."

"He's Darby's math tutor. My little brother is this math genius. Which obviously is so not me. Did you know I flunked the algebra test? But Mr. Savard gave me extra credit to do to make it a pass so I can stay on the squad. There's like a zillion questions I have to turn in on Monday. Except I don't know if I'm going to be able to do them all."

God, she was prattling. She bit her lip to shut up.

The misty glow of Aunt Huck's neon sign welcomed them. Johnny tossed his unlit cigarette in a trash can. Inside the entry, Livey used the pay phone to call her dad, who said he'd be there in fifteen minutes.

"Don't forget, Dad," Livey warned. "I'm stuck here all alone with a boy I don't know." She smiled at Johnny as she said that, but it wasn't entirely a joke.

"Let's get you warm," Johnny said. He opened the inside door for her. Only a few people were in the booths. "There's a heat vent in the back," he said, taking her arm to lead her, but she stubbornly swung into a side booth overlooking the parking lot so she could look out for her dad. Johnny slid into the seat opposite her.

Livey was still shivering, the cold fog having bitten deep, but the smell of food made her stomach growl. The matronly waitress came over, with only a twitch of her eye registering surprise at Livey's wet appearance.

"A cup of hot cocoa, and can I get a hamburger quick, like under ten minutes? No fries."

"Honey, the way our chef cooks, five minutes."

"Do you want anything, Johnny?" He started to shake his head but she said, "I have to see you eat something or I'm going to think you're a creature of the night."

"The same," he told the waitress. After she left with the order, he said, "Creature of the night, hunh? I'm a creature of the daytime, too. I'm your basic twenty-four-hour creature."

"When do you sleep and where is your den?"

He yawned hugely. His teeth were perfectly white and perfectly straight and perfectly human with their back molar fillings. He patted the vinyl seat. "I could sleep right here."

There he goes, being evasive again, she thought, then sternly told herself, *I am not curious about him, I am* not *going to pry.* She opened her purse to sponge her wet money with a napkin. She frowned at her ruined cell. "Now I have to get everybody's numbers again."

He took it from her and hit the on button.

"Typical," she said.

"What?"

"If a girl can't get it to work, then a guy thinks he can."

He cupped it in his hand for a moment and then handed it back. The Nokia logo flashed onto the screen.

"How'd you do that?" she asked.

He shrugged. "I'm a guy."

She fiddled with the keys. "Yeah, but it's still wrecked. I'm not getting any signal." She was ticked off about that, but also relieved that Johnny hadn't gotten it working again. That would have been just too weird.

The food arrived as quickly as promised. Livey's soggy clothes and damp underwear were uncomfortable, but she was already warm enough to throw off the towel. They were probably seated by another heating vent. She sipped the cocoa and took a bite of her hamburger.

Johnny didn't touch his, but kept his hands upright around his plate, as if afraid somebody was going to steal his food. She was finally going to say something when he drenched his burger in ketchup and started to chow down. He finished before she did, and sat back in the booth, watching her. He played with a toothpick. His sleeve cuffs had ridden up onto his wrists, and the edges of his tattoos peeked out.

"Where is this Bob staying?" he asked.

"Why are you so interested in him?"

"Is he staying with you?"

"He's a mathematician. They're like this tribe, we get them staying at our house all the time. It's nothing to worry about." She wiped her fingers with a napkin and reached for his wrist, to tug the cuff higher up his arm. "What kind of tattoos do you have?"

He snatched his hands back. "Don't you ever do that," he said softly.

"Sorreeee," she said, surprised by his reaction. Headlights flashed in the window, and a green Montero Sport rolled into the lot. "There's my dad," she said with enormous relief and waved her arm to get the waitress's attention.

Johnny put down a hundred-dollar bill on the table. He swung out of the booth and got to his feet. "Let's go."

"But the change—"

He shook his head with sharp impatience. "Plenty more where that came from." He ushered her out the doors. Once more the cold damp cut through her wet clothes. She hurried out to the car, idling in the lane. Darby was in the passenger seat. She yanked open the front door to tell him to get in the back, but went silent with surprise. Bob was at the wheel.

"We told Dad we'd get you," Darby said. "He was busy with this idea. You know what he's like."

Bob was looking past her, studying Johnny with wary interest. Johnny stared right back at him for a second before opening the rear door for Livey. She got in without saying a word. He kept the door open and bent down to say to Bob, "I hear you're visiting."

"That is correct," Bob replied with a courteous smile. "Three days. I have made certain promises."

Johnny nodded and closed the door with a solid thud.

Darby peered through the window at Johnny. "Is that your boyfriend?"

Livey smacked him on the back of the head. "Don't be stupid, genius."

Bob hit the accelerator with a heavy foot, jerking Livey against her seat as she turned to look out the back window.

Johnny was striding around the corner, the fog lit like a halo around him.

An hour later, Livey settled gratefully into bed. Her dad and Bob were in the living room, still working away at the stupid Riemann Hypothesis.

Wiles limped out of her closet and jumped on the bedcover. She absently stroked his fur. What a weird evening. Her mind darted about, from the TETRA KUIZ game to Taylor pushing her into the pool.

To Johnny Magnus.

No, she was not going to think about him.

The way he'd been leaning against the car, as if waiting for her . . .

No, she was NOT going to think about him.

Taylor. Taylor would require some delicate handling on Monday. As in, *You better buy me a new phone, or else.*

The way he'd snatched his hands back and snarled at her. What were those tattoos he had?

God! Stop thinking about him! Okay, Chantelle and Alain. That was interesting.

A hundred-dollar bill? More where that came from? Like drugs? Were those gang tattoos? No. That was too ordinary. Nobody could have gotten a policeman to walk away like Johnny had. Those eyes of his . . .

From the top of her dresser, her ruined cell phone rang. She bolted upright, pillow toppling to the floor, and stared at the stab of light coming from the phone's viewer. Wiles opened his eyes for a moment and peered at the phone before shutting them again. That calm reaction reassured her. She picked it up. Caller ID said it was Chantelle.

She answered. "Hi."

"Where'd you go? I was trying to call. That sure was some drama."

"My cell died on me. I'm home."

"Me too. Just now. Alain drove me. Kissed me good night. Gentlemanly."

"That's good."

A sigh. "Livey. Not good. I didn't want gentlemanly."

They chatted for several more minutes about Taylor and Derek and what Livey should do. Livey didn't really want to talk about it, at least not yet, so she finally faked a yawn that turned into a real one and said she had to go to bed.

After she hung up, she stared at the phone in her hand. It must have dried out.

Still, she remembered the way Johnny had held it in his hand.

What if it rang again, the call from an unknown number?

Would she answer?

But it didn't ring.

22

THUMP-THUMP-THUMP.

Livey opened a bleary eye. The thumping came from the living room.

She put her pillow over her head. She was *not* going to get out of bed. Getting up before ten on a Saturday was immoral and certainly should be illegal.

THUMP-THUMP-THUMP.

With a muttered curse she got out of bed and put on her robe.

In the living room, Bob was exercising. He had somehow found one of her mother's ancient Jane Fonda aerobic tapes, which was playing soundlessly on the TV. He wore a leotard that looked identical to Jane's too, complete to the high cut on his thighs. Probably some sort of European metrosexual fashion.

It was waaaaay too early in the morning to be seeing this.

"Good morning, Livey," he said brightly as he high-kicked. He didn't sound out of breath at all. "I have turned off the sound so that it does not disturb you. Is Jane not simply marvelous?"

Livey grunted and trudged to the master bedroom. She pounded on the door. "Dad! I think Bob is ready to do some math!"

But her dad wasn't in. Bob said that he'd gone off to the college to get some old papers for them to look at.

There was no point trying to go back to sleep. Besides, she had Mr. Savard's makeup homework to do. After a shower, she settled down at her desk. Friday night's fog had turned into gray mist, the weather matching her mood as she struggled through the first few problems.

The doorbell rang. Livey gratefully abandoned her algebra to answer.

A white man in a black suit and a black woman in a gray suit stood on the landing. A third person, a man, smiled over their shoulders at Livey. He had short gingery hair and wore a red bow tie and had eyes that looked empty all the way to the back of his skull. Parked on the curb was a long black car.

"Is this the home of Dr. Jerry Ell?" the woman asked.

Livey kept her hand on the doorjamb, her arm blocking the way. "That's right. He's at the college. What do you want?"

The woman flashed a badge billfold, showing a gold shield and laminated ID card. Livey stared at the big blue letters. FBI. "I'm Agent Geisler," the woman said.

The man did the same. "Agent Deakin. We have a warrant to search for a trunk belonging to Ludavica Ell." Without waiting for a reply, the agents pushed past her into the house. The man with the red bow tie meandered in behind them.

Agent Deakin reached for the pull-down stairs to the attic.

Livey ran for her cell phone in the bedroom. Forget her dad—she dialed her mom, who sounded pleasantly surprised over the background woofing of the black Labradors she and her husband kept. "Hello, honey. What's up?"

Livey quickly explained. She could hear the two agents in the attic.

"Ask to see the warrant," her mom said. "And keep this line open."

Livey intercepted the agents as they were awkwardly hauling the trunk down the stairs.

Darby and Bob had heard the commotion. They stood in the doorway to Darby's room. The man with the red bow tie studied Darby with mild interest.

"What's going on?" Darby asked.

Livey ignored her brother. "Can I see the warrant?" she asked the two agents.

They put down the trunk and looked at the man with the red bow tie, who nodded. Agent Deakin pulled out a piece of paper from his jacket pocket. Livey read it to her mom over the phone. It specifically mentioned the contents of the trunk, and was signed by somebody in the Attorney General's office.

She also gave her mom the agents' names. When she asked the man with the red bow tie for his, he smiled and said, "Two out of three will do."

"Holy cow," Darby said. "You guys secret agents?"

Mr. Bow Tie winked at him.

In the background, Livey could hear the Slimy Jerk asking her mother what was going on. Then he took the phone. "Good morning, Godeliva," he said. He always used her full name. "Is there a gentleman there wearing a red bow tie?"

"Yes," Livey said without looking at the man.

"There is nothing to worry about," the Slimy Jerk said, using his smoothest voice. "Your great-aunt was involved in top secret research—"

"That was ages ago—"

"And some top secrets remain top secret. Let the agents do their job—"

Livey hung up on him.

"You guys carry guns?" Darby said.

"Wouldn't be secret agents if we didn't," Agent Deakin said.

"Can I see?"

"Only if we have to shoot you," Agent Geisler said.

The two agents went through the contents of the trunk, flipping through pages.

"Nothing here, sir," Agent Deakin told Mr. Bow Tie.

Mr. Bow Tie asked Livey if this was everything that had been in the trunk. Livey thought of the book that Darby had taken. But she was still annoyed with the Slimy Jerk telling her what to do, and in her own house at that.

"As far as I know," she said. "Isn't that right, Darby?" Telling him in sister-code to keep his mouth shut.

Agent Geisler said conversationally, "I have a daughter about your age. She's on her high school debate team and is the world's best liar. So what isn't here?"

Darby got the old book from his room. The volume fell open in Agent Deakin's hands to a well-thumbed page, one with scribbling on the margins.

"That's it," Mr. Bow Tie said.

Agent Deakin snapped the book shut and handed it over. "It's all Greek to me."

"Some of it *is* Greek," Darby said helpfully. "Math uses a lot of Greek symbols. Zeta, gamma—"

"He's just making a joke," Livey said, wishing her brother wasn't so naive.

Mr. Bow Tie fixed his empty gaze on Darby. "Is this all? Anything else we should know about?"

Darby bit the inside of his cheek and glanced at Bob.

Bob chuckled. "We are working on the Riemann Hypothesis."

"And who are you?" Mr. Bow Tie asked.

Livey had had enough. She said, "The warrant doesn't say anything about the trunk. You can take the books and stuff, but not the trunk. You have to leave that."

"Now, young lady," Agent Deakin said, "we need it to carry the books."

"No way. The trunk's a family heirloom."

"It is?" Darby said.

"It's not in the warrant," Livey repeated.

"I think we have ourselves a budding lawyer," Mr. Bow Tie said. "Would you mind giving us some garbage bags, then?"

Darby got a couple from the kitchen and helped the agents load the bags.

"You can put the trunk back up in the attic," Livey told them.

Agent Deakin hoisted one of the garbage bags. "Sorry, hands are full."

"I shall do it," Bob said, and dragged the trunk by one handle up the stairs, the trailing edge going *bump-bump-bump*. The agents hauled the bags out to the trunk of their long black car.

Darby watched from the front door. Mr. Bow Tie gave him a casual wave as Agent Deakin opened the car door for him.

"What top secret was in that book?" Livey demanded after they'd driven off.

"No idea."

"There's this girl who's on the debate team and is the world's best liar," Livey said. "What top secret was in that book?"

"Just this idea Aunt Ludy had."

"And you're working on it?"

"It's only math."

Livey glanced up at the attic. There was a scraping sound, Bob shoving the trunk back into place. "With him?" she said, keeping her voice lowered.

"Livey, it's just *math*."

Darby had a point. What could be so secret about math? Still, there was something going on here that made her feel uncomfortable. "You'd better be careful," she said, closing the door. "Or else they might come and take *you* away."

23

SILAS AND MARIA DJUREK stepped out of their house with their two Labradors and their leashes. It was a sunny Saturday morning in a quiet suburb of Washington, DC.

"I'm surprised you don't have to work," Maria said.

As a matter of fact, there was work for Silas to be doing, but he had promised to spend the day with his wife, and such promises he took seriously.

As they put the dogs on the leashes, Maria asked, "Why were there federal agents at my children's home?"

"Ludavica's original work still remains classified," Silas said. "She had material in the attic."

Maria watched the dog on her leash lift a hind leg to a sidewalk lamppost. "That was information I confirmed for you."

"That's right."

"Why do I feel manipulated? Why do I feel there's something going on I should know about but I don't?"

Silas exhaled deeply. "Darling, you know I can't tell you."

"Are Livey or Darby in any danger?"

"Why would they be in danger?"

"That's not an answer."

"No, they are not in any danger whatsoever. We have the materials we were looking for and put them under lock and key. And darling, I was thinking about Christmas. Perhaps it would be better to go to Disney World with your children. I know I can never buy their respect, but it would at least be a neutral venue."

Maria took her husband's arm as the dogs strained on the leashes. "That's a good idea. Livey might have to grumble on principle that she's too old for the place, but she'd be secretly delighted. Darby, too."

Later that afternoon, Silas was chauffeured to his club in Georgetown. He bypassed the lounge and headed for the rear, where an ordinary door opened to a small back garden of trees and bushes, the weather kept out by a skylight. On the portico, Silas put on an olive robe and lit an oil lamp, which he took out to the garden and placed before an ancient tetraktys, a waist-high slab of badly weathered sandstone, eroded pegs marking the triangle. There were several other people there, in quiet meditation. Silas recognized a couple faces but no one was here to be greeted.

Silas composed his outer self and prayed.

But he had lied to his wife about the danger to her son, and inwardly he felt like a small boat in a gale, with a gray, gray mist howling all around him.

24

LIVEY'S CELL PHONE buzzed. It was Mandy.

"Livey, you know that TETRA KUIZ game we were playing at the party?" she said. "I was having some gas, and, you know, one escaped. That's why I got all embarrassed and left. So if you hear any rumors about me, they aren't true, and would you tell Ashlyn to stop spreading them?"

Livey said she would. *That explains one mystery*, she thought as she hung up. She waited for Taylor to phone and apologize, which didn't happen.

Johnny didn't phone, either. Why would he? He didn't even have her number.

And there was no way she was going to give it to him either.

Her dad returned from the college, his briefcase stuffed with printouts of old papers. In the living room, he and Bob continued their work on the Riemann Hypothesis, filling up the whiteboard. Darby sat on the couch and watched, keeping an eye on Bob in a way that reminded

Livey of Coach Mazur, ready to jump in and help a flyer in trouble.

She pulled him aside. "Why do you keep watching him like that?"

"Um, he's Italian, you know. They have different electricity and plugs and things. I don't want him accidentally starting a fire."

"For Pete's sake," Livey said, and was about to state the obvious, that Bob was a capable adult, but then she realized that Darby might have a point. A mathematician *and* an Italian could be a dangerous combination.

Outside, wind began to shake the trees, and the mist condensed into rain. The living room board filled up, and Livey's dad brought in the whiteboard from his bedroom and the garage. Soon those, too, were filled. He and Bob moved to the whiteboard in the kitchen. Having skipped breakfast, Livey was eating a bowl of Cheerios at the counter. She studied Bob out of the corner of her eyes. She hadn't made up her mind about him. He was a combination of charming and weird and something else she couldn't quite put a finger on. Maybe it was because she couldn't figure out who he reminded her of. It was right there, on the edge of her mind.

"Let's take the big oh function," her dad was saying, scribbling on the bottom of the board. He ran out of space and, without a pause, continued writing on the fridge.

"Dad!" Livey said. "Puh-leeze!"

"Perhaps it is time for an intermission," Bob suggested. "I am hungry."

Jerry suggested one of the sandwich places at South Farm Square. Bob was delighted with the idea. "I do so love a good peanut butter and jelly."

Jerry laughed. "You can have that here. We'll get a real deli sub."

Darby got his rain jacket from the hall closet. "They have great avocado sandwiches," he told Bob.

With the house empty, Livey checked on the guest bedroom. She wasn't snooping, honest, she only wanted to make sure that everything was okay. She noticed that Bob's toothbrush—a child's SpongeBob at that—was still in its package on his dresser. God, he hadn't used hers or Darby's, had he? But at least he'd made his bed, so perfectly that it looked like he hadn't even slept on it.

The closet was empty. Beside the dresser, the shiny aluminum suitcase lay flat on the floor. She opened it. Half the contents were new clothes, identical black trousers and white shirts. The other half was filled with packaged TETRA KUIZ games.

She was still staring at them, trying to figure this out, when a voice came from the doorway. "Are you snooping?"

She whirled around. It was the little girl, holding a closed umbrella that was dripping wet, although she herself looked dry, her hair sticking up all over.

"Haven't you ever heard of a doorbell?" Livey demanded.

"Is Darby home?"

"He went out to get something to eat. Here, let me take your umbrella; it's dripping everywhere." She took it out to the porch, leaning it against the planter.

The girl had followed her. "What about Bob? Is he here?"

"He went out too."

"Has he been good?"

What sort of question was that? "Yes, he's almost house-trained," Livey said. Out of politeness, she asked the girl if she wanted a snack or something to drink.

"You got any manna?"

"Like in the Bible?"

"That's all I eat. It's really good with peanut butter. Oh, glazed doughnuts, too, but only Krispy Kreme." She perched herself on the edge of the sofa like royalty. Wiles limped out of Livey's room and jumped up onto her lap. He purred loudly as she petted him.

The girl was autistic, Livey decided. Another strange element to a strange day that wasn't sitting right on its hinges. It got more crooked when the guys returned from lunch. The girl nodded her head in royal greeting to Livey's dad, but stuck out her lip at Bob in a suspicious squint.

"Hello, my dear," Bob said with a graceful bow of his head.

Wiles growled. "The cat doesn't like you," the girl said.

"It is most unfortunate that the creature's symmetry is ruined," Bob replied.

"You leave him alone."

"Certainly. I am a canine person myself. Canis Major is my constellation, I have discovered."

"Bob's still busy helping my dad," Darby said. "He's here only two more days, isn't that right, Bob?"

"Indeed," Bob said.

What a strange conversation, Livey thought, but only two more days of Bob was good news.

At the bookstore, her dad had bought poster paper and a stand to keep doing math. He quickly filled the first page, spouting jargon to Bob, and then flipped to a fresh page.

From the kitchen, Livey noticed Darby gesturing to the girl, who followed him to his bedroom. After a few seconds, Livey drifted down the hall. Darby had closed the door, but there was a chink where the lock had been that she could peer through.

He stood at the foot of his bed, holding a shiny brass compass.

"I just found out this morning," he said to the girl. "It doesn't point north. It always points to the notebook." He was referring to the Shedd Aquarium notebook, which was on his bed. Transferring the notebook to his desk, he held out the compass. "See? Pointing right at the notebook. Do you have any idea why?"

"Nope."

"You sure? I thought maybe you would, because you're a—"

"Your sister," the girl said quickly.

"What about her?"

The girl was staring at the door. "I bet she's snooping. Bossy sisters always snoop."

Livey scooted into her bedroom.

A moment later, her dad knocked on her door and announced that he was going with Bob and Darby to the college to continue their research there.

"We are on the verge of a breakthrough," he said excitedly.

And this would be about the zillionth time, she thought. "What about the girl?"

"I don't know. She took off."

After they left, she phoned Chantelle.

"It's been totally bizarre around here," she said. "You try living in a house of mathematicians."

"You do realize that right now you could be with Derek at the mall?"

"Would you forget about him?"

"Ooo-kaaay."

"Besides, I have all that algebra makeup."

"Then you better do it. Call me back when you're done."

Livey reluctantly returned to her algebra. It was so unfair Mr. Savard had given her so much to do. If she had Johnny's number, she could call him and ask him to explain some of the problems. That wouldn't be cheating. After all, as Mr. Savard's student assistant, it was his job to help explain things.

There were two Magnuses in the phone book, one living in the ritzy north side of town, the other in the Evergreen apartment complex. She paced the room, her cell phone in her hand. Should she or shouldn't she?

"Oh, for Pete's sake," she said, annoyed at herself. She dialed the first number. An old woman answered. No, no Johnny living there. The second person, a man, said no and slammed the phone down.

Sitting down at her computer, Livey did an Internet search for "Johnny Magnus." Google tossed out the usual random assortment of Johnny Magnuses, but no teenager in River Oaks. Facebook and MySpace threw up blanks.

Of course none of this meant anything. And she wasn't even really curious.

But if there was a God, then He would give her understanding of algebra.

Or send somebody who could.

Half an hour later, the doorbell rang again.

"Sheesh, this place is like Union Station," Livey muttered.

She opened the front door, and gaped at Johnny Magnus. His hair was dry, although a few raindrops glistened on his black hair like diamonds. Behind him, the Beetle was parked by the curb.

"What are you doing here?" she said.

"Not even a 'hi'?"

"Hi. What are you doing here?"

"Last night you were complaining about all the makeup you had to do for Mr. Savard. I thought you'd like some help."

She didn't know what to say. She stepped back to let him in. He took a look around the living room and kitchen. "You alone?"

She realized with a tightening of her skin just how alone she was.

He must have noticed. "You want me to come back later?"

"Let me get my stuff; we'll work out here."

They sat side by side at the kitchen counter. He led her patiently through the problems, not telling her what to do but letting her make the decisions for herself. He still smelled like clean earth, but mixed with pure rain, although his clothes were dry. Veins ran blue underneath the pale skin of his hands. He had a tiny scar between his right thumb and finger. She'd never noticed that before. She wanted to touch it but she didn't dare.

Pointing to a line in her workbook, he accidentally brushed her hand and yanked it back so fast that she looked up at him.

He was looking down at her, his jaw muscles clenched. His black irises were hard and shuttered, no green glints to them.

She suddenly felt very much alone again. Her heart began to pound. Then she noticed the tiniest of cracks in his gaze, as though he were trying to hold back some unbearable pain. She remembered what he had said about the moonbow, the longing in his voice.

"What's wrong?" she said.

"You have no idea," he replied softly, his jaws still tight.

She was silent for a moment. "Maybe I do." Speaking hesitantly at first, she told him about her mother falling in love with another man and leaving the family. Abandoning them.

"Every night I cried my eyes out," she said. The words were now tumbling out, tripping over themselves. "Then during the day I put on my brightest cheerleader smile. Pert and bubbly and cute. I had to be strong, especially for Darby. Last year my mom started reaching out to me again, and at first I didn't want anything to do with her. But she's still my mom. Always will be. Even though it hurts."

She had never told anybody this. Not even Chantelle, her Best Friend Forever Plus A Day. And here she was telling Johnny Magnus, practically a stranger, sitting there with duct tape around his boots, listening to her without expression.

"Well," she said, cutting herself off in embarrassment, thinking that she was telling him *too* much. "I'm hungry. Want a snack?" She poured them glasses of milk and brought over the last of Mrs. Blink's chocolate cake. He cupped his hands over the glass, and then around the cake, like he'd done at the coffee shop.

"Are you saying grace when you do that?" she asked.

He looked startled, and then laughed. "Nah. Just a habit." He took a nibble of cake. "So how's your houseguest?"

The change in topic threw her. "Bob?"

"You haven't kicked him out of the house?"

"You know, this is weird. You're the second person asking about him today. There's this strange girl who visits my brother. I think she's autistic. She won't tell me her name or where she lives. She was asking about him too."

"Yeah?"

"And guess what? He's got a bunch of those TETRA KUIZ games. I wonder if he's a salesman for the company."

Johnny took another nibble. "Or the inventor."

"You think?"

He shrugged and then looked down. Wiles was rubbing his head against his ankle. "Well, hello there, kitty." He poured some milk into his plate and bent down to put the plate on the floor.

"No, don't," Livey said. "We don't feed Wiles at the table. He's too spoiled as it is."

Johnny held the plate above the floor, listening to her, but then put it down anyway.

She couldn't believe it. "Johnny, I just asked you not to do that."

"I know."

She got off her stool, took the plate away from Wiles, and washed it off in the sink, trying to control her anger. Had she really spilled her heart out to this jerk about her mother? She wished she could take it all back. All the way back to opening the front door so she could tell him to go away.

"I think we're done," she said.

"There are still four more problems."

"I'll do those on my own."

"Okay." He got up to go. In the front hall he said, with a ghost of a smile, "Remember, a minus times a minus is a plus. Just something you have to get used to."

God, he was such a total aggravation. She slammed the door shut after him.

25

SUNDAY MORNING, LIVEY chased down the beeping alarm clock. What a waste of perfect sleeping-in weather, gray and drizzling, with occasional rain bursts spattering against her window. But she had to finish those last four algebra problems and write her earthquake paper.

Dressed in old sweats, she yawned down the hall, heading for the kitchen counter, where she'd left her algebra. Bob wasn't doing his aerobics, thank God. He was in his academic tweed and seated at the dining table. On a plate before him was a slice of bread spread with Skippy Super Chunk peanut butter. On the peanut butter he was placing Cheerios, one by one, making a triangle of them.

"Ah, Livey, a question for you, if I may," he said. He turned the back of the cereal box to her. On it was a contest promo blurb, promising the winner a trip to Italy. Bob pointed to the accompanying picture of the Leaning Tower of Pisa. "If this tower were straight, would you not be even more willing to go see it?"

"Could be upside down for all I care," she mumbled. After toasting a bagel, she sat down at the counter and started in on her algebra.

Bob perked up. "Are you working on a proof?"

"Just some stupid algebra."

"Perhaps I may be of some assistance."

"Sure. Maybe *you* could explain to me why a minus times a minus is a plus."

There was a silence. She looked at him. He was staring at her with a horrified expression. "It is?" he said.

God. Mathematicians and their sense of humor. She gathered up her work and took it into her bedroom, where she struggled with her xs and ys. In the final problem, she noticed, there was even a z thrown in.

Maybe she shouldn't have gotten in such a huff with Johnny.

But she'd *told* him not to feed Wiles, and he'd done it anyway. In her own house!

After a while, making no headway on the problems, she took a break. She did a special wash and dry of the Riccis' towel, which she put in a plastic bag and then in a old day pack. She phoned the Riccis' residence. A maid told her they had gone to the River Oaks Community Church service, which she knew, Mr. Ricci being a deacon, but she just wanted to make sure. Of course, she could have taken the towel directly to the Riccis' house and given it to the maid, but she decided to catch the Riccis leaving the service and return the towel directly to them. If she just so happened to see Johnny Magnus there, then no big deal, all that meant was that she just so happened to see him, as her only purpose to be at the church was to return the towel. That was all. She shucked on a raincoat, tugged the hood tight, and, with a frown of distaste at the cold rain, rode off on her bike.

The church was a mile away, a spot of heavenly architecture along Oak Creek. Cars packed its sprawling, landscaped parking lot. Livey got there a few minutes before the main service let out. She rode up and down the lot, her bike tires splashing through shallow puddles, and then found what she really hadn't been looking for, honest, just happening to spot a brown Beetle tucked away in a long line of gleaming cars.

The youth church met in the back Annex. She leaned her bike against a hedge and stood in the doorway of the admin building. From this spot, she couldn't see worshippers leaving the main sanctuary, but that was okay. If she missed the Riccis, she could return the towel to them another time.

The Annex doors burst open. Teens rushed out, many from other towns. People drove for miles to attend this church. After the exodus eased, Johnny sauntered into the open, still wearing those jeans and black cotton shirt and those God-awful taped-up boots. He held a closed umbrella and a Krispy Kreme box.

Just as she thought. Only there for the doughnuts.

He didn't head for his car but stood by the set of doors that led to the children's Sunday school classes. Soon the doors opened, and loud kids spilled out. Many darted along the canopied walk toward their parents, already turning the corner from the main sanctuary.

A little girl in a white crinkly dress turned the other way, running in an awkward knock-kneed gait toward Johnny.

It was Darby's friend, the autistic girl.

What was going on here?

Johnny handed the box to the girl. She opened it and picked out a glazed doughnut, which she munched as they headed across the parking lot to the Beetle.

Livey ran after them, her sneakers slapping on the wet pavement. She slowed to squeeze between two parked cars. Johnny and the girl were about twenty feet away. Livey blinked rain out of her eyes. Even though the drizzle had gotten heavier in the last few minutes, Johnny didn't have the umbrella open. Weren't they getting wet?

Her footsteps were loud and squishy. Johnny whirled around, clicking the umbrella's button, which popped open over him and the girl.

They stood still, watching Livey with unblinking gazes.

"Hi, Johnny," Livey said. She nodded at the girl. "And hello to you
too. So you two know each other, do you?"

"Of course," the girl said. "He's my brother."

A raindrop ran down Livey's nose. She wiped it off. "God, Johnny,
how come you didn't tell me yesterday? You sat right there when I was
telling you about her coming over to visit my brother and you didn't
say a word."

"You didn't ask."

"So what's your sister's name? She won't tell me."

Johnny looked down at the girl. "Should I tell her?"

She bit her lip and then sighed hugely. "It's Aether. Not *either*. A-E-
T-H-E-R." She crammed the rest of the doughnut in her mouth.

Livey wiped more raindrops from her face. She said to Johnny,
"Your sister plays with my brother at Lincoln Park. She's alone a lot. I
don't think that's such a good idea."

"Why not?"

"She's what, five? You just don't let little girls play alone like that."

Johnny didn't reply.

"Do you guys live near the park, then?"

"Not really," Johnny said.

Livey felt confusion and anger starting to build. "How do you get
to the park, Aether?"

"The train, sometimes."

"For Pete's sake, Johnny, she goes on the train by herself?"

He still kept silent, watching her carefully.

"Aether, you don't have parents or a guardian?"

She shook her head, left once, right once, then back to center. "Not
in Illinois." She pronounced it *Illi-noise*. "I live with Johnny."

Livey closed her eyes. "Okay. I don't want to pry into your private lives. But . . ." She opened her eyes and looked at Johnny again. Now there was subtle amusement playing across his face. That did it. She exploded. "You dumb idiot, it's irresponsible. Something could happen to her. She could get hurt. And I'll tell you something else. Those moms at the park? If they know this, they'll call family services, and they'll take your sister away. Seriously. They're really strict about that here."

"Like the cops."

"I'll call family services myself!" Livey yelled at him.

"Boy, she's bossy, isn't she?" Aether said.

Livey gritted her teeth.

Johnny put his hand on his sister's back and pushed her toward his car. "Livey, you don't need to be concerned."

"He means butt out," Aether said, and fished another glazed doughnut out of the box.

Livey stomped back to her bicycle and pedaled home as fast as she could. In the garage, she ripped open the plastic bag and wiped her face dry with the Riccis' fluffy towel.

26

AT RIVER OAKS COLLEGE, the math department's hallway was as long as a bowling lane, but everyone called it the Continuum Corridor. On the wall were framed copies of papers by famous mathematicians. The originals, donated by a rich alumnus, were kept in a vault.

Darby studied a scrap of paper on which Isaac Newton had scratched a list in black ink. The great man's handwriting was terrible. The numbers he'd jotted down didn't have anything to do with science. It was a grocery list with shopping expenses. And right there at the bottom, you could see that one of the world's greatest mathematical minds had added wrong.

Darby had once tried to comfort his sister with this fact, but she'd only thrown her pencil at him.

In an empty lecture hall, his dad wrote on the blackboards with a *rat-rat-tat* of the chalk. Bob had left an hour ago, telling Darby that he had to return to deep space to secure his black hole. "I do not wish for Aether to became angry at me and kick my leg again," he said, smiling.

He evaporated into his elemental form of triangles and zipped off into Hilbert space. Good thing nobody had been in the hallway. But this being the math department, maybe nobody would have noticed.

Jerry rushed out, stumbling over the last step by the door. "Where's Bob?"

"Dad, he left an hour ago. He said he had to go, remember?"

"But, my God, he has to see this." Jerry rubbed a hand through his hair and then down his face. "I can't believe it."

"What?"

"Come here!" He ran back down the lecture hall aisle and stabbed the chalk on the final lines that he had scribbled on the side blackboard. "We haven't proved the hypothesis. We've *dis*proved it! We have shown that there *must* exist a zero off the critical line!"

Darby had only seen his dad this upset one time before, when his mother hadn't come home from that conference.

"But that's just as good. You'll be just as famous."

Jerry threw up his hands. "Famous! Who cares about famous? It's a disaster! The Hypothesis must be true. It simply must!"

He began to wipe the blackboards clean with huge sweeps.

"This doesn't help, Dad," Darby warned. "If you've disproved it, you've disproved it."

"I shouldn't have listened to Bob," Jerry whispered.

Back home, Jerry shut himself in his room. Darby could hear his father's heavy tread, back and forth, back and forth. Boy, he really *was* upset. Darby waited for Livey to ask him what was wrong with their dad, but she was distracted herself. For once she didn't drag everybody out and sit them down at the table for dinner. Instead Chantelle came over, and she and Livey holed up in Livey's room.

Darby made a PB and J sandwich. When night had fully fallen, he put on a jacket and took his notebook out into the damp darkness.

Behind him, a long black car pulled out from the curb and followed at a walking pace. Darby heard its purring engine but was too preoccupied to take further notice. When he turned off the sidewalk onto the path leading to Lincoln Pond Park, the car stopped.

The park was deserted, streetlamps glistening on the wet paths. As Darby walked past the Lincoln statue, he absently trailed his hand along the President's bronze knee and then slipped through the pine trees that circled the picnic tables. Wiping one bench dry with the hem of his shirt, he sat down and opened the notebook.

"Good evening, Darby," a voice courteously said.

Two men had moved in from the shadows. The man who had spoken wore a bow tie. Darby couldn't make out the bow tie's color, but he knew it was red, because he recognized the man. He was one of those secret agents who'd been to the house to get Aunt Ludy's books. The one with the dead eyes, which at night looked even more dead. As he approached Darby, Agent Deakin kept watch in the background.

"What do you have there, son?" Mr. Bow Tie asked.

"Nothing," Darby said, whipping the notebook under his jacket.

"Now, Darby," Mr. Bow Tie scolded. "I asked you before if you had anything more to give to us, and you said no. I believe that notebook belongs to us."

Darby gulped, trying to keep his heart in place. "It's mine."

"It would be best if you just handed it over, like a good little boy."

Darby slipped his finger inside the notebook, to the last page of the proof. "Q.E.D!" he whispered.

The man stepped closer. "You have no idea what we can do to little liars like you."

Footsteps rang. Agent Deakin gasped and whipped out his gun as the statue of Lincoln took off his top hat and gave a bronzed bow. "Oh, do put that weapon away, sir. It is of no use against me. And a ricochet can be deadly to yourself." To Mr. Bow Tie he said, "Instead of the notebook, please have this."

He dipped a hand into the top hat and pulled out a TETRA KUIZ game board, which he pressed into Mr. Bow Tie's hands, making sure that the man's thumbs were on two of the metal stubs. He did the same to Agent Deakin. Neither man resisted. After a second, Lincoln returned the game board to his top hat.

Mr. Bow Tie blinked and straightened the wings of his bow tie. He said to Agent Deakin, "You are wrong. Warner Brothers made the better cartoons. Consider the subtle existentialism of Daffy Duck and compare that to the vapid sentimentalism of Donald Duck."

Agent Deakin shook his finger. "How can you say that? Donald Duck is one of the great patriotic Americans of all time. . . ."

The two men wandered off into the night, vehemently arguing the virtues of the two cartoon ducks.

Darby watched them, his knees trembling with relief. "Phew, thanks," he said to the bronze statue. "I mean, that is you, Bob, isn't it?"

The metal Lincoln sat down across from him. "A convenient form to take, especially considering handguns were present. Although the ants on my feet are most annoying." He nodded at the notebook. "It was fortunate you called me. Take good care of that, would you? I would hate for anything to happen to my proof. Those two gentlemen will not recall this evening—I tidied up their memories—but they might be back."

"Can you become anything you want?"

"If I borrowed the complex conjugate of the mathematical equation that represents your existence, I could even become you."

As Darby thought about this, various opportunities presented themselves. He grinned. "Whoa. Think of the tricks we could pull on Livey."

"Would she find them humorous?"

"Of course not. That's why it would be fun. But look, my dad. Why I came out here to call you. He just *dis*proved the Hypothesis. He's really upset."

"Is that not as remarkable an achievement?"

"But it's like a pastor proving there is no God. Maybe he made a mistake. Could you look over his proof?"

Bob gave a long, bronze-sounding sigh. "Darby, what is true is true. Truth, elegance, beauty: and the greatest of these is truth." He fingered his metal hat. "This world is a mess, Darby. There is so much ugliness and inelegance and asymmetry. I have been thinking that perhaps I am here for a purpose, to make it a better place."

"Wait a sec. You promised Aether you'd be leaving. You have found your black hole, haven't you?"

"Near Sirius. The Dog Star. But it is no longer there. I have taken the liberty of moving the singularity to a more secure place."

"Then you better go like you promised. But first, tomorrow at school. Julian and the Boys' Club. They're the opposite of truth and elegance and beauty. They're bullies."

"What do you wish me to do?"

"I was kind of thinking of Julian dancing the funky chicken in his underwear in front of everybody."

"The funky chicken?"

"Just embarrass him big-time."

"Would you like to be king of the Boys' Club?"

Darby hadn't thought about that. "That'd be awesome."

"Indeed it would. I must go, Darby. There are people worshipping me, which places upon me a tremendous responsibility." He put on his top hat and strode away on his long legs into the shadows.

Darby sat there for a moment longer, stroking the cover of the notebook. Imagine, him being king of the Boys' Club!

For once, he couldn't wait for school the next day.

27

LIVEY LAY ON her back on the carpet, hugging a pillow to her chest. Chantelle sat cross-legged on the bed above her.

"And then he puts the plate down anyway!" Livey said. "After I told him not to! God, he's so annoying."

Chantelle sucked on her cheek, and then released it. "You know what I think?"

"What?"

"I think you're falling in love with the one guy you should *not* be falling in love with."

"You're crazy."

"Johnny this, Johnny that, and how mad he makes you. Sounds like love to me, girl."

Livey threw the pillow at her.

After Chantelle left, Livey rummaged through the fridge. Talking about Johnny had given her a craving for some chocolate, but the box was empty. "Darby!" she yelled. "Who ate all the chocolate?"

He called out from his room, "Abraham Lincoln?"

"Fun-nee." Darby didn't like chocolate. It had to have been Bob. Some houseguests could be pigs. In her bedroom, her cell phone chirped. There was only one person who phoned this time on a Sunday night. She ran and answered it without checking caller ID. "Hi, Mom."

A silence. "Not quite."

She plopped down on her bed. "Johnny. What do you want?"

"To see you?"

She found it hard to breathe. "Are you asking me out?"

"Sort of. If you don't mind climbing out your bedroom window."

She glanced at the window. Johnny stood in the back flower bed, a cell phone to his ear, looking at her. "My God, Johnny, have you been peeping at me?"

"I don't peep. I look."

"What if I wasn't decent?"

"Then I wouldn't be looking."

"Haven't you ever heard of a front door?"

"It's more fun sneaking out. I'm not going to stand out here all night. Hurry up."

She hesitated and then slipped into her sneakers and got her jacket. She had to admit there was a touch of thrill in sneaking out of her bedroom window, even if there was no real need to be sneaking at all. Johnny helped her over the back fence into the alley, where his Beetle was parked. He chucked his disposable cell into a garbage can. "Out of units," he told her. "You should be honored I used the last to phone you."

"You're such an insufferable jerk, you know that? And how'd you get my number anyway?"

"Deceitfully."

"Figures."

"The whiteboard in your kitchen. In the corner it says 'L's cell.'"

Livey groaned. "My dad. He's a mathematician but he can't remember numbers. It's like he can count one two three four and after that it's *n*."

Johnny opened the door for her. She wrapped her arms around herself. "Where are we going?"

"For a ride."

"Can I trust you?"

"Trust me to what?"

"Bring me back safe?"

"Get in."

She got in, thinking, *this is really stupid*. He closed the door after her. She could feel her pulse clogging her throat. She wished she'd brushed her hair.

Once he was behind the wheel, he opened the glove box. Within was a box of Hershey's chocolate bars. "Want one?" he said, a sly undercurrent to the question, as if he knew she'd wanted some chocolate.

She shook her head, way too nervous to even think of eating.

He gunned down the alley. The clouds had cleared enough to allow a glimpse of the white moon, which looked as though a drop of bleach had spilled on the black sky. He didn't speak, and she didn't either. For once in her life, she had no idea what to say.

Her cell phone rang. Chantelle's caller ID.

"Aren't you going to answer?" he asked.

She turned her phone off. After a few blocks she said, "Chantelle thinks you're bad news."

"Chantelle's right, but for the wrong reasons."

She wiped her sweaty palms on her sweatpants. "What are the right reasons?"

He didn't reply. They were on President. This time of night, the traffic was light. The Beetle's speedometer needle had stuck at fifty, but it seemed to Livey they were going much faster. Johnny whipped onto Butterfield Avenue and after a mile braked hard to turn off onto Old Farm road. A big sign said OBERLUND FOREST PRESERVE and underneath that NO PUBLIC ENTRY ON THIS ROAD.

"Johnny, didn't you see that sign?"

"We're not the public."

The road was roughly paved and had no streetlights. It wound round the side of the marsh. The car's feeble headlights lit up trees and reeds. Here and there moonlight glittered on the water. At a stand of prairie pines, Johnny swung onto a smaller track. The Beetle's tires crunched on gravel as Johnny drove deeper yet into the most remote area in the county.

Livey's heart really began to thud. She wondered if Johnny could hear it.

He parked in a weedy area by a settler's old wooden house, long abandoned. The State wanted to tear it down, but conservationists were fighting a court battle to keep it. In the moonlight Livey could see shutters hanging loose, and the few windows that still had glass were badly cracked. The chimney had toppled, and the roof sagged in the middle.

Here she was, looking at just about the loneliest, spookiest house she'd seen, with a boy she didn't know at all in the seat beside her. She turned her phone back on, the little beep loud in the car, ready to dial 911.

"Livey," Johnny said, "I would never do anything to hurt you. I would never let anybody else hurt you either."

A small part of her told her that this made him *more* dangerous to her. But her heart quieted.

He opened his door. "We have a short walk."

She got out of the car. Damp weeds scraped her ankles. She followed Johnny across the lot to a path that led into a tangle of woods.

He held out his hand to her. With his warm fingers wrapped reassuringly around hers, she entered the woods. The cold did little to dampen the smell of rotting leaves. An animal rustled in the underbrush, and she jerked to a stop.

"Only a raccoon," Johnny said.

"How do you know?"

"I know what raccoons look like."

He had seen it, in this darkness?

"You see better at night with your peripheral vision," he said, as if reading her thoughts.

He walked slowly to allow her to keep up, but with no hesitant steps. This was a trail he obviously knew well. Livey felt like she was on the edge of a storybook, about ready to fall into some fantasy world. But when she checked her cell phone, it still held its full signal.

The trail opened up into a small clearing. The tall trees blocked the lights of the town. Johnny glanced up at the moon overhead. "Two days to full, but it's bright enough," he said. With the night cleansed by rain, the moon's light cast shadows.

Johnny led her to a fallen tree with a flat trunk like a platform. "We'll sit up here. It'll be another minute."

She jumped up and hugged her knees to her chest. Johnny sat cross-legged beside her. "What are we waiting for?" she finally asked.

He pointed to the eastern sky. "That."

She didn't see it at first, but then saw an arc of muted light that strengthened into banded shades of gray. The arc brightened even more, and faint blushes of color stole into the gray.

A moonbow.

"My God, it's beautiful," she breathed. She didn't know how long she sat there, mesmerized, but all too soon the angle of the moonlight changed and the moonbow faded away.

In Livey's heart was something special that had never been there before. A gift that Johnny had given her. She touched his arm. "Thank you."

He was turned to her, looking at her in such a way that she realized he hadn't been watching the moonbow at all.

"I've seen much better ones," he said, "but never with anyone like you."

Her heart began to skid. She found herself leaning ever so slightly toward him. He was leaning too. For a fleeting second, a rule of gravity came to mind, a leftover from her mom's physics about the attraction between two bodies growing larger the closer they were.

"Livey," he whispered, "I'm not who you think I am."

"I know," she whispered back, already feeling the warmth of his lips before they touched hers. "I had you wrong from the very beginning."

Livey wanted to stay here with him and wait until the next moonbow, however long that took. She kissed him again. He tasted like buttered gold and sweet lava.

"Oh, yuck," a voice said.

Livey jerked away. Aether stood in the clearing by the bench, her arms folded across her chest.

"Aether, butt out," Johnny said.

"Don't tell me you've fallen in love with her."

"None of your business."

"I suppose you've fallen in love with him, too?" she demanded of Livey.

"Well," Livey said, with dazed wonder, her bones lighter than air, "come to think of it, I guess I have."

"This is really, really stupid."

"Talk about ruining the moment," Johnny said, rising to his feet and extending his hand to Livey. "I'd better get you home."

Aether skipped ahead of them on the trail and disappeared.

"Johnny," Livey said worriedly, but he hushed her.

"She'll be okay. Believe me."

At the weedy parking lot, before Livey got in the car, she took another look at the ruined house. Through a cracked window came a soft glow.

"I get it," she said. "This is where you and Aether are staying."

"Sometimes. We're flying under the radar." He held up a hand. "No questions. I'll tell you what I can when I can, I promise."

In the car he opened the glove box and handed her a Hershey bar. She slowly savored it on the drive home. It was the best, most divine chocolate she'd ever had.

28

AS DARBY DREAMED of crowns, he was rudely shaken awake. Why did his stupid sister always have to wake him so early? "Go away," he grumbled.

"Where's Bob?"

Holy cow, it wasn't Livey. Aether was standing on his bed, shoving his shoulder with her foot. She held an early morning edition of the *Sun Times*. "Look at this."

He sat up and put on his glasses. On the front page was a breaking news article with a photo of the Tower of Pisa, lit with powerful floodlights. Lots of people in various uniforms were milling about.

The Tower wasn't leaning anymore. It was perfectly straight. "Possibly a local seismic event," an expert was quoted as saying. "We are all baffled and horrified."

"That stupid Bob," Aether said. "He can't do this."

Darby got out his notebook from his desk drawer. "Q.E.D!"

Triangles swam out of Hilbert space and then settled onto the carpet as Bob, wearing an unfinished suit jacket marked with chalk, the arms not yet sewn. "Now what? You are interrupting. I am at a fitting. I have found a tailor in Hong Kong who is a worshipper of me and who makes the most elegant clothes—"

"This!" Aether said, pointing to the picture on the cover.

"Ah. That. At first it was only a minor annoyance, but then it increasingly irritated me. Like an ant in my shoe. Therefore, I removed the ant."

Aether shook the paper. "You can't go around doing this!"

Bob took the paper and studied the picture. "Permit me to say that I did a most excellent job. It is elegant, as it should be."

"Put it back the way it was and then go."

"Now, now, my little seraph. Allow me one little mark of my presence in this universe. A sign that something true and beautiful and elegant was here."

Darby said, "Aether, I've invited him to attend my school for the day. He can't go yet. After school, okay?"

She frowned.

"Hey, I was the one who proved him," Darby said.

"A beautiful mind," Bob added.

Aether blew air. "All right. Just today. You're gone by evening. I have to get back to more important stuff than keeping an eye on you."

Bob looked offended. "What could possibly be more important than I?"

On the school bus, Darby sat in Julian's seat, ignoring the others' incredulous stares.

"What are you doing in my seat?" Julian said when he boarded.

"You don't own it."

Julian's face went blank with disbelief, and then hardened. "Get up."

As Darby pushed by Julian, he said, "Lunchtime. We'll see who gets to sit there."

"What did you say?"

"You heard me."

A profound silence settled on the bus. Then everybody pulled out their cell phones and began texting their friends, spreading the word that at lunch Darby was going to fight Julian for his seat on the school bus.

As they got off the bus, Roz said to Darby, "You might be smart, but this is real dumb. I'll sweet-talk Julian out of it, say you weren't thinking right."

"Just stay out of it," Darby coldly said.

Later in his classroom, Darby listened to Mrs. Essex as she pointed out the Pacific Ring of Fire on the world map. She was getting her subduction zones all mixed up, but Darby had learned not to correct his teachers.

A voice whispered in Darby's ear. It was Bob. "Your land masses are very untidy. I could rearrange them if you wish."

"Whoa," Darby said, alarmed. "The Tower was bad enough. Better leave everything alone."

"Australia, then. Who would notice?"

"The Australians, that's who. Just leave the world alone, okay?"

Darby became aware of a peculiar silence in the classroom. Everybody was staring at him. His ears grew hot enough to fry eggs. "Um, I'm practicing dialogue for a story I'm writing."

Julian announced, "Darbielle is not only Einstein, he thinks he's J. K. Rowling, too."

"That's enough," Mrs. Essex said, silencing the laughter.

After a moment Darby heard Bob's voice. "That boy. He is Julian?"

Darby gave a tiny nod.

"An odious brat."

Darby smiled.

Lunch was going to be *great*.

◪ ◪ ◪

Darby had just finished his sandwich when Julian strolled around the corner of the alley. The Boys' Club followed, along with a crowd of other students.

Darby didn't mind. He wanted an audience. He took his notebook out of his bag.

Julian stopped, arms folded across his chest. He didn't speak. Roz slipped past him and up to Darby. "This is so not good," she said in a low voice. "You say you're sorry, I'll help you get out of this."

"I don't need your help, you big fat traitor. You have cellulite for brains."

Her face turned bright red.

Darby smiled at Julian. "As for you, you know what you are? You're a sphincter."

Julian frowned and glanced at his friends. Karim shrugged. "That Egyptian thing?"

"Not Sphinx, *sphincter*," Darby said smugly. "It's the medical term for the hole in the middle of your butt. But you're too stupid to know that, you stinky sphincter." With Bob to help him, Darby could say whatever he pleased. Boy, it felt good to be dissing Julian.

Julian clenched his fist. "I'll make you a new Sphinx."

Darby held up the notebook. "Q.E.D!"

Nothing happened.

Julian's fist began to swing. Darby took a step back. "Bob! Q.E.D!"

Darby noticed too late that Bob wasn't materializing to stop the punch. Julian's knuckles slammed into his cheek. An explosion of light accompanied the painful crunch, and then Darby was falling backward into a garbage can.

MR. SAVARD HELD out his pink palm. "Your makeup?"

Livey pulled her workbook out of her bag, realizing with horror that she hadn't finished the last four problems. She'd been so light-headed about Johnny that she'd completely forgotten.

Mr. Savard flipped through the pages. "Not doing these problems means a maximum possible score of eighty-nine percent. You need ninety."

"Can't you please give me one percent for the effort?"

He wagged his red pen at her. "A deal is a deal."

Normally she would try to charm him, but the moonbow night with Johnny had changed her. "I'll report you."

His pen stopped wagging. "Are you threatening me?"

"You've been picking on me ever since school started."

"I've been trying to get you motivated."

Johnny, who'd just entered the classroom, glanced over Mr. Savard's shoulder. "I'd give her the extra percent."

Mr. Savard rotated his red pen toward Johnny. "Are you telling me what to do?"

"A gesture of good will," Johnny said. He was looking right at Mr. Savard.

He handed Johnny the pen. "One percent for effort. Grade the others."

Livey brushed by Johnny, her hand deliberately bumping his. The touch made her heart pump moonbows, and her skin hummed with purples and greens and blues. The way everyone was looking at her, she was sure they knew she'd fallen in love with Johnny Magnus.

During the class, she didn't hear a word Mr. Savard said. Johnny filled her senses up to the brim. Why hadn't she ever noticed before how handsome he was? Those high cheekbones and deep eyes and square chin. The black stubble added the right touch of mystery.

She wrote a note saying she'd be in the library for lunch, and slipped it to him after class. Picking a secluded study table by the library's rear windows, she daydreamed about moonbows. She wondered where Johnny was from, the whole mystery of who he was.

She glanced at her watch. Where was he? What was taking so long?

The shelf of books in front of her parted and in the gap appeared a face, wearing a clown's red ball for a nose.

"I am the oracle of the library," Derek intoned. "Ask me anything and I will answer."

She'd been avoiding both Derek and Taylor all morning, but despite herself, and maybe because being in love with Johnny made her happy, she laughed. "Why is a minus times a minus always a plus?"

"A minus times a minus is a plus, the reason for this we need not discuss."

"For the first time ever, some sense!"

"Naturally. I am the oracle of the library. Now I have a question for you. Derek Mankowski would like to ask you to the homecoming dance. What is your answer?"

Again she laughed. This was probably one of the most original ways ever to ask out a girl.

"Well?" he said, wriggling his nose.

"I'm honored, Derek, really, but I think Taylor wouldn't be too happy."

"She doesn't have anything to do with this."

The intercom came to life. "Will Godeliva Ell please report to the admin office."

She glanced at the speaker. "That's me."

"Godeliva?"

She picked up her schoolbag. "My real name."

Derek's huge grin popped the clown's nose off his face. It rolled onto the carpet by Livey's feet. "You mean that lady who rode naked on a horse?"

She threw the nose at him. "Some oracle you are. That's Lady Godiva."

"The homecoming dance?" he called out after her.

She paused and made a regretful face. "Sorry, Derek, but I've already been asked." Well, not yet, but that was just a technicality. And if Johnny didn't want to go the dance, then she wouldn't go either. Watching moonbows instead of dancing was perfectly okay with her as long as it was with him.

Hoping to bump into Johnny on the way out, Livey didn't exactly hurry to the office. Why hadn't he shown up? And why did the front office want her?

At the office, Mrs. Otto, the receptionist, quickly hid the romance novel she was reading and handed her one of the phones. *Your mother,* she mouthed.

Mom? Livey thought. Her mother never phoned her at school. She took the phone. "Mom, what's wrong?"

"Newton Academy phoned me. It's Darby. He's been in a fight."

"Oh my God. Is he okay?"

"He seems to be. But not the other boy. They can't get hold of your father, and neither can I."

"Darby's been in a fight and the *other* boy's not okay?"

"Where's your father, do you know?"

"Did you try the college?"

"Not there. And his cell doesn't answer."

"You know Dad, he always keeps it off."

"Then what's the point of having one? He's your *father*. He needs to be contactable if there's a family emergency. That man, I swear."

Not so long ago Livey would have sarcastically pointed out that her mother hadn't been so contactable herself when she'd run off with the Slimy Jerk. But she kept silent.

"I've asked Mrs. Blink to go there," her mom continued, "but I'd feel better if you went too. I know how responsible you are. I've already talked to your school. They'll have someone drive you over."

Livey handed the phone back to Mrs. Otto, who said that one of the counselors would take her.

The counselor was Mrs. Shetty, a middle-aged Indian woman who had a red dot on her forehead and wore saris. Livey was silent during the ride, thoughts tumbling around in her mind. Why hadn't Johnny shown up at the library? What kind of trouble had Darby gotten himself into?

Mrs. Shetty's gentle voice broke in. "Is there anything you want to talk about, Livey?"

Livey hesitated and then said, "You know Johnny Magnus?"

"I do."

"What do you know about him?"

"There are some students you see and they carry a certain image on the outside, but you know they are full of surprises. He is one of them. You, Livey, are another."

"I am?"

"And you've fallen for him, haven't you?"

"You can tell?"

Mrs. Shetty's laugh was as light as incense smoke. "A special counselor's trick."

"I love him," Livey said. "I love him, I love him. I can't help it, but I do."

"If you could help it, it wouldn't be love."

"You know, my mom fell in love and left us, and now I understand a little better."

Mrs. Shetty nodded at this as she pulled into Newton's lush campus. Mrs. Blink's ancient Dodge was parked in one of the visitor's slots, so Livey thanked Mrs. Shetty and said she'd get a ride back to school with their housekeeper.

As Livey hurried through the front door, she wasn't aware of Mrs. Shetty watching her with a smile that was both happy and sad. How wonderful that such a lovely girl was in love. Such a shame that it had to be with a boy who, she was quite certain, would break her heart.

At the front security office, Livey showed her ID and signed in for a pass. The guard pointed the way to the admin office. In the reception area, Darby sat with Mrs. Blink, both of them side-by-side in two corner chairs. Her brother slumped on his elbows. A scratch on his forehead was red with disinfectant, and a red lump marked his cheek. There was a small cut on his lower lip, which was turned down in a scowl.

"My God, Darby."

The woman sitting on the opposite sofa uncrossed her legs. "My

God, indeed. You should see what he did to my poor Julian."

Livey recognized the woman. Mrs. Bostick was one of those country club and charity moms, and even in golf clothes she looked polished to an inch of her life. She wore a gold necklace, its pendant a tiny gold version of that TETRA KUIZ game board.

Another boy limped into the lounge, escorted by the school nurse. He held an ice pack to a badly bruised eye, the other arm cupped around his ribs. His lips were swollen.

Mrs. Blink's heavy brows rose a fraction.

Way to go, Darby! Livey thought exultantly.

Darby's scowl deepened. He didn't seem very triumphant.

Mrs. Bostick cooed over her son. "Oh, my poor baby."

"You'd better have a dentist check Julian's loose tooth," the nurse said.

The two boys were summoned into the principal's office. Mrs. Bostick glared at Livey, and Livey smiled right back with her pert and bubbly cheerleading smile. She'd never been more proud of her brother in her life.

A few minutes later, the principal appeared and announced that both boys were being suspended for a week. They could go home right now.

Mrs. Bostick stood and glared at Darby. "You . . . you . . . violent little plagiarist."

"I am not a plagiarist!" he said, glaring right back.

Livey stepped between them.

The Bosticks left. Darby took his time getting his schoolbag that he'd stuck in the corner of his chair. The Shedd Aquarium notebook fell out, and he slammed it back into the bag.

As he slunk down the hall, Livey finally said, "What's wrong with you, Darbs? You won a fight with a bully twice as big as you."

"Thirty percent," Darby muttered.

"What?"

"He's not twice as big as me. He's approximately thirty percent heavier in mass, ten percent taller in height."

"Compared to you he's a heavyweight. And you won. So why the long face, horse?"

The old joke didn't raise a smile. Darby's cut lower lip began to quiver. "He said he was a friend. He said I didn't have to worry. But he wasn't even there. He didn't even help. Not one little bit."

"Who on earth are you talking about?"

Darby glanced away.

The security guard at the desk held up a hand. "Excuse me, Miss Ell, but do you know that young man out there? He says he's waiting for you."

She looked out the double doors. Her heart did a handspring as she saw Johnny leaning against one of the fancy pillars.

"It's okay, that's my boyfriend," she said.

"My goodness, Livey," Mrs. Blink said, pressing a hand to her chest. "Did you say your *boyfriend*?"

Livey didn't bother explaining. "You go home with Mrs. Blink," she said to her brother. "I'm going back to school with Johnny."

As they exited the double doors, Johnny straightened. He nodded politely at Mrs. Blink, quickly eyed Darby, and then said to Livey, "I missed you earlier."

She gave him a smile that burst up from way inside her and helped Darby into Mrs. Blink's car. Mrs. Blink was studying Johnny with the same concentration she gave her Arlington Park racing forms. She whispered, "He doesn't look your type at all, Livey."

"What type is that, Mrs. Blink?"

She patted Livey's forearm. "He needs fatting up. We'll have him over for dinner."

Livey waited until Mrs. Blink drove off before quickly kissing

Johnny on the cheek. "How'd you know I was here?"

"Heard your name on the PA and asked the school office."

"They told you?" The school office was very tight-mouthed about student information.

"I put on my most charming manner and threatened Mrs. Otto I'd tell her the ending to that novel she was reading if she didn't tell me where you went."

With a laugh, Livey got into the Beetle. Johnny closed the door after her and slid into his seat. As he started the car, Livey repeated what Mrs. Blink had said about having him over for dinner. "What's your favorite food? She's a great cook."

"What about you?"

"I make a killer PB and J."

At the gate, he stopped for traffic. "That'll do for me."

"What brand of peanut butter?"

"I don't know. Jif?"

"My God," she said dramatically. "A traitor to the great cause of Skippy Super Chunk!"

"I didn't know you could make a cause out of peanut butter."

"In our house you can."

He didn't reply, still watching the heavy traffic for a gap, his hand on the gear shift. She placed hers on his, marveling how small her hand was compared to his.

He gently shook it off. "Livey, please, I'm trying to drive."

That stung. She sat back and studied him. "How come you weren't in the library?" she asked.

He bit his cheek. "Aether was right. It's not a good idea."

There was a horrible sucking feeling in her chest. "Why not? Last night . . . were you just playing games?"

"Livey. That's the last thing I was doing, playing games. I've never shown a moonbow to anybody else."

"So what is it?"

"I have to tell you something. That clearing we were in last night, at certain times like full moons, a group of people meet there."

"What does that have to do with us?"

"I'm getting to that," he said. "It's the Pythagoreans who meet there."

"Those ancient Greek guys Mr. Savard talked about?" she asked, even more confused.

"He's one of them."

"He *is*?"

"We wear robes and pray before the tetraktys."

"*We?*"

"Haven't you ever wondered why Mr. Savard picked me to be his student teacher's assistant?"

Livey imagined him in a robe with a hood, those dark eyes glowing in the night. The image was so strong that goose bumps broke out on her forearms.

The traffic cleared. He hit the accelerator and swerved around a sports car. "Livey, the truth is, like I said, I'm not who you think I am. I'm working for somebody."

"You're an undercover agent?" she asked incredulously.

He tapped his fingers on the wheel. "Let's just say for somebody pretty important. Your brother's managed to get himself involved in something. That Bob guy isn't who you think he is either."

Livey stiffened. "My God. Is he dangerous?"

"Not in the way you're thinking."

"What do you mean, not in the way I'm thinking? I mean, he's practically a stranger. Staying in our house!" She got out her cell and dialed her dad. "Come on, come on, answer!" No answer. In frustration and fear she slapped the dashboard. "My stupid dad, inviting strangers to stay with us."

Johnny took her hand, folding his long fingers around hers like he was cupping a small bird. His touch calmed her. He released her hand as they approached a stop sign. Instead of rolling through it, he came to a complete rule-book stop. There were no other cars. Under the pale skin of his face the muscles twitched, as though he were thinking about something, trying to make up his mind.

"That's one hundred dollars we've saved," he said, and then drove on. At a second stop sign, he again came to a full stop. "That's two hundred." And then at the third sign on President, before they turned into the school's student lot, he did it again. "Three hundred." He pulled into an open parking spot and said, "Check your right pocket."

Patting the pocket of her jeans, she felt something. She stuck her hand in and withdrew three brand-new hundred dollar bills. She stared at them and then at Johnny. The green flecks in his eyes were sparkling, and a color had crept into his pale face, but unlike any color she had ever seen on a person. It was as though underneath his white skin the high bones of his cheeks were glowing.

"Me and Aether don't have to worry about money," he said in a soft voice. "We don't have to worry about where we live. We don't have to worry about lots of things that you have to worry about. And we're here to help. Just so you know."

Livey shoved open her door. She tried to get out. Something was keeping her in her seat. The seat belt. Johnny unbuckled it for her. She scrambled out as fast as she could and threw the money down on the seat. "That was just a trick," she said. "You planted them."

"I didn't want this assignment, but where I come from, you obey." That soft voice seemed to fill up her ears, her blood. "And the very first time I saw you made it even worse. You make me want to break the rules, Livey. That's why Aether was right. That's why it's not a good idea."

She turned and ran.

ONCE HOME, DARBY went straight to his room and hurled the notebook at the da Vinci poster. "Some friend you are."

Triangles shimmered and settled. Bob tugged on the cuffs of an elegant pinstripe suit jacket and shook back his hair, which had been cut and styled. He looked like he was ready to go on TV or meet the president or something. "No need for a temper tantrum."

"You promised you'd help. But you didn't even show up."

"I was indeed there. You do realize I was getting a hair and body treatment when you summoned me. One of my worshippers has a spa in Arizona. Elegant place." Bob critically examined Darby's hair. "I should get you an appointment."

"You let me get punched out."

"And you punched back, quite successfully. Do you not see? I did not need to help."

Darby thought of how his fright had turned to fury, and the way he had bounced out of the garbage can and charged Julian. He remembered Julian on the ground underneath him, and he remembered his quiet, efficient rage as his fists pummeled and punched; he remembered Julian screaming for him to stop, Roz sprinting for help, the janitor pulling him off Julian.

"Now you know something about yourself that you did not know before," Bob continued. "That you can win your own battles, and be crowned the king of the Boys' Club by your own efforts, which is the best way to be a king. Therefore, I helped you in the way you most needed help, did I not?"

Darby fingered the little cut on his lip. "But this still hurts."

"I can fix that," Bob said, reaching out a hand.

Darby stepped back. "Whoa. Wait. How?"

"By rotating the mathematical element that represents your lip through a symmetrical Hilbert space."

Darby fingered his lip and winced. "All right," he said. "Be careful."

Bob squeezed Darby's lower lip. There was a stinging sensation and then a numbing cold that was immediately replaced by flooding warmth as Bob let go. "There go you, my boy."

Darby touched his lip. The cut was gone. He looked in the mirror, stretching and flexing his lips. "Holy cow," he breathed. He had a sudden idea. "Can you do my ears?"

"Certainly." Bob held Darby's ears with both his hands. Again there was that bitter cold and rushing warmth. Bob stepped back and studied the result, looking pleased. "There. Elegant and symmetrical."

Darby excitedly rushed back to the mirror. His joy turned instantly to disbelief. His ears were tidy and evenly placed, and his glasses were no longer lopsided on them—that was true, but not in the way he wanted. "Bob, you put them on *backward*."

"A trivial symmetry."

"No, it's not! Put them back the way they were."

"And undo my handiwork? I think not."

"Bob, put them back!"

"My dear temperamental boy, please do not be such an ungrateful brat."

The door opened. In a panic, Darby draped a towel over his head.

Aether marched in, taking a bite out of something that looked like a soggy cracker, spread with peanut butter. She instantly spat the bite out into the wastebasket and tossed the rest. "Yuck, the manna's gone bad," she said, wiping her fingers on her shirt. "And Darby, why do you have a towel over your head?" Before Darby could react, she plucked it off and inspected his ears. "I told you he was dangerous."

"My little seraph," Bob said, "have you not heard of knocking?" Then his face lit up. "I say, how about a knock-knock joke? Knock-knock."

"Knock it off. You said you would go. So go."

"Now, my dear, the joke first. Knock-knock."

She growled with exasperation but played along. "Who's there?"

"It is I."

She rolled her eyes. "It is I who?"

"It is I, the Alpha and the Omega Function."

"Is that supposed to be funny?"

"It is elegant humor."

"It's stupid. Go, like you said. Now."

"Wait!" Darby exclaimed. "He's got to fix my ears first."

"I am not of this universe, my sweet seraph, so you have no authority to command me."

Aether eyed the notebook, splayed on the carpet where it had tumbled. She darted forward with outstretched hand, but Bob beat her to it. He opened his mouth and dropped the book into the black space beyond his sharp triangular teeth. "There. No more annoying Q.E.D.s."

"Give it back."

"I think not, my dear. Not only do I have much work to do here, I also have people praying to me. I cannot abandon them. I am that sure you, of all creatures, will understand."

With that he shimmered away.

"Now see what you've done?" Aether told Darby.

"My ears! Can you fix them?"

Aether shook her head.

"But you're an angel—"

"How many times—"

"Sorry, sorry. A seraph. You guys heal, right?"

She glanced skeptically at his ears. "I haven't learned that far. I might put your feet there by mistake."

"Ask somebody else."

"Then they'll know Bob didn't leave. I'll be in trouble." She sat down on the edge of the bed, kicking her feet. "What a mess this has turned into."

Darby cupped his hands over his ears. "We have to do something!" he wailed.

"The only way to get them fixed is to get that notebook back. If you have it, you can command him. And that's the only way to get Bob to leave, too, before he starts fixing things up too much."

Darby slumped on the bed beside her. "What are we going to do?"

"I don't know."

"But you're the seraph."

"Darby, if I knew everything, I'd be You Know Who."

"Can't you ask your older brother? He's a seraph like you, right?"

"He's too in love with your sister."

This made Darby forget about his ears for a moment. "He is?"

"He's breaking all the rules, falling in love with your sister. And she's in love with him, too, and she doesn't know who he really is. It's gonna be like the *Titanic*."

That was Livey, Darby thought. No ordinary boy for her. Her first boyfriend had to be an angelic being. He absently scratched his ear in bemusement and then rerealized his predicament. "We have to do something! I can't live like this forever!"

"There's plastic surgery. Like on those TV reality shows. You could be famous."

"I don't want to be famous, okay? I just want my ears back. And you want Bob gone, so this is your problem too."

She swung her legs. "This is all your stupid great-aunt's fault."

"No, it isn't. It's *your* fault. You should have stopped Bob. But no, you were playing hide-and-seek—" Darby abruptly went silent as his gaze fell on the framed photograph of his great-aunt. "I know! My Aunt Ludy. I bet she could help."

31

DURING CHEERLEADING PRACTICE, Livey was in a fog. What had been moonbows and mystery was now misery and menace. She was in love, and it was hurting.

In the gym, everybody seemed so far away, their voices coming from a great distance. Even when Chantelle and Trish held her up in the Liberty, she barely felt their grip.

That bad bruise when she'd fallen—Aether had told her it would get better, and it had, almost immediately. . . .

The rain that didn't get them wet . . .

I only eat manna . . .

The way Johnny had been waiting for her at the party and the way the drowned cell phone had started working after he'd held it . . .

And it wasn't possible for any ordinary person to predict in advance when a moonbow was going to appear. . . .

The money in her pocket . . .

We don't have to worry about things you worry about. . . . We're here to help. . . .

Understanding slammed into her so hard that she collapsed out of the Liberty and staggered over to sit on a bleacher. Chantelle squatted in front of her. "You all right? You're white as a ghost."

No, I'm not all right, Livey thought in a daze. *I've fallen in love with a . . . with a . . .* Her mind refused to cooperate. How could it be real? It was her heart that provided the word: *I've fallen in love with an angel.*

How could she even begin to explain such a thing? She would sound crazier than Aunt Ludy.

And if Aether and Johnny were angels, then what did that make Bob?

She finally realized who Bob reminded her of.

He was the guy in Darby's poster, down to each strand of that hair.

She rocketed to her feet. "Oh my God," she gasped. "I have to get home, right now."

32

AFTER CHANGING INTO corduroy pants and a camping shirt, Darby rummaged in his closet for his winter earmuffs to hide his ears. He found an old reggae knit cap instead, a gift from Aunt Ludy that she'd knitted herself. Even with the ragged stitching, it was much better than the earmuffs. He pulled it down over his backward ears.

In his daypack he put the explorer set Bob had transformed. The compass needle tilted up on its axis, tapping the glass. The notebook was still out there somewhere. Maybe not in ordinary three-dimensional space, but the compass was still pointing the way.

What else? He picked up the TETRA KUIZ board game. He didn't see any reason to bring it along, except that it had been in Hilbert space with the explorer set. Maybe it could do something helpful. If it didn't, then he could throw it away, or chop it up into firewood. He slipped the board game into the daypack.

He also added a pair of socks and a clean pair of underwear. The last thing he packed was the bathroom's first-aid kit. That guy on TV who did all that surviving the wild stuff was always putting tree sap on cuts and eating leaves to eat to stop diarrhea, but a first-aid kit was a lot easier.

Mrs. Blink had gone grocery shopping, so he sent Aether into the kitchen to make peanut butter and jelly sandwiches and to fill up a couple water bottles. While she did that, he wrote a quick note to his sister.

Livey, I've gone out with Aether to do something important. I don't know how long I'll be gone, but don't worry. She's not really a girl, she's a heavenly seraph, sort of like a guardian angel. And maybe I shouldn't tell you this, but so is her brother, your boyfriend.

He slipped the note on her computer keyboard, and a few moments later, he and Aether left the house. As they hurried across Lincoln Pond Park to the commuter station to catch the train to Elgin, he spotted a long black car with tinted windows turning the corner. "Uh-oh," he muttered.

Grabbing Aether's hand, he broke into a run, trying to get to the station's platform before whoever was in the car could spot them. Too late. As they ran up the stairs to the platform, the car swung into the commuters' parking lot.

On the platform, the mayor, Miss River Oaks, and members of the River Oaks Chamber of Commerce were waiting to greet the year's hundred thousandth commuter for a River Oaks promotion. A brass band stood by, and a video crew was recording the event.

Down in the parking lot, Agent Deakin opened the back door for the man wearing the red bow tie. Darby tried to hide among the small crowd of passengers waiting to board, but Mr. Bow Tie spotted him and wriggled the fingers of his hand as though saying *hi*.

In the distance, the arriving train blew its whistle.

Mr. Bow Tie and Agent Deakin headed for the stairs. Mr. Bow Tie pointed his finger at Darby, smiling a dead-fish smile.

"Those guys?" Darby whispered to Aether, with a quick jerk of his chin. "They're government agents. They want the notebook too. We have to stop them. Actually, you have to stop them, because I can't. I don't have any powers."

"I'm not allowed to do anything bad."

"Well, how about doing something good for *me*? And quick!"

Aether stood on tiptoe to whisper into the ear of one the welcoming committee members.

The train came to a stop with hissing brakes. Mr. Bow Tie clamped a hand on Darby's shoulder as the train doors opened. "I think you better come with us, young man."

The band broke into loud, trumpeting song. Miss River Oaks and her entourage marched up to Mr. Bow Tie. "Congratulations, sir!" The video camera team closed in.

Mr. Bow Tie let go of Darby's shoulder. "What? Wait, wait, you got it wrong. I didn't get off the train." But Miss River Oaks was draping a flower lei over his neck as the mayor approached with the key to the town.

Darby and Aether slipped onto the train just as the doors closed. Mr. Bow Tie glanced at him through the window, his strained smile for the mayor turning into a quick snarl at Darby. Darby wriggled his fingers at him as the train carriage lurched forward.

"Phew, that was close," he said to Aether. "Thanks. That was quick thinking."

"What was?"

"Back there. What did you tell that man?"

"Oh, that. His zipper was down."

"Hunh?"

"You told me to do something good, right? His zipper was down, so I told him."

"But that's not—oh, never mind."

The three women across the aisle were giving them looks and whispering. One of the women leaned over and asked them where they lived and where they were going.

Aether told her to mind her own business.

The woman jerked back as if she'd been scalded. "Children these days," she said to her traveling companions. "No manners."

At the Elgin stop, Darby and Aether transferred to a local bus. On the bus, a teenage boy with a bully's bored look on his pimply face sat in the back. He eyed Darby and then moved forward to say he really liked Darby's reggae cap.

Darby told him to mind his own business.

The boy pinched the cap from Darby's head. A look of horror blossomed on his face. He threw the cap at Darby and backed away, saying, "That's just gross, man."

Darby could feel his ears burning as usual, but backward this time. He crammed the cap back on.

At Elgin, he and Aether got off at a stop near the community college and walked several long blocks to the Silverwood Home for Mental Health. The criminally insane were locked up in the secure wards at Elgin's state psychiatric hospital, but Silverwood looked like a charming bed-and-breakfast, with spacious lawns and old oaks whose leaves were starting to change color. Yet the patients here were no less locked up. Even more securely, since this was where the government kept a lot of people with top secrets in their crazy heads.

Like Aunt Ludy.

Darby halted before the wrought-iron gates, lacquered black and garnished with painted grape clusters. These gates were open during the day, and were only for show. The real gate was the guarded lobby entrance, a short walk down the tree-lined drive. A woman was entering, the double doors swooshing open. Beyond the doors, Darby could see the armed guard at the front door counter and beyond him another armed guard at the metal detectors.

Every time he and his family had visited Aunt Ludy, they'd been screened and checked.

"We have to think of a way to get in," he told Aether.

"Easy." She marched to the lobby doors, which silently whisked open.

The first guard looked at them. "Yeah?"

Aether asked, "Did our mom just come in here? In a green dress and big hair?"

"That was your mother?"

Aether pouted. "She left us behind at the bus station. Again. *She* should be put in here. Come on, Darby."

As they trotted across the foyer to the metal detector, Darby whispered, "You can't do bad things, but you're allowed to lie?"

"That wasn't lying. That was acting."

The detector caught the metal in Darby's backpack and buzzed.

"Hold up there," the second guard said.

"It's okay," Aether said.

"I don't think so. Let's have a look."

"It's okay," Aether repeated, emphasizing the last word. She did something with her eyes, made them go narrow as if boring a hole right into his head. He plopped back down on his seat and stared at the metal detector.

"It's okay," he said. "It's okay it's okay it's okay it's okay. . . ."

Darby glanced over his shoulder at the guard as they rushed to the lounge. "What did you do?"

"I'm not real good yet at hypnotizing. He might get stuck there for a while. Where's your aunt's room?"

Darby led her through the visitor's lounge and up carpeted stairs and then down a hall toward his aunt's room. An orderly spotted them. "Hey, you, you're not supposed to be in here!"

They were passing a restroom. Aether pushed Darby into it.

"This is the women's!" Darby whispered.

"Shut up." She made a circular motion with her hand around them. Something like a bubble of air formed around Darby. The orderly barged in and looked right at Darby and then poked her head into the toilet stalls. "Where'd they go?" she muttered. She ran back out.

"I'm invisible?" Darby said.

"It's more fun acting," Aether said.

Darby peered into a toilet stall. "Just like the men's."

"You want to use it?"

He stepped back in embarrassment. "No."

In his cocoon of invisibility, Darby confidently walked to Aunt Ludy's room. The orderly was not in sight, and nobody else was in the hall. He opened the door and entered, Aether behind him.

Aunt Ludy was in a wheelchair by her bed. Wisps of frizzy white hair floated loose around her aluminum hat. Her black eyes peered suspiciously from their sunken wells at the door opening and then closing. "Who's there?"

"Me, Darby," Darby said.

He pulled aside the bubble of air. He was expecting Aunt Ludy to be astonished at his sudden appearance, but she only grinned, showing her mottled gums. "My dear boy! How wonderful to see you. Do give us a kiss."

He dutifully pecked her leathery cheek.

"I remember knitting that cap," she said. "Let me see." Before Darby could react, she plucked it off his head and frowned at him. "What on earth's ever happened to your ears?"

"That's what we're here about," he said. "We're in a bit of trouble, Aunt Ludy."

"Who's 'we'?"

Aether appeared out of her bubble.

"And who are you, my dear?"

"Her name's Aether. She's a seraph."

Aunt Ludy nodded as if she saw seraphs all the time. "And what trouble are you in?"

"You know that Thingamabob Conjecture of yours?"

"Oh, dear. I don't like the sound of this."

"Darby proved it," Aether said.

"Oh, my. Now he exists. He's dangerous."

"I know," Darby said, fingering an ear.

She sucked her lips and chewed her gums for a few seconds. "Perhaps you've made a mistake in the proof. If we could find one, then he'll go poof!"

"I didn't make a mistake," Darby said indignantly.

"He promised me he'd go back to his universe after he was proved," Aether said, "but he's cheating. He's swallowed up Darby's proof. We have to go find it. It's in Hilbert space."

"Is it, now? What a coincidence. I have a Hilbert space machine." She got up from her wheelchair and shuffled to her closet. From the back of the closet, she pulled out a folded cardboard box the size of a mini-fridge, which Darby unfolded for her. She told him to lay it on its side, the bottom facing the wall. Equations were scribbled on its sides. From behind a dresser, Aunt Ludy retrieved a three-foot plastic pipe attached to a leather belt. The pipe was a sheath for her walking cane, which she pulled out and showed to Darby. The cane was wrapped in gold foil, with aluminum flakes glued at intervals. "Do you remember this?"

"Your fractal sword."

"This is the new, improved version. You'll need it. Put it on."

Darby strapped the belt around his waist.

Aunt Ludy pointed to the box's open top. "Off you go, then."

Darby stared at the opening, his heart thumping. "Ladies first," he said to Aether.

She shook her head. "Unh-unh. Boys lead the way."

Darby tugged on his cap. Taking a deep breath, he got down on his hands and knees and crawled into the box.

LIVEY BURST THROUGH the front door. "Darby, are you home?"

Bob stood in the foyer, folding a sheet of notebook paper which he tucked into the inner pocket of an immaculate pinstriped suit coat. A gold A-Ω emblem was pinned to the lapel. His hair had been styled.

Livey backed up a step. "Stay away from me."

"Pardon?"

"I don't know who or what you are."

"Now, Livey." He sounded so reasonable, and looked so real, that doubt crossed her mind. Maybe he only just sort of kind of looked like that guy in Darby's poster.

"Where's Darby?" she asked.

"A most excellent question, one that I am wondering myself. Ah, my ride is here. If you will excuse me?" He picked up his suitcase and marched out to the street, where a prim Honda Civic, with ALGBRA vanity plates, had pulled up. Mr. Savard got out and helped put away the suitcase with lots of bowing and scraping.

After Livey closed the front door, Mrs. Blink poked her head around the kitchen corner. "Some houseguest. He was in your room."

"He was?" She rushed to her bedroom. On her computer keyboard was a note, written in elegant script. "Thank you for your hospitality, my dear Livey." It was signed "Bob A-Ω"

She barged into her brother's room and stared at the da Vinci poster. There was no mistake. Bob was the spitting image of da Vinci's *Vitruvian Man*.

She ran back to the kitchen, where Mrs. Blink was washing vegetables. "Where's Darby?"

"I don't know. I went to the market and he was gone when I came back. And the peanut butter is empty and half a loaf of bread is gone."

Livey sprinted to Lincoln Pond Park. Darby wasn't there. One of the moms said she'd seen Darby trotting across the park with that little girl he was always playing with. Darby's backpack looked heavy, she said.

Livey sat down on a bench and stared at the Lincoln statue without really seeing it. Where could Darby and Aether have gone? She tried to convince herself that her brother would be home by dinner, but she doubted it. He was doing something stupid and probably dangerous.

"Johnny," she whispered. "I need you."

No Beetle rattled up the street.

She thought of the old abandoned house out in the marsh. Were Darby and Aether planning to camp out there? It didn't seem likely, but on the other hand, nothing else came to mind.

She raced on her bicycle to the Preserve and the broken-down farmhouse. The weedy lot was empty. A faint swampy smell clung to the air. The only sound was the chirping of crickets. A black bird circled overhead, as though watching her.

She leaned the bike against a stunted apple tree. The front door of the house was tilted off its hinges. The floorboards in the room beyond were warped, and graffiti was sprayed on the walls. Crumpled in a corner was a tattered sleeping bag. Opposite the sleeping bag, stairs with several treads missing led up to the attic.

"Darby? Aether?" she called out.

Outside, she heard the harsh cry of the bird.

She checked the other rooms. Empty. Climbing the creaky stairs, she came to a gaping hole where three treads were missing. She wasn't a cheerleader flyer for nothing. She crouched and jumped to the next step. It cracked under her weight. She grabbed the railing, but the rotten wood gave way. As she toppled backward to the floor, her ankle caught and twisted in the railing's balustrade. The pain brought tears to her eyes, clouding her vision, so when she saw the man at the top of the stairs, she wasn't sure exactly how he got to her side. Had he floated down on his own black shadow?

He knelt beside her with a scraping of boots, his winter overcoat draping on the floor. His eyes were streaked with red. His stubble hair looked like burned straw, his teeth were cracked, and he smelled like rotting garbage. "Oh, did you hurt yourself?" he asked.

She scrabbled away on the palms of her hands, dragging her hurt foot, groaning from the pain of it, while still managing to say, "Get away from me."

"But you need help. I'll help you. I'll help you good."

Livey's back hit the wall. She couldn't go any farther. She was more scared than she'd ever been in her life. "Johnny!"

The man chuckled hoarsely. "Johnny? Who is this Johnny? Can he help you like I can help you?"

Another shadow spilled through the front door. Johnny appeared. "Hello, Rotgut."

Rotgut stood. "You," he spat.

"Yup. Me."

Rotgut slowly grinned. "You just want her for yourself."

"Sure I do. *You're* certainly not going to touch her. Leave."

"You gonna make me?"

Johnny threw out his hand. Light flashed. With a pained cry, the thing called Rotgut flew backward, turning into shadow that flapped out the broken window.

Still trembling with fright, Livey held her arms out to Johnny. He knelt beside her and let her hug him tightly. "It's okay, you're safe," he said.

"Who . . . what was that?"

"That was one of the bad ones," he said softly. "They're around, especially wherever there's trouble. Like vultures. But he's gone. He won't bother you anymore."

She buried her face in her hands.

"Hey, you don't have to cry."

But she wasn't crying. She was laughing. She lowered her hands. "I can't believe it. I know who you are, Johnny, and I just can't believe that I've fallen in love with an angel."

"Oh, boy," Johnny whispered.

"And you love me, too."

His smile slid into her blood and made it hum. "It's still not a good idea."

She leaned forward, and gasped from the pain shooting through her ankle.

"Let's have a look at that," he said. She was still in her gym clothes. He carefully rolled down the sock on her right ankle, which was already swelling. "We should get you to a doctor," he said. "But I've broken so many rules, what's a few more?" He put both his palms on her ankle. Warmth flooded through her foot. He murmured something in a strange language that sounded like a flute's haunting notes. The warmth turned into heat that was nearly unbearable, making her hiss.

"That should do it," he said, releasing her ankle.

She tentatively flexed it. It no longer hurt. The swelling was gone. "Wow," she said. "Some girls have personal trainers, but *I* have a personal healer."

"What are you doing here?"

"Looking for Darby and Aether. They've gone off somewhere. And Bob, too, with Mr. Savard. He's not human, is he?"

"It's a long story," he said. "I'll tell you in the car."

His Beetle was parked out on the lot. She hadn't even heard it pull up.

Using a length of grimy rope, he tied her bicycle to the rounded roof. As they drove off, he told her the story, starting with her Aunt Ludy and the Pythagorean circle during the H-bomb test and the intelligent math function that got stuck in the regular Einsteinian universe.

"Aether and I were assigned to guard this alien math thing. An intelligent, aware, conscious mathematical object. Your brother calls him Bob, which is as good a name as any. With everything going on in this world, the big battle of good versus evil, Bob was the least of everybody's worries. He wasn't doing any harm. Our job was pretty boring. And it got Aether out of everybody's hair, so to speak."

"And you?" Livey prompted.

He was silent for a moment and then said, "I was involved in something else, something much more important, but I disagreed with my superiors and got reassigned."

"You can disagree? I thought you were all obedient and everything."

"There's a lot people don't know, and a lot of what they think they know is wrong. Thousands of years of myths add up."

She squeezed his hand, to reassure herself that he was real, he was here.

"Now, Bob wanted your aunt to prove him so he could go back to where he came from. That's what we wanted too, and that's what Bob promised us. He can't lie, you know. Nothing to do with ethics, it has to do with his identity as a mathematical object. In math, what's true is true and stays true. But your aunt, she didn't trust him. She didn't trust any of us, either." Johnny shook his head and chuckled. "She can be as stubborn as a two-headed mule. She decided she had to go crazy in order to help save the world from Bob."

"How did my brother get involved?"

"Your great-aunt wrote the Conjecture in the margins of one of her old books which he found—"

"The one in the attic! FBI agents came and took it away."

Johnny shucked a cigarette out of his pack. "That's another complication. But your brother, when he was four, he came across that conjecture and because his mind was so flexible and unprejudiced, he was able to communicate with Bob, play with him as a make-believe friend. Darby grew out of that, but this idea of Bob was already stamped on his mind."

Livey put the palm of one hand over the fingers of her other. "Time out," she said.

"Yeah?"

"Your cigarettes."

He looked puzzled. "What about them?"

"You never smoke them. Is that because smoking is a sin?"

His brows and mouth twitched and then he burst out laughing.

"What's so funny?"

"Sorry, I wasn't laughing at you." He crushed the cigarette in the ashtray. "Look, the reason you shouldn't smoke isn't because it's a sin, it's because it ruins your health."

"So that's why you don't actually smoke?"

Now he looked sheepish. "I suppose I better explain something. I don't really have to smoke, just like I don't really have to eat. The essence of the food, not the actual meal, is what I need."

That explained his strange eating habits, Livey thought, the way he cupped his food with his hands. "So you actually are smoking when you have a cigarette in your mouth?"

"Kind of, but it doesn't do me any harm. I just like the taste."

"Well," she said primly, "it's a good thing you don't light up, because I wouldn't kiss you. It'd be like licking an ashtray."

"In that case," Johnny said, "I'll obey the spirit as well as the letter of the law." He chucked the pack of cigarettes out the window.

Livey shook her head. "I can't believe you did that. You just littered. Now go back and get it and throw it in a garbage can."

Johnny sighed and reversed the Beetle to get the pack, which he tossed into the backseat.

"Now, what about Bob and Darby and Aunt Ludy?" Livey asked.

Johnny continued the story. "So we have Darby already impressionable when it comes to Bob, right? This is when Mr. Savard gets involved. He's a minor elder of the Pythagorean Brotherhood. He finds a paper with your aunt's Conjecture and starts to fiddle around with it. That tetraktys does have supernatural power, you understand, so he starts communicating to Bob through it. This doesn't prove Bob, but it does make him more active, and he starts to reach out to Darby, who is Bob's best bet to be proved. Aether and me, we knew this, things were getting critical here, so that's when we became who we are in this life. In your lives." He fiddled with the silver cross on his necklace. "I've only become a mortal a couple of times. I never expected to fall in love. I had no idea what it could do."

"Are you sorry?"

"Are you kidding?"

Livey thought of something else. "How old are you?"

"In human years? Almost eighteen. Old enough to attend council but nobody listens to you; they pat you on the head like you're a young one and think you have nothing to say."

"Guess what, it's the same down here."

"Anyway, Darby proves Bob. But Bob's taken a liking to being worshipped by Mr. Savard and other Pythagoreans and so he doesn't really want to leave."

"But he promised he would, right? I mean, I thought you said he can't lie."

"He's learning how to fudge. He *will* leave, but he thinks it's his duty to fix up the world first." Johnny's face hardened. "Your Aunt Ludy was right about him. He's become a danger."

"Aunt Ludy!" Livey exclaimed. "I bet that's where Darby and Aether went, to go get her help."

34

IN THE SUNROOM of the Bostick residence, decorated with prize orchids, Bob and Mr. Savard took afternoon tea with Mrs. Bostick. She fussed and twittered and showed them an expensive orchid, a potted blue Vanda, and promised to name her next new cultivar after Bob. *Phalaenopsis Alpha-Omega.*

"But this orchid is simply a tangle of roots," Bob observed.

"It isn't flowering. It's gorgeous when it flowers."

"What elegance is there to a flower without flowers?"

She put a hand to her chest and twittered. "Oh, you," she said.

The maid brought fancy cakes but Bob asked if he might have a PB and J sandwich instead. "I have taken quite a liking to them," he said.

As he nibbled on the sandwich, Mrs. Bostick spoke of the horrifying assault on her son, Julian. "That boy Darby Ell is a menace to society," she declared. "I wouldn't be surprised at all if he ends up in jail."

"He is indeed a menace," Bob replied, although not in the way Mrs. Bostick was referring to. He was sensing vibrations in Hilbert space. Darby and that odious little seraph had found a way in and were searching for the Book, the glorious proof of his magnificent self.

Not that he worried. Not only was Hilbert space infinite, but the clever little lad had been dumb enough to bring along a tetraktys, which made tracking him much easier. Furthermore, Bob had hidden the Book particularly well, and with superb wit. His worshippers would do well to put away their crass comedy and study the elements of Alpha-Omega humor.

There was much to do on this planet. The Tower of Pisa had merely been a minor exercise, but there were other, more serious things. There was, for example, the problem of Standard Reference 2387 at the National Institutes of Standards and Technology. This was the national standard for peanut butter, which laboratories and true peanut butter lovers could order, three six-ounce jars for $501. It wasn't the price that bothered Bob—what did he care about money, except of course that the dollar bills were poorly designed? No, it was that one would expect the national standard to be the most elegant of peanut butter, with super chunks, not creamy. This definitely required fixing.

There was also the annoying untidiness to the speed of light—299,792,458 meters per second. An ugly number. Something must have gone wrong in the creation of this universe. Surely it was intended to be an orderly 300,000,000 meters per second. He would have to do something about this soon.

But in the meantime, there was Darby and that detestable seraph to take care of. Just in case.

"May I see your son?" he asked Mrs. Bostick.

Leaving Mr. Savard to his cake and tea, she led Bob to a bedroom with the curtains pulled. Julian lay in bed. Bob asked to be left alone with him, and Mrs. Bostick withdrew.

Julian had drawn a remarkable likeness of Darby on a piece of cardboard, which he had taped to his closet door. In his hand was a pellet gun. He took aim. *Thwock!* Another bull's-eye. Darby's ears were in tatters.

"Excellent marksmanship," Bob said.

"I wish I could do it for real," Julian muttered.

"Do you, my dear young man? Darby is trying to steal something of mine, and I need you to stop him."

Julian lowered the gun. "Yeah?"

Bob bent to a terrarium and gazed at the insects within. "Remarkable creatures. You collect them?"

"Well, I don't eat them. What's this about stopping Darby?"

On the table by the terrarium were a TETRA KUIZ board and the super-duper vacuum bug collector that Julian had bought at the Shedd Aquarium gift shop. Bob inspected the gun-shaped collector and pulled the trigger. The barrel sucked air into its transparent trap. "Interesting," he said. He rotated the gun into and then out of Hilbert space, and aimed it at the antique oak clothes tree by the closet. He again pulled the trigger. The clothes tree quivered, and then *shwuuucked!* across the room, shrinking as it did so. Bob peered at the trap, which now contained a miniature antique oak clothes tree.

"How did you do that?" Julian asked in amazement.

"I have my ways," Bob said. "Would you like to catch Darby and add him to your collection? Perhaps put him on that twig in there?"

Julian blinked and then smiled. "Better than shooting off his ears."

Bob picked up the TETRA KUIZ board and asked Julian to put his thumbs on two of the pegs. Julian did so. His eyes widened. "My ribs are better, and my toothache's gone!"

"Darby is in Hilbert space," Bob said. "You need to go after him."

The mention of Hilbert space did not confuse Julian. The metal studs presented to his mind a fantastic landscape of adventure, and also of a very tiny Darby begging for mercy. Julian grinned in anticipation. Then, in the landscape he was seeing, he spotted a flitting creature, a creature that was possibly unfriendly and hungry. "Can you send Rosalind Arbito with me?" Rosalind was big and slow. Anything chasing them would catch her first.

"As you wish. I shall pay her a visit later. As for you, I need to swallow you, but do not be afraid. You will not be harmed."

Bob opened his mouth wide as the bed, and scooped up Julian and the bug collector and the TETRA KUIZ.

As Mr. Savard drove Bob to Roz Arbito's house, Bob considered his options.

There were many Pythagorean circles he needed to visit in his elemental form as the Alpha and the Omega function. Yet it was entirely fitting that he also take the form of the humans he was saving, and become one of them. To borrow the complex conjugate of a mere drawing served its purposes, but there was no need to limit oneself to only that manifestation.

The human senses were limited, but quite exquisite. The taste of Skippy Super Chunk, of which there was an abundance at Darby's residence, was there not? Livey needed assistance with her algebra, did she not? And he was here to help make this world a better place, was he not? If her mind was inelegant, then he could make it elegant, could he not? And with Darby gone, his bed was empty, was it not?

Thus the idea came to him. He saw that it was elegant, and was pleased.

35

LIVEY NEEDED TO go home and change first before driving out with Johnny to see Aunt Ludy. She also had to come up with some story to tell her dad. He believed pretty much anything she told him, but even so, this one would be tricky. Plus, there was the problem of how to get in and see her. The Home was strict about scheduled visits.

But then again, she had her own personal angel to help, sitting right there in the car beside her.

Dusk was quickly thickening. As Johnny turned onto Beechwood, the streetlights came on. And there, shuffling through the glow by Lincoln Park, was Darby, hands thrust in his pockets.

"Johnny! Stop! Look who's here!"

Johnny pulled over. Livey got out and ran over to Darby to give him a hug.

He squirmed. "Please unhand me."

She ruffled his hair and let him go. "Where were you?"

"A random walk." He adjusted the glasses on his nose.

"Hey, the cut on your lip," Livey said.

Darby touched his lower lip, pinching it a little. "It stings."

She had thought it was gone, but no, the cut was there, scabbing over. The shadows must have tricked her.

Johnny leaned out the car window. "Where's Aether?"

Darby shrugged. "I do not know. She never tells me where she is going. I am hungry." He headed for the house.

"You want to have dinner with us?" Livey asked Johnny.

"I'd better go look for Aether."

"Can't you sense her? You don't have, like, a psychic connection?"

"It's more difficult when we're not our other selves. She needs to use her powers first. And she goes her own way a lot. Which means I'd really better go look for her before she gets into some kind of trouble."

Down at the end of the street, a pale white moon had ghosted above the houses. "Does she go to that meeting with you?"

"Sometimes." He frowned. "And Livey, if you get tempted to go out there, don't. It's dangerous. Just stay home with Darby."

"All right."

He parked the car and untied her bicycle from the roof. She got on, but didn't want to leave him. He removed the necklace and cross from around his neck and draped it over her head. He didn't say anything. There was no need for words.

She rode home on a cloud and stayed there, even when Darby hogged all the hot water.

Mrs. Blink noticed. "Is it that new boyfriend of yours?"

"He's an angel," Livey said.

She harrumphed. "They all are at first."

At dinner, Livey ate a double portion of pot roast. If falling in love was supposed to take away your appetite, it sure wasn't working for her.

Darby scraped the last of the peanut butter out of the jar and had a sandwich for his dinner, announcing that from now on all he would eat would be PB and Js.

Her dad was moody and quiet, so much so that the announcement of Darby's fight at school had gone right past him. Something had gone wrong with his Riemann Hypothesis proof.

"Truth is truth, Father," Darby said. "You must accept that fact."

Father? Livey thought. Since when did Darby ever call their dad "Father"?

"I wish Bob hadn't run out on us," Jerry grumbled. "It's his fault."

Darby carefully folded his napkin and placed it on the table. "He helped you as you asked. You cannot pick and choose the result."

"I should have been a garbage collector. I shouldn't have gone to school. I shouldn't have married your mother—"

Livey let her fork drop. "Dad!"

"Excuse me. I'm going to go lie down."

Darby did the dishes while Livey talked to Chantelle in her bedroom about Johnny. "He's an angel, he really is."

"You got it bad," Chantelle said.

"I know," Livey said.

After they hung up, the house felt too small for her. She felt all bouncy and excited. Plus all that dinner she'd eaten needed to be worked off. She decided to walk to May's Market and buy more peanut butter for Darby's lunch.

Darby was just finishing up the dishes, holding a plate in his hands. His back was to her, and from the hallway she only had a partial view, but had she really seen what she thought she'd seen?

"Darby! Did you just lick that plate?"

He turned to her. "Am I a dog? I most assuredly did not lick the plate."

Livey examined the dishes. All squeaky clean. They couldn't have been any cleaner.

"Do you wish for me to do the laundry?" Darby asked.

She laughed at the idea. He would probably flood the utility room with foamy suds. "You don't even know how."

"That is true. I do not. Algebra, perhaps? Do you need my help?"

"God, Darby. No thanks. I'm going to May's to get some stuff. Be back in a minute."

"I shall go with you."

That surprised her. "But you hate shopping."

"I do? Yes, I do. Yet you are my sister. It is my obligation to help."

She frowned at him. "You have been, like, so weird! Talking funny and everything. What side of the bed did you wake up on?"

"Which inertial frame of reference are you employing?"

"Oh, for Pete's sake," she muttered. He was just trying a new way to annoy her, but she wasn't going to let him. "Get your jacket and stay out of my way."

May's Market was a small family chain, more expensive than the bigger supermarkets, but it was within walking distance, in South Farm Square. Livey and Darby walked down Beechwood and past Lincoln Park. Livey kept touching the cross on her neck. It was the best gift anybody had ever given her.

"Listen, that Bob guy," she said. "Doesn't he remind you of anybody?"

She'd been wondering how much to tell Darby. This was a start. Hadn't Darby noticed that Bob was exactly the same guy as the one in the poster he saw every morning when he woke up?

Darby nodded. "He reminds me of Jesus."

"Jesus?"

"His hair. The world he must save. The name Bob is a palindrome, did you know? The same forward as backward. An elegant name. The longest known sensible palindrome is approximately five thousand words long. It begins with 'Star? Not I. Movies . . .' and ends 'I vomit on rats.' Have you ever vomited, Livey?"

"Just shut up, okay?"

At the shopping center, a van was unloading children to see a special Monday evening show at the theater. Many were in wheelchairs. Livey knew the group, as the cheerleaders had done a fundraising for their organization last year. She greeted Mrs. Chastain and then hugged Suzi, one of the girls in the wheelchairs. Darby darted in and gripped Livey's arm, tugging her away.

She resisted. "This is my brother, Darby."

Suzi smiled as best she could. "Hi, Darby."

Darby yanked harder. Livey followed him to the corner, wondering what this was all about. He nodded at the group. "What is wrong with them?"

"What? Nothing's wrong with them. Some people are tall, some people are short, and some people are in wheelchairs."

"They are not elegant."

"Darby! Do you say that about Wiles when he limps around?" Livey was shocked that her brother would say such a thing. It was not like him. Something about her brother had changed. Maybe he wasn't trying to annoy her on purpose. Had Bob hypnotized him or something? "Why are you acting so weird? Did Bob do something to you?"

He blinked and looked hurt, just like he always did. Livey's doubt vanished. She hugged him. His ears turned red, and that typical Darby blush further reassured her.

At May's Market, she got a jar of Skippy's Super Chunk. Darby had been right behind her, looking bemused at the racks and shelves. Now she couldn't find him. She looped around the aisle and found him at the butcher's section, staring aghast at the refrigerated meat display with its moist red slabs of freshly butchered beef.

"Holy cow," he said to Livey. "Do you eat this?"

"Well, you do like yours well-done—"

Without warning, he vomited into the display case. The two elderly women at the section screeched and rushed away. The butcher behind the counter yelled, "Jeez, kid!"

Livey froze with shock and embarrassment. A manager in a red May's apron rushed up. "Dammit, if you're going to be sick, be sick outside."

Darby heaved again. The manager pinched his shoulder and swung him around. Darby winced from the pain of his grip. Livey's embarrassment turned to anger. She swatted the man. "Let him go! It's not like he planned it."

"He just ruined all that meat. Now we'll have to throw it out."

From around the back aisle appeared another man. Livey recognized him at once by his red bow tie. He was one of those federal agents who'd been to the house. He showed the manager a badge and hauled Darby out the front door.

Livey ran after him through a cashier's lane, forgetting about the jar of peanut butter she hadn't paid for. The manager was now shouting at her, and one of the bag boys tried to tackle her. She threw a ten-dollar bill at him and ran out of the store, frantically calling for Darby.

But her brother was gone.

36

ON THE MARSH'S graveled road, Livey pedaled her bicycle into a gusting wind. It seemed to her as if the swaying trees were trying to scrape the full moon from the sky. The abandoned house came into view, the roof tracing a jagged outline against the whitewash of moonlight. She got off her bike and hid it behind a bush. The luminous dials of her watch said it was five minutes to midnight. She crouched down to watch and listen. More than a dozen cars were parked in the lot, including a Honda Civic with ALGBRA plates. No Beetle, though. The flush of warmth from her hard ride faded, and despite the sweater she was wearing, she began to feel cold.

She hadn't planned on doing this. Her first instinct at May's Market had been to call 911, but then she sat down on the curb outside the store to think it through. A federal agent had taken Darby away, no doubt because of Aunt Ludy's Conjecture and that proof he was working on. The cops wouldn't be able to do anything. Besides, she'd have to start explaining things, about the proof and

RICHARD LEWIS

Bob, and they'd probably lock her up with Aunt Ludy.

From the market, she had gone back to the house, only to find that her dad wasn't home. He was probably at the college working on that stupid proof. As usual, he didn't have his cell phone on, and the department number only gave her a recorded message. She paced the living room, debating whether to call her mom. But if she did, then sure as anything, the Slimy Jerk would get involved. Livey knew he worked at the NSA, which was another top secret federal agency. What if he was friends with Mr. Bow Tie?

That wasn't her only concern. There was Darby. Grossed out by beef and throwing up in a meat display? He loved Mrs. Blink's special T-bones. No, Darby wasn't really behaving like Darby. Her initial suspicion had been correct. What if he'd been, well, *possessed*? Could Bob do something like that?

That was when she suddenly realized something. She slapped her forehead with the heel of her hand. *Stupid, stupid, stupid,* she thought. *I have an angel for a boyfriend. If anybody can help me, it's Johnny.*

She knelt at the sofa and prayed. Surely God would relay the message. But Johnny didn't show. After waiting awhile, she finally decided that she couldn't wait any longer. She had to take action herself, which meant going to where Johnny would be.

So here she was, picking her way along a trail through a moonlit wood. For courage, she cupped Johnny's cross in her palm.

She began to hear a murmured chanting. Through the thinning branches by the clearing she saw people in robes gathered in a half circle before the fallen tree. Moonlight drenched them. She spotted the profile of Mr. Ricci's handsome face. Mrs. Bostick was there was well. But she couldn't tell if Johnny was among the others.

In the front of the gathered Pythagoreans, an unrobed man knelt on the wild grass, his head bobbing loosely on his neck. Two burly Pythagoreans stood guard on either side of him, and in front of him was Mr. Savard, his hands clasped behind his back.

Beside Mr. Savard was a folding card table, and on the table was a TETRA KUIZ game board, its metal studs brightly reflecting the moon.

Mr. Ricci stepped forward and bowed to Mr. Savard before handing him a squat jar. Mr. Savard turned to the table, holding up the jar in both hands. He chanted, "O holy tetraktys, root of all wisdom and creation, we come to you in humble adoration. And come to us, o divine Spirit of Number, and grant us knowledge. Reveal thyself, o blessed number!"

Shimmering triangles flowed up from the metal studs and began to swim in lazy curves, their forms appearing and disappearing, casting a trailing wake of rainbow colors. Livey was mesmerized by its beauty.

"Bow before me," a voice said, seeming to come from everywhere in the moonlight, "for I am the Alpha and the Omega function who blesses you and makes you perfect."

Mr. Savard placed the jar on the table and knelt on the ground, as did the others.

One of the triangles opened up, revealing a darkness that closed around the jar. Just before the jar vanished, Livey recognized the label: SKIPPY SUPER CHUNK.

The triangle creature spoke again. "That which is inelegant in your lives, make elegant. That which you cannot make elegant, dissolve into nothingness, for nothingness is absolute elegance. Mrs. Bostick, this means your Vanda orchid. It does not possess the beauty it should. Burn it."

Mrs. Bostick stiffened. "But it wasn't flowering yet! You haven't really seen it!"

The voice spoke softly but carried a sharpness that made Livey's skin pucker. "I am the Alpha and the Omega function. I have spoken."

Mrs. Bostick bowed her head.

"And now we have an initiate," the thing said. "Bring him forward."

The two burly Pythagoreans lifted the kneeling figure. Livey recognized him then—the agent with the red bow tie. The two men each took one of his hands and put a thumb to the TETRA KUIZ board. The man jolted and then began to babble. "O most holy Alpha and Omega, I repent and kneel before thee."

Livey watched in astonishment and fright. If that was the man who'd taken Darby away, then where was Darby?

"Johnny," she whispered. "Where are you?"

And from behind her came a replying whisper. "Keep as quiet as you can. We have to get out of here right now before they realize you're here."

37

LIVEY AND JOHNNY quickly and quietly retreated through the woods. Once they were in sight of the abandoned house, Johnny said, "I told you to stay away."

"I was looking for you." She briefly explained about Mr. Bow Tie taking Darby. The same Mr. Bow Tie who had crumpled to the ground, babbling like his mind had been short-circuited. "What was that triangle sharky thing?"

"That," Johnny said grimly, "was Bob. The real him."

"You mean that thing was living in our house the whole time? Oh my God. Does he have Darby, too?"

"I don't think so."

"So where's Darby?"

"I bet you'll find him back home at your house wondering where *you* are," Johnny said as they skirted the parked cars.

"You think?" Livey said, relieved by the thought. "I hope so."

"How'd you get here?"

"Rode my bike."

Johnny didn't want to waste time tying her bicycle to the roof of the car, and he didn't want to leave it there either, in case somebody from the Circle spotted it. With Livey's reluctant permission and his promise that he'd come back and get it later, he chucked it into a space of clear water in the marsh bordering the gravel road.

After the splash cleared, the handlebars remained above the surface.

"That wasn't so smart," Johnny said.

"No, it wasn't," Livey agreed.

"Close your eyes, real tight. No peeking."

"Why?"

"Just do it."

She closed them, but not all the way.

"I mean it, Livey."

Something in his voice made her squeeze them shut. She felt a swoosh of heat and heard a sizzle.

"You can look now."

The bicycle was gone. A residual patch of steam floated away from where it had sunk.

"What did you do?" she asked.

"What I had to do."

"Am I getting my bike back?"

"A brand-new one."

"But I liked that one! I had it since middle school. You have no idea how hard it is to get a bike with a seat that fits."

"You're getting your driver's license next semester anyway."

"But I still want my bike."

"All right, all right," he said, opening the Beetle door for her, "I'll get a special one with the best seat you ever sat on."

She got in. "Why couldn't I watch you do what you did back there?"

He started the engine and drove off. "Just best you don't."

"Do you do magic very often?"

"Let's not call it magic. I use those powers as little as possible. It draws attention."

Livey thought again of Bob, the restless triangles, always on the move. "Can Bob possess people? I mean, Darby's been acting really weird. Not like himself." She described her brother's behavior, and was telling Johnny about the episode at the meat counter as he turned onto Beechwood. He parked in front of the house and reached over the seat to get one of those TETRA KUIZ boards.

She had a sudden thought. "This isn't going to turn into *The Exorcist*, is it?"

"I'm not sure what's going to happen."

She took a deep breath. "Oh, boy."

When they entered the house, Darby was chasing Wiles around the living room. "Hold still, you idiotic creature!" Darby snarled.

With a yowl, Wiles jumped up into Johnny's arms.

Darby glared. "And what a nuisance *you* are, Johnny my boy."

Livey cupped her mouth with her hands. "Oh my God," she said, her voice muffled. "He *is* possessed."

Cradling Wiles in one arm, Johnny extended the TETRA KUIZ board toward Darby, as though holding up a cross against a vampire. "Tell her who you really are."

The metal studs seemed to act like magnets, tugging on Darby's glasses and clothes and then skin, which dissolved into the same shimmering, oily triangles that Livey had seen in the clearing. They flowed and swam and curved. Wiles hissed and spat. Livey stared speechless, on the verge of fainting.

"Bob took your brother's identity," Johnny said.

"Then where's Darby?"

"Where is he, Bob? Where's Aether?"

"And why should I tell you?" Bob said.

"Because you love truth and beauty and cannot tell a lie."

"They are in Hilbert space."

"Bring them back!" Livey cried. "Right now!"

Several of the triangles curved in what looked like a sharky smile. "Do not worry, my dear Livey. He will be brought back unharmed, I assure you, although his ego might be, oh, shrunken somewhat by the experience."

"What are they doing in Hilbert space?" Johnny asked.

"Looking for the Book."

"What book is that?"

"My dear Johnny, it is true I cannot lie, but I do not have to answer your questions, either."

"I know!" Livey exclaimed. "It's that Shedd Aquarium notebook, isn't it? Darby was always scribbling it in."

The triangles swam more vigorously. "They will never find it. I have hidden it most cleverly and elegantly."

Johnny's skin began to brighten, his eyes began to glow. "You promised you would leave."

"Indeed. And I will. Once my work here is done."

"Now."

There was laughter that sounded like a tinkling of metal chimes. "You have no authority over me. I have no tawdry soul for you to possess, for I am perfection. Livey, my dear, do you have any idea who Johnny is, this boy to whom you have given your heart?"

"Sure. He's an angel. And you'd better do as he says."

Again that laughter, but louder. The triangles swarmed around Johnny, covering him until he and Wiles vanished in a glow of colors. A moment later, Wiles popped back into view, twisting to the floor, where he stood frozen for a second.

His front leg was normal, like the others, no longer mangled. He stared at it, and then hissed, shaking the leg as though trying to get it off him. He rolled over and scratched and batted at it with his other paws. He shot upright in the air and darted under the couch, no longer limping but scuttling sideways, refusing to use the leg.

"Do you doubt my goodness now, Livey?" Bob's voice said. "Do you now see? I heal and perform miracles. And as for the angel of your heart, observe!"

The triangles lifted.

Johnny stood there as before, but shirtless, and for the first time Livey saw his tattoos. They were magnificent—red, glowing, exuding heat. And Johnny himself was the most gorgeous being she had ever seen, but she backed away in terror.

For he wasn't an angel at all, but a creature of unholy beauty.

38

THE TRIANGLES STREAMED out the front door into the night, but Livey didn't notice. Her senses were overwhelmed by Johnny's terrible beauty. His hair flowed like black silver, and his colorless skin was like marble frost, his tattoos glowing red and black and red again. His warrior's belt and kilt were woven of night and shadow and lightning.

Livey backed away even more, bumping into the sofa.

He held out a hand. "Livey." His voice reverberated through her.

"Stay away from me."

Pain shot through those magnificent eyes. "I couldn't tell you. How could I tell you? Even when you said you didn't care who or what I was, I knew that wasn't really true."

"But I thought you were an angel!"

"I am."

"No you're not!"

"One of the rebels. Better to stand tall in hell than bow low in heaven. But Livey, I would never hurt you."

"Could you hurt me?"

Those eyes grew shuttered and that mouth she'd kissed fell grimly silent. A second passed, two. "Yes."

Her heart was shattered, her mind in pieces. How foolish she'd been! And Darby—

"My God," she whispered. "Aether. What's she done to Darby?"

Johnny took a step toward her.

"Stay away!"

"Aether can be the most infuriating little angel, but she's one of the star bright ones, one of heaven's favorites. She could never hurt him."

The door to her dad's bedroom opened. "Livey, is that you?"

She instantly moved into the hall to block him. Too late. He frowned in his mild, puzzled way over her shoulder. "And who are you?"

Livey took a deep breath and turned around. Johnny was his old self again, wearing that cotton shirt that covered his tattoos, his skin pale and tight on his bones. "I'm Johnny Magnus, sir. Livey's boyfriend."

Her jaw dropped. Boyfriend? Under those pretenses he'd made? God, what a lying, arrogant, insufferable . . . devil!

"Boyfriend, hunh?" her dad said as he shook hands. He yawned and glanced at his watch. "I'd better do my fatherly thing and tell you next time I want her home by midnight."

"Yes, sir. I'm sorry. It's just that tonight is the full moon. A beautiful evening."

Jerry walked over to the living room window and pulled the curtain to look for himself. "So it is. Want some coffee?"

"No, sir."

He headed toward the kitchen. "Can't sleep, so might as well wake up. That damn Riemann disproof."

The doorbell rang, followed by loud knocking. "What the . . . ?" Jerry said. He changed direction and opened the door.

A woman and a man stood on the porch. The woman's suit was rumpled, her eyes tired but alert. Livey recognized her as Agent Geisler, but her attention was riveted on the man. His suit was immaculate, his gaze crisp and sharp.

"Hello, Jerry," he said. "Sorry about the hour."

"Silas?" Jerry said in disbelief.

Livey was as dumbfounded as her dad. The Slimy Jerk was *here*? At *this* time of night?

"May I come in? It's about Darby. He was seen at Silverwood, visiting Ludavica. This has become a matter of national security, to be frank."

Jerry stepped aside. The Slimy Jerk nodded at Livey. "Hello, Godeliva." He eyed Johnny quickly but curiously.

Before Livey could shoot her dad a warning glance to shut up, Jerry said, "And this is Johnny, Livey's boyfriend."

Silas's attention returned for another quick but more assessing glance. Livey wanted to die. She knew that the Slimy Jerk would report back to her mom, and that there were going to be a gazillion questions.

"That your Beetle out front?"

"Yes, sir."

"I used to own one in college. Those were the days, Beetles and the Bee Gees and Birkenstocks."

Silas and Agent Geisler took seats in the living room, Silas settling back in the sofa as if he owned it. Agent Geisler sat on the edge of hers, ready for any danger, but when Jerry asked if they wanted coffee, she became distracted. "God, yes. Please."

Johnny caught Livey's eye. With a tiny jerk of his chin, he gestured for her to go to her bedroom, and then said, "Thanks, Mr. Ell. I'd better be going." She instantly understood—they had to get out and find Darby before these guys did. She'd sneak out her window and join him on the street. Sidling away to the hall, she grabbed her coat from the rack.

"I don't suppose your son is home?" she heard Silas say.

"Livey?" her dad called out. "Is Darby in bed?"

"Sound asleep," she called back. "And I'm going to do the same."

She locked her door and climbed out the window. Bending low, she hurried to Johnny's Beetle, where he was already waiting. Parked in front of him was a plain sedan with government plates. She got in the Beetle, and Johnny eased the car away and down the street. Livey looked behind them. Nobody was running out of the house chasing them—at least not yet.

"What they really want is Darby's notebook, don't they?" she said.

"They're NSA. Codebreakers. No code will be safe if they have it."

She looked at Johnny, who looked like Johnny, but in her mind she could still see that terrible angel underneath his skin, that appalling beauty in his eyes.

"Why did you tell my dad you're my boyfriend?"

"Aren't I?"

"No!"

"That's what you told Mrs. Blink."

"That was before I knew who you were."

"So I had to use a little camouflage to blend in. But I'm still who I always was. I'm still the same me you knew."

Could you hurt me?

Yes.

"I have a soul," she said.

"A beautiful one."

"You could possess it."

"I'm not one of those ugly demons, Livey."

"You could possess it," she repeated.

A longer silence. "Yes."

"And you want to."

In the moonlight angling through the side window, she could see his jaws clench. "From the first moment I saw you."

She leaned against her door, as far away from him as she could get. He reached out for her hand.

"Don't touch me." She undid the necklace clasp and tossed the cross in his lap. "The only reason I'm still in this car is because of my brother. You're going to help me find him."

His sigh sounded like the ragged breath of a wounded animal. He clenched the cross in his fist, hard, as though wanting it to pierce him. Despite herself, she wanted to . . . she wanted to . . . she didn't know what she wanted to do. He tried to attach the necklace clasp around his neck with one hand while steering with the other.

She suddenly leaned across and did it for him. Her fingers, brushing his skin . . .

"Thank you."

"Doesn't that cross, I don't know, burn you or something?"

"Sometimes."

After a moment she said, "What now? How do we find my brother?"

"Can you drive?"

What did this have to do with anything? But she answered, "My dad let me practice with ours."

He patted the Beetle's gear shift. "A stick shift?"

"Never tried. Why?"

He pulled into City Hall's big parking lot, empty this time of night, the neat white lines glowing under the perimeter lights. "Because this car isn't just a car," he said, "and for the first part of getting to Darby, you're going to have to learn how to drive it."

IN HER ROOM at Silverwood, Ludavica Ell struggled to turn her wheelchair.

A man with a red bow tie had shoved the chair into the corner, trapping her there. He squatted before the cardboard box. "The boy went down this, did he?"

"I'm not telling you a thing," she snapped.

"You don't have to. The Conjecture's been proved." He began folding up the box.

"Leave that alone."

The man smiled and tucked the flattened box under his arm. "No exit now." With a pleasant nod, he opened the door.

"Bring that back!"

He paused and turned back to her. "You were the first to know the Alpha and the Omega function. Do not reject him. Believe in his elegance and beauty, Ludavica Ell, and eternal glory will be yours."

She spat at him.

He smiled sadly and then left, the door closing after him with a soft click.

Ludavica stopped struggling. Somebody would soon come along to get her turned around, and she would tell them about government agents taking her Hilbert space machine, but nobody would believe her.

She adjusted the hat on her head, as though tuning it. "Darby," she said, stern as a great-aunt can be, "keep calm, don't panic, and you'll be fine."

40

AS THE MOON drifted below City Hall's tower clock, Livey tried again. She slowly released the clutch while stepping on the accelerator. Once more the Beetle lurched and then died. She hit the wheel in exasperation.

"Almost," Johnny said from the passenger seat. "A bit more gas when you feel the clutch engage."

He was patient and encouraging. The supernatural weirdness of the situation—a fallen rebel angel was teaching her to drive some sort of otherworldly vehicle, for Pete's sake!—had given way to the present moment and her determination to drive a stick-shift Beetle.

She put the gear in neutral and restarted the engine. "All right, this time's the winner," she said. She let up on the clutch. The Beetle lurched as before, but she added a touch more gas. The car kept going. She whooped. "I did it! I did it!"

"Now shift into second."

He'd already shown her the gear changes, working the plastic skull that was the gear shift knob, but she'd forgotten. "Where's second again?"

He put his hand on hers. She stiffened. "Relax," he said. "I'm not going to bite you. Okay, when I say 'now,' ease off the gas and clutch it . . . now!" He led her hand through the shift and then let go.

"Now the same for third," he said.

Third gear she remembered. Right and up. But she said, "Could you show me?"

So he would put his hand on hers again.

And this time, did he let it linger for just a second? Or was that only her wishful thinking?

He told her to brake to a stop and repeat the process. Her feet and hands coordinated more smoothly. After shifting into third and taking a wide turn around the outer ring of the lot, she asked, "What does this car turn into?"

"You'll see."

"And you know where Darby is?"

"I'm sure he's with Aether. If she uses her powers I'll be able to find them."

"If Aether is one of the good ones, and you're not, then how come you're working together?"

"A temporary truce. Nobody on either side wants Bob here, even though he wasn't a real big concern. That'll soon change. Okay, pull over and stop and I'll show you reverse."

She halted in the dark corner by the City Hall loading dock.

"And Aether really is your little sister?"

"Put in your words, yes. She's really my little sister. We chose different sides. You could say she's the white sheep of the family. If I could do it all over again . . ." His voice trailed off, but Livey could hear an echo of anguish. He took a deep breath. "I'm proud, and part of pride is accepting the consequences of your choices."

She squeezed the steering wheel to keep from hugging him. "But you're still good. I know you're good. I couldn't have fallen in love with somebody who wasn't—" She stopped, realizing what she was saying.

He turned his head and stared out the window, looking away from her.

"Johnny?"

With his head still turned he said, "For reverse, you press the gear down, like you're trying to push it through the floor, and then to the left."

"Johnny."

"What?"

"Look at me."

"Who's possessing who?" he whispered, but he turned and looked at her. Tears glittered in his eyes.

"Could you become your real self?" she said very quietly. "For me?"

He didn't say anything. As a gust of breeze blew a scrap of old newspaper across the windshield, he changed, transforming into that darkly radiant angel, frightening in his power and beauty.

But those tears had not vanished.

He was still Johnny.

She slowly leaned toward him.

He shook his head. "Livey. Please."

"Don't be scared," she whispered, and kissed him.

With her finger, Livey traced a marking on Johnny's arm. His colorless skin was soft on the surface, but hard as marble underneath. The marking was solid to her touch, yet looked like a crack that cut into the deep core of him. They gave to him the darkness of his beauty. He had a fragrance like night wind from deep space, carrying a hint of wine and bitter chocolate. Nothing at all like that creature Rotgut.

The seats in the Beetle had been too uncomfortable, so they had moved to the loading dock to watch the lowering moon.

"I'm a lucky girl," she said.

Johnny smiled his gorgeous smile. "How's that?"

"I got to fall in love with you twice. With a driving lesson thrown in."

"Other people might say you never learn."

"Two wrongs make a right. Or, hey, a minus times a minus is a plus."

He laughed. She loved hearing him laugh.

"I could stay here forever, but I suppose we'd better go find Darby," she said. "That was the whole point of me learning how to drive, right?"

"That's right."

"But why can't you drive? I mean, I'd love to, but you're better at it. Well, sort of better, considering the way you drive."

"Hey, now," he said. "I'm going to be busy making sure you stay safe where we're going, and I can't be driving while I do that. And I also have to keep an eye out for trouble. For instance, that."

A black car with probing headlights had appeared, and was trawling the far end of the parking lot. A police cruiser cut in from the side.

Livey smiled. "We'll show 'em what your old Beetle can do."

"There's only one problem. You can't survive—not as you are."

"So what do I have to do?"

"It's what I have to do." He put his hands on her shoulders and looked in her eyes. His were in shadow, but glowed softly. "I have to possess your soul to protect you."

She didn't flinch. "All right."

"Livey. I'm one of the *rebels*. Things can tempt me. Your soul is beautiful, but fragile. It can be . . . dangerous."

"I trust you." She pulled him to her. "Quick, then."

It was no ordinary kiss. There was at first an intense joy and flush of love that rapidly turned into excruciating pain. *I'm sorry,* she could hear him say in her mind, could feel his hurt for hurting her, could sense that he was doing this as fast as he could, and, what was most awful, could tell he was struggling with an immense desire to slow the process and enjoy it.

She blacked out from the agony.

When she came to, she was floating a short distance above the Beetle. She could see right through the roof, could see herself sitting in the driver's seat, turning the ignition and gunning the engine. The passenger seat was empty.

Johnny? she said. She wasn't sure if she was speaking.

Right here. His voice, in her mind.

I felt like I died.

Almost. That's your body down there. Your soul is up here. With me.

Ohmigod. I'm having an out-of-body experience? She realized that she wasn't just out of her body. Her conscious self was wrapped up within Johnny. She was totally helpless, but she felt no danger. It was like she was snuggled underneath her blanket on a cold rainy day, warm and secure.

Back the car up, Livey.

The conscious Livey willed the Livey down in the car to move the gears, but she didn't know how to reverse. *We didn't get to that part.*

She sensed his sigh. *I didn't want to do this, so you'll have to excuse me.*

She felt him take control of her will in order to move her body. This feeling she didn't like. She resisted.

I have to do it this way, Livey. I'll only do the bare minimum, promise. We have to get going.

She relaxed, allowing him to control her will. He got her to move the gear shift and smoothly reverse the Beetle.

The police cruiser spotted the movement and zoomed across, sirens wailing, lights flashing. The black government car cut across from the other side of the parking lot. The cruiser slid to a stop in front of the Beetle. Johnny expertly made her hit the brakes before the cars collided.

The Slimy Jerk got out of the government sedan and walked over to Livey's door.

Up to you now, Johnny said to her.

She used her will to roll the window down.

Dr. Djurek bent to her. "Where's Darby?"

"I don't know," she said, speaking out loud to him.

"You need to come with me."

"Just like Darby went with that guy of yours with the red bow tie?"

"You have to trust me. I'll explain."

But she didn't trust him. No way would she trust him. *What do I do now?* she asked Johnny.

You've always been a polite person, right?

I try to be.

So this is what you do.

Johnny took control again. The Livey in the car smiled pleasantly. "You know what, you Slimy Jerk, if you were any dumber, you'd have to be watered once a day." With that, she gave the Slimy Jerk the finger.

Two dark dots appeared on Dr. Djurek's handsome cheeks.

The real Livey was aghast. She struggled against his hold on her. *Johnny! You promised!*

Come on, you've always wanted to do that.

True.

But enough, Johnny said. *Now we really got to go.*

The Livey in the car gunned the engine and popped the clutch. The tin-sheet Beetle plowed into the cruiser and shoved it aside as though it were a dandelion. Another cruiser appeared and hit its siren, racing after the Beetle.

Sorry, pal, you don't have a chance in hell, Johnny murmured. *Okay, Livey, second gear, now third, and fourth.*

She moved smoothly through the gears.

Now step on it.

She pressed on the accelerator.

Her body was slammed back against the seat. If her life hadn't been wrapped up in Johnny's being, if he hadn't been fully concentrating on protecting her, the acceleration would have killed her. Not only that, but in an instant the Beetle was no longer a Beetle, and the road was no longer anywhere near City Hall.

Instead, she was at the wheel of a gorgeous, sleek sports car that was racing up into the velvet night, its hood throwing off a sparkle of blue and green and gold.

Turn left.

She banked the sports car and gasped. The Space Station hung in the star-strewn darkness. Within the station, a female astronaut floated behind a big porthole, looking out.

Give her a wave.

Livey waved madly. *Does she see me?*

That would be fun, but no, in this form, the car isn't visible and neither are you.

A sports car? I would have thought a chariot with golden wheels and black horses with flying manes.

That's so old-school. All right, see that other knob there? Push it in.

What's it do?

It's Hollywood special effects.

She pushed it in. Space began to fold up around her, like a road map. Even with her life safe in Johnny's hold, she felt a giddying disorientation that spiked into terror, as though she was tottering on the edge and was going to fall through the cracks into a void without depth.

Calm down, we're just space tunneling.

Then space unfolded to its familiar three-dimensional form. Her terror eased into wonder. The car was now zooming past a blue sun and heading for a white planet that looked like a pearl in the black velvet oyster of deep space.

I'm going to ease you into your body, Johnny said. *I'm still going to have to hold you a little while you're in your body, because you can't live out in space. Is that okay?*

Sure. Then, thinking about it for a second, she added, *thanks for asking.*

A silence. *It's hard. I'd like to keep you forever.*

I wouldn't mind.

You're just talking. You have no idea what that would mean. He sounded grim, and she sensed the darkness in him that he was controlling only because he loved her. It was frightening, but not like before, because it was exhilarating, too. *Okay,* he said, *here goes.*

She thought she'd slip down into her body, but that wasn't what it felt like. Instead, it was like waking up after a deep sleep and rising up into her senses. She even yawned, but it was one of those shake-off-the-cobwebs yawns. Her senses had never been sharper. The steering wheel under her hand, the pressure of her seat belt across her waist and chest, the low humming of the engine under that sleek hood, and even the smell of empty space, cold and brittle.

Johnny was sitting in the seat beside her, grinning at her. She could feel him in her heart and humming in her blood, his supernatural powers making sure she stayed alive.

"We're going to land on that planet."

"Is that where Darby is?"

"No. I have to wait for Aether to use some of her powers so I can figure out where they are. She's such a stubborn little brat sometimes." His smile changed, tinged with sadness. "She can get me madder than a dunked cat, but I love her, you know. I'm not a very good rebel angel myself, loving her like that." A moment passed, then he became all business. "All right, you'd better let me take over the wheel; landing this thing can be tricky."

She thought they'd have to switch seats, and the thought of space-walking to the other side delighted her, but to her disappointment the car itself transformed, her wheel morphing into the dashboard and reappearing in Johnny's hands.

Unlike space vehicles easing their way into the Earth's atmosphere, Johnny aimed the car and charged straight down, a fantastic shower of sparks and multicolored plumes streaming off the hood. The planet's mother-of-pearl surface loomed closer and closer. Johnny made sure her seat belt was snug and then said, "Ready?" He pulled the car up and did a couple roller-coaster loops. She whooped. When he straightened out, he was going only a few miles an hour, two feet above the level ground.

He grinned. "You forgot to buy the ticket—"

He was cut off by a jolt. The car smashed into a boulder and fell with a jarring thud onto its wheels.

"Whoops," Johnny said. "That was the worst landing ever."

The car had changed back into the Beetle, its front hood badly crumpled. Livey barely noticed. It seemed as though the crash had knocked her senses out of whack. She felt off-kilter, disoriented and lonely. Then she realized that Johnny was back to being Johnny, in his jeans and cotton shirt. He wasn't a part of her heart anymore.

"You okay?" he asked her with sudden concern.

"You left me," she said.

He took her hand. The touch restored some sense of balance to her. "No need for that here. And honestly? I don't want to do too much of it. I could get dangerously addicted to you." He opened his door. "Let's inspect the damage."

She got out and circled the car with him. "Good thing the engine's in the back," he said. "Otherwise we might just be stuck here."

Livey wouldn't have minded, not if it was with Johnny, but she did have to remember that the whole point of this was to get Darby safely back home. The ground underneath her sneakers was scaly and dusty, like a mix between talcum powder and crushed mother of pearl, and had a sheen to it under the blue sun, which was quickly setting across a distant purple sea. The air was as warm as a young summer day. She stretched her arms over her head, bending her back, flexing her muscles against the planet's gravity, less than Earth's. She pretended she held pom-poms and pranced through a cheer. "Go Eagles go!" Because of the lessened gravity, she really got some elevation on her jumps.

She laughed. "That better give us the championship. Nobody else has a cheerleader cheering from outer space. Where is Earth anyway?"

He pointed up and to the east. "*Way* over there."

She took a few deep breaths . . . and then stopped. "Is it okay to breathe this air?"

He kicked the layer of the shining dirt, some of which billowed in a puff of dust. "Oxygen bubbles up. Atmosphere's about the same as Earth's." He took her hand and helped her climb one of the pearl boulders that had a flattened top. "We'll watch the sunset from here."

Near the shore of the sea, a column of water spouted into the air, the pink mist drifting away. "Was that a whale?"

"More oxygen. There's no life on this planet. If you want to know, there's no life anywhere else in this universe. Only Earth."

"Really? Those E.T. people are sure going to be disappointed. But why not?"

"Because the Garden of Eden was pretty much a disaster, and the Haloes don't trust us not to do the same. There's been a kind of diplomatic conference going on about this for, oh, a really long time, and nobody can come to an agreement."

"The Haloes?"

He grinned and with his finger drew a circle around his head. "Sometimes we call them the Holy Haloes."

"And what do they call you guys?"

He curled two fingers on either side of his forehead. "The Horns, of course."

She laughed. "It sounds so, I don't know, Xbox-ish."

"Our seniors aren't so amused by our irreverence." Then his humor sank away. "But it really isn't a game, you know. And you and me, we're breaking the rules. Big-time."

She held his arm close to her side. "I'll take all the blame."

"You're lucky. You can ask for forgiveness. Not me. Not ever." There was no bitterness to his words, but behind the matter-of-factness she sensed a longing made more awful yet by the certainty it would never be fulfilled.

"I'll ask forgiveness for you," she said.

⧐ 41 ⧏

DARBY STOOD PANTING on the edge of an immense cliff, trying to catch his breath as he wiped sweat from his face with his dirty cap. The wool stank. He was tempted to chuck the thing off the cliff, but then he wouldn't have anything to cover his ears later, so he tucked the cap in his pocket instead.

The cliff looked like smooth, yellow sandstone and stretched into the unseen distance on either side of Darby. In front of him, it plunged to an infinite depth.

Aether peeked over the edge. "That sure is a long way down."

Darby couldn't look. It made his head swim.

The compass had led them this way and that through Hilbert space, but this was as far as they could go. Being in Hilbert space had been like a feverish, disjointed dream. At first there'd been a desert that seemed endless, the horizon coming no closer. Following the compass, Darby was taking a step on a sand dune, his leg muscles aching with the effort of slogging through the soft sand, when the next step he found himself in a rain forest jungle, with sharp spiky plants slicing his arms. After jumping into a jungle stream to get away from Julian and Roz, he and Aether had been swept around the corner and onto an iceberg.

Or at least that's how Darby had perceived it with his altered senses.

But now he and Aether had come to this cliff. In front of him were the twinkling stars of the Einsteinian universe. Despite the white hot Hilbert sun over their heads, precisely and forever at noon, outer space hung in front of them like an inky black curtain.

The compass was pointing straight ahead. After all that hiking and sweating and aching and bleeding and trying to stay away from Julian in the weird geometries of Hilbert space, the notebook and its proof were somewhere out there in the regular universe.

Oh, that Bob. Maybe he couldn't tell a lie, but he sure could be tricky.

Darby glanced behind him, at what looked like a steep, rocky trail, dotted with large yellow boulders arranged in a geometric series. Any minute Julian and Roz would appear. Darby hadn't been able to shake them off. Julian had his bug collector's vacuum gun with him, and back in the rain forest jungle, Darby had seen what it could do. Julian had known Darby was watching with his binoculars from his hiding place. "Hey, Darbielle, look at this!" Julian had yelled. He aimed the gun at Roz, who was standing about ten feet away. The gun went *shwoop!* and with a scream Roz was sucked into its barrel. With his binoculars, Darby could see a tiny Roz in the transparent trap, pounding her fists against the sides. Julian hit another button, and Roz popped out of the trap, expanding to her full size, looking woozy. "But you, Darbielle, I'll keep insect size," Julian yelled. "I'll put you in with my praying mantises."

Darby had his fractal sword, which Hilbert space had turned into a real sword, its edge an incredibly sharp fractal pattern of vanishingly smaller triangles, but the sword was useless against that vacuum gun. How come Aunt Ludy hadn't made a cardboard laser blaster for him to take along?

And how was it that Julian was able to stick so closely to their trail?

On the cliff, Darby pushed his glasses up on his sweaty nose. "What now?" he said to Aether, trying not to let his voice tremble. "Do we jump?"

"I don't know. I don't fly real good."

"What do you mean you don't know? You're the angel."

"A seraph!"

His fear and frustration came bubbling out. "I don't care. You've been the most totally useless angel ever."

"I haven't been useless," she said indignantly. "I've been giving you moral support."

He showed her the dried blood scabs on his arms where the sharp jungle leaves had cut his skin. "What about these? You wouldn't even heal them."

"I told you, blood makes my head spin."

"What good are you, then?"

She pointed to a spiral galaxy. "At least I know where we are."

Darby aimed the binoculars. The lenses pulled hundreds of thousands of light years into focus. There jumped into view a stunningly gorgeous blue-and-white planet.

Earth.

Darby lowered the binoculars with a groan. "Oh, man. We had to go through all this just to go back to where we started from?"

"Maybe it's in the past," Aether said. "Maybe the Book is being guarded by T. rexes and giant spiders."

Had they time traveled? It was possible, Darby had to admit. The mathematics allowed it.

"Or maybe it's in the future," Aether continued. "You could be married and have kids. I wonder what your wife is like. Probably screechy and bossy."

"Just shut up, would you?"

Aether fell into a hurt silence.

On the still air there came Roz's gasping voice. "Why can't we take a break? Please, Julian. Just five minutes rest."

"You can rest if you want, I don't care," Julian said, sounding hardly tired at all.

"But you'll leave me behind."

"Then keep walking."

Darby clutched the handle of his fractal sword. "Aether, pray or something."

"You told me to shut up."

"Then un-shut up!"

"Don't yell at me."

"I'm not yelling."

"Say you're sorry for telling me to shut up."

"I'm sorry," Darby said through clenched teeth.

Aether harrumphed. "There's these big, giant halls I used to play hide-and-seek in. Some of them are shortcuts back to Earth."

Darby heard a rustle of falling pebbles, and Julian emerged from behind a large boulder, as cool as Indiana Jones. Behind him trudged Roz, her face red and sweaty.

"There you are, Darbielle," Julian said. Then he laughed. "Whatever happened to your ears? Oh, they're so cute. I'll name you *homunculus auricle backwardii.*"

As Julian aimed his vacuum gun, Darby's mind was going a million miles a minute. Shortcuts . . . big giant halls . . . a memory of his mom explaining that some of the extra hyperspace dimensions of Einsteinian space-time were huge . . .

In desperation, he swung his sword, not at Julian but at the yawning black space beyond the cliff. The sword's fractal edge sliced through the normal three dimensions, opening a jagged tear. With his free hand, he grabbed Aether's elbow, and jumped headfirst into the hole. He could feel Julian's vacuum gun tugging hard on his legs, almost sucking off his sneakers, and then he was through, falling into absolute darkness.

When Darby came to, he was lying on his back on a dusty floor of some kind and was smelling a powerful ammonia stink. But it was still pitch-black. "Aether?" he said.

"Right here."

"Where are we?"

"A cave."

Darby jerked upright and rummaged in his daypack for the flashlight. There was a moment of panic when he didn't find it, but a deeper grope located it at the bottom, underneath the TETRA KUIZ board. He turned it on. Its bulb cast a weak glow, but enough for him to see the irregular, rocky contours of a cave. Twenty feet overhead, bats clung to the rocks, chittering and squeaking.

The flashlight died and remained dead despite Darby's frantic shaking. The batteries had run out. "Bob isn't as perfect as he thinks he is," he said. "Now what?"

"Not a problem," Aether said, and began to glow, her body radiating a soft white light that illuminated the cavern.

"Wow. You're like neon!"

"If I turn on full, you wouldn't be able to look at me."

"So where is this? Are we on Earth?"

"Earth bats don't have four eyes," Aether said. "You took the wrong shortcut."

"Well, excuse me. I didn't have much of a choice." He shoved his sneakers back on tight and picked up the sword, which had fallen to the dusty ground. "Let's slice open another hyperdimension."

"If you do that here, you'll end up on Pluto. The shortcut to Earth is this way." She began to move toward her left, glowing without casting any shadow.

Darby heard something. "Wait!" he whispered urgently. He tilted his head. Roz's faint voice drifted into hearing, saying something about the awful bats.

"Don't go that way. They've gotten ahead of us."

"Your ears are on backward, dummy. You're hearing behind you, not in front of you."

Darby had forgotten about his ears. He glanced the other way, and saw a tiny flickering of light. Julian must have brought matches. *And,* Darby thought, *his vacuum gun must be able to suck holes to the hyperdimensions.*

The bigger cave split into several smaller ones, each crammed with sharp stalagmites and stalactites. Aether unhesitatingly picked one tunnel. "We have to run, like, really really fast to get through here."

"Why?"

"See those sharp thingies? They're teeth. Ready? Set? Go!" She sprinted, twirling around and sometimes over the stalagmites and under the stalactites. Darby followed, but not as quickly, so that he could marvel at what he was seeing. He'd never seen real stalagmites and stalactites before. Which was which? *That's right: Stalactites stick tight to the ceiling.*

Then he realized that the stalagmites and stalactites were slowly coming together.

That got him going.

He came to the last pair, the narrow gap between them closing. He tossed his sword through and frantically squirmed between the points. The top one snagged on his backpack. The bottom one pressed into his stomach. He yanked desperately, ripping the daypack loose, and tumbled clear.

He lay there for a moment, catching his breath and letting his fright settle, before getting to his feet, sword at the ready. "I cut here?" he asked Aether.

She nodded her small chin. "Right here."

Darby double-checked with his compass. "Are you sure? The compass is pointing that way."

"This is the shortest shortcut." Darby hesitated. She scowled. "I know this place like I know the back of my hand. Hurry up."

Darby swung. This time he heard the noise the blade made, a low bubbling hiss. The three dimensions of ordinary space split open, like stretched rubber ripping. He jumped through with Aether, and found himself in the middle of an enormous room with marbled floors, a space so huge Darby couldn't see any walls. Rows upon rows of enormous carved columns rose to a ceiling so high there was pinkish mist floating way overhead.

"Are we in New York somewhere?" he asked uncertainly, sheathing his sword.

"Um," Aether said, looking around with a frown. "I don't think we're on Earth yet. We're still in the hyperdimension."

"Wait a sec. Don't tell me you're lost."

"I'm not exactly *lost* lost, I'm just not real sure where we are."

He threw up his hands. "'Don't worry,' you said. I told you the compass was pointing the other way, but you wouldn't listen. Oh, no, not you. 'Trust me,' you said, 'I know the shortcuts.'"

"So this is a long cut. We'll still get there."

Three columns over, about a hundred yards away, a portion of space seemed to shimmer and distort and thin out. Beyond the thinning ripple, Darby could see Julian and Roz. He grabbed Aether and darted behind the closest column. Peering around one of its carved niches, he watched Julian step into the hall, with Roz stumbling after him. Julian was holding a TETRA KUIZ, aiming it as though it were a homing device. Could it actually be one? Darby got out his own TETRA KUIZ board and aimed the triangle of metal pegs at Julian. The pegs began to softly hum.

So that's how he's tracking us, Darby thought. The two TETRA KUIZ boards were signaling each other. Darby put his on the floor.

"Darby," Aether said.

"What?"

"Look. Over there."

He glanced where she was pointing. Fifty feet away in the same corridor was a magnificent bull the size of a small car. It seemed to be made of crystals, shining and twinkling, the tips of its gleaming horns looking as sharp as spear points. It stood very still, except for its tail, which tick-tocked back and forth. Its eyes were fixed on Darby, who thought, *There exists a hall, containing at least one bull, of which at least the front half is glass. . . .* He stood and slowly backed up.

"Is that thing safe?" he asked Aether.

"It's a lot safer than you are."

The bull snorted and charged. Darby rolled out of the way, trying to withdraw his sword. One of the horns narrowly missed him. The bull turned and charged again. Darby got his sword out just in time. Spinning around, he jabbed the tip in the bull's back. The prick didn't cut, but shattered, like a BB shot into a window. The creature bellowed in pain.

Darby glared down the length of his sword at the creature. "Leave us alone."

The bull sprinted away.

Leaving the TETRA KUIZ board on the floor, Darby retreated with Aether to an adjacent column. He peeked from behind it, watching as Julian trotted over to Darby's board. Julian nudged it with his foot.

"He figured it out, that stupid Darbielle."

Roz leaned wearily against the column. "Can't we just go home?"

The bull sprang into view again. Roz shrieked. Julian whipped out his vacuum gun, but he was kneeling awkwardly, and the gun fell from his hand. The bull charged Julian with lowered head, those sharp horns leading the way. Julian tried to scoop up the gun, but instead knocked it against the column, sending it skittering out of reach. He grabbed Roz and pushed her into the bull's path, giving him time to run the other way. One of the creature's horns caught Roz under her right arm. She flew through the air and fell in a heap. The bull turned around, again aiming its horns at her and snorted. She scrabbled backward. Blood soaked the side of her blouse. "Julian!" she screamed. "Julian! Help!"

Darby raced silently toward the bull, his sword lifted high. Rotating the handle, he swung the sword as hard as he could. The flat side came thwacking down on the creature's rump, the skin of which cracked into a spiderweb. With a sharp bellow, the bull spun around. Darby swung again, this time with the sword's sharp side, slicing off one of the horns. It fell to the floor and shattered. The bull blinked its big eyes in stunned surprise at the shards, and then slunk off with a despairing moan.

Darby knelt by Roz and ripped the sleeve of her blouse. From a deep wound in her armpit, blood oozed in rhythmic pulses. Her face began to glaze over with shock. She groaned. "Julian, help me."

"Aether, come here!" Darby yelled.

Aether inched up behind him, her face turned sideways and scrunched up in distaste.

"Do something," Darby said.

She peeked. "All that blood. Yuck."

"I'm not joking, Aether. Heal her."

"Okay, okay." She squeezed her eyes shut tight and felt blindly for Roz's arm. Darby took her small hand, holding it tight, and put it on the wound. She made a distressed noise and tried to pull away, but Darby forced her hand to stay in place.

"Quick, she's losing a lot of blood."

"I have to think of good stuff to make this work. Um, manna with peanut butter. Vultures, but only when they're flying. Cute mice. Riding tigers. Mud. Moonbows with Johnny. Playing on the swings with Darby." Her hand began to glow. Roz's blood stopped flowing. The wound in her side grew shallower, the raw red flesh turned pink, and then was normal skin once more.

Aether looked at the blood on her fingers. "I think I'm going to be sick," she said faintly. Darby wiped her hand on his shirt. Then he helped Roz sit up against the column and held his water bottle up to her mouth so she could drink. She gulped greedily. When she was done, tears blossomed in her eyes. "Why did he run away?"

Aether harrumphed. "He's a coward. Why are you his friend? You should be Darby's friend."

"I thought she was, once," Darby said. He could still feel the sting of her betrayal.

Aether scrunched up her nose, studying Roz, and then smiled gleefully. "I know why! You like Julian. You like him a *lot*."

Even with all the blood she lost, Roz's face still managed to turn bright pink.

"Do you kiss him?" Aether asked. "Johnny kisses Darby's sister. It's yucky."

Darby startled. *Livey, kissing a boy?*

From behind them came a voice. "Her father's a domestic. Our gardener." Julian had reappeared, with the gun in his hand. "We treat them kindly, but we don't patronize. Drop that sword, Darby, and get away from her."

Aether shoved past Darby and thrust her sharp chin at Julian, her hands on her hips. "Why are so you mean to him? What's he ever done to you?"

Julian looked thoughtful. "What's he done? You should hear my parents. Darby scored higher than you, Darby was better than you, Darby this, Darby that. Not to mention him beating me up. That's what Darby's done to me."

"It's not his fault. And leave us alone. We have to get to back to Earth before Bob fixes everything."

Julian wriggled the gun barrel. "His name is the Alpha and the Omega. He's going to make me the greatest scientist the world has ever seen."

"You?" Aether snorted. "You're dumber than a roll of toilet paper."

Julian slapped her across the cheek. "Get out of the way, or else I'll add you to my collection."

Aether put a hand to her cheek. "Now you've done it," she said. Her skin began to glow. "Darby, close your eyes, tight."

Darby reacted instinctively, throwing himself toward Roz and clamping a hand over her eyes while squeezing his shut. Even so, a searing white light exploded through his eyelids, and a hot wind ruffled his hair.

Julian's screams were high, thin wisps of sound. Darby peeked. Aether's form was still radiating a white light too brilliant to look at. Julian was staggering away from his fallen gun, scratching and rubbing at his eyes. The skin on his face was red, as if badly sunburned.

"You shouldn't have slapped me," Aether said, her radiance fading.

Roz had backed up against the column, as though trying to force herself inside the marble in order to hide. "Who—what is she?"

"A seraph," Darby said. "Don't call her angel. She gets mad. And," he added, "I guess it's not a good idea to get her *really* mad."

42

THE BLUE SUN sank into the purple ocean, casting no sunset color. Livey had seen far better sunsets on Earth, but she didn't care, not when she was with Johnny.

A large moon the size of Earth's rose in the middle of the eastern sky, followed by two more, spaced equally apart on either side of the first. They were full moons, shedding a soft white light. As twilight quickly faded, the planet's soil and all the pearl boulders began to glow with opal colors.

"It's beautiful," Livey murmured.

Johnny smiled and said nothing.

Then, without warning, a dozen moonbows appeared in the sky, from little crescents of delicate pastel hues to enormous ones of stronger color that spanned the horizons.

This beauty stunned her.

Johnny lay down, hands behind his head. "I like to come here sometimes and just watch. Just because I am who I am doesn't mean I can't enjoy how awesome it is."

"Thank you," she said, her heart full of wonder. She kissed the back of his hand and then the cracked markings on the skin of his wrist. They tasted bitter. She pressed her lips harder to his skin before letting go.

He smiled. "Shakespeare could write a play about us."

"Not him. He had sad endings. Ours will be happy."

Exhaustion overtook her. Johnny retrieved a blanket from the car, and she stretched out beneath it. He sat beside her, clasping his knees and gazing out to unseen distances.

Sometime in the night, she woke. The moons were low, the middle one a fat bubble. The moonbows lingered only faintly. Johnny was asleep beside her, his head resting on an arm. In his sleep, he was his real self, the markings on his skin only slowly pulsing, looking shallow and not deep. His face was calm. *Angelic,* she thought, trying to memorize every feature.

As he slept, he suddenly smiled, as though in joyous astonishment. The tattoos faded, his skin becoming whole and pure again. Livey couldn't breathe—something was happening to him, something wonderful. She wanted to wake him, but whatever the spell was, she didn't want to break it.

His eyes opened. There was no sleepiness in them, only that radiant joy. The radiance eased, and the tattoo markings slowly returned to his skin.

"I was dreaming," he said.

"You looked beautiful."

"We *never* dream."

"What was it about?"

He sat up. "I'm not sure—"

The pearl boulder vibrated. A blanket of dust rose from the ground. Several boulders rolled off a cliff and into the sea.

Above them, the faint moonbows fractured.

"An earthquake!" Livey exclaimed, trying to get to her feet.

"More like a universe quake," Johnny said, scanning the horizons and the stars with narrowed eyes. "Bob's changing the speed of light."

Then he added, "Got her. Aether's used her power. She's in trouble. Let's go."

43

DARBY SHEATHED HIS sword and inspected the vacuum gun. Its barrel had melted. He took a bearing on his wrist compass, which pointed in the opposite direction from where Julian had vanished. "Maybe we'd better go get him first," he said to Aether.

"Let his sins find him out," she muttered.

"Aether, look at your T-shirt."

She looked down at the sequins that said OD IS LOVE. "That's Him, not me. But I guess I should—" She was cut off by a grinding rumble. The floor began to tremble, and the columns started to quiver.

"Uh-oh," Aether said.

High above them, a chunk of marble cracked off a pillar and came crashing down. Darby yanked Roz and Aether out of the way. The chunk shattered into pieces, spraying Darby's leg with shrapnel. He pulled out his sword, swinging at the air, and opened a portal, but smoke and flame billowed out. Something was happening to space-time geometry.

"Do something," he told Aether. "And do it quick."

She closed her eyes and folded her hands. "Dear God, I haven't been a very good seraph, I know, but I think you'd better help us."

In the distance, an entire column shattered with a roar and a cloud of dust. A crack appeared on the shaking floor. Even the air seemed to split—but it wasn't from the quake. A brown Volkswagen Beetle appeared from the split, bouncing along the undulating floor. It braked to a stop beside Darby.

Livey was behind the wheel, and beside her was the guy Darby had seen before at the coffee shop and then at Newton Academy. Livey's boyfriend. The boy bounced out of the car and pulled his seat forward so Darby and the others could get in the back. Darby caught sight of his ears in the sideview and instantly grabbed his stinky cap out of his pocket and crammed it back on his head.

"Quick," Livey said.

"You can drive?" Darby asked with suspicion.

"Get in!"

Roz clambered into the back. The guy picked Aether up, kissed her on the cheek, which she instantly wiped off, and then tossed her into Roz's lap. Darby threw his sword and sheath onto the floor in the back and hopped in, squeezing beside Roz.

"I knew Johnny would come," Aether said happily.

Johnny swung into his seat. Livey put the car in gear.

Darby suddenly cried out, "Wait! Julian—we have to get him!"

Livey released the clutch. "We don't have time!"

Grabbing Johnny's shoulder, Darby hauled himself forward and slithered out the front passenger window. He ran through a thickening cloud of dust to his TETRA KUIZ board, hoping it would help him locate Julian, and quick. But he didn't need the board. Julian staggered around a column that was starting to crack with loud snaps, his burnt face covered with dust. He fell to his knees. Darby looped his hands under Julian's armpits and dragged him toward the car. Another chunk of falling stone nearly hit them.

Seeing what was happening, Livey moved the car forward so he didn't have to drag Julian as far. Johnny jumped out and opened the front hood of the Beetle, where the luggage space was. "He's going to have to ride in here."

With all the dust billowing from collapsing columns, it was getting hard to see. The floor was really shaking now. They inelegantly chucked Julian into the space. Johnny slammed the hood shut.

With the added weight, the Beetle struggled to gain acceleration down the hall. The columns collapsing behind them were catching up.

"Faster!" Darby yelled at Livey.

"I'm going as fast as I can."

He leaned forward to shout in Johnny's ear, "Why did you let her drive?"

"Just shut up, Darby," Livey said in a tone of voice that told him she really meant it.

The car picked up speed. The columns falling behind them reminded Darby of toppling dominoes, snapping at the car's back bumper. Roz buried her face in her hands.

"Cool," Aether said, looking out the back window.

"You're an angel," Darby said. "You don't have to worry about getting squished flat like a bug."

"Can't we go into space again?" Livey asked Johnny. Her face was pale and strained.

"Too many people." He spoke to Aether in a language that sound like a haunted flute, and nodded at her reply. "Keep going. This hyperdimension will take us back to Earth. We'll blast out somewhere. That's all we can do."

44

DR. MARIA DJUREK fidgeted before a bank of monitors in the Fermilab main control room. Dr. Karls babbled about the experiment that was underway in the four-mile-long particle accelerator, but she wasn't hearing a word.

Early yesterday, when she heard from Jerry that Livey had gone missing, she'd immediately pulled strings to get on one of the NSA's private jets to Chicago, where Silas was waiting for her. Her husband seemed quiet and strained. At River Oaks, he stayed in the car while Maria entered her former home. Not the same house, but still her former home.

She had vowed she was going to keep her head and her emotions under control, but upon seeing Darby, sweet lovely Darby—my, how big he'd grown!—she'd swept him into her arms. He had patted her back and told her not to cry, and in the next breath explained that Livey had run away with her boyfriend.

Livey, running away with a boyfriend! That just didn't sound like her, she blurted.

With that, her ex-husband Jerry's haggard face sharpened with slicing amusement. She felt her face grow hot. Because, of course, she had run away with Silas, which was the very last thing everybody expected Maria Ell to do.

Maria had pestered Darby with questions about this boyfriend. Darby's answers had deepened her anxiety.

"He is a rebel," Darby had said. "I am afraid he will be a bad influence on her."

Then, too, there was the police report, of Livey driving a brown Beetle, a boy in the car with her, and plowing the Beetle into a police car in order to escape.

That evening, in the hotel room with Silas, she blew up at her husband, who had been uncommunicative and distant all day, at a time when she needed his support the most. "I know they aren't your family," she yelled at him, "but they are still mine!"

He sighed and asked her to sit down. He had something to tell her, he said. He paced the room. He took a deep breath and began, "I have only ever made two vows in my life. I made the lesser vow when I married you."

She went brittle at that, anger threatening to break her into a thousand pieces.

"But now I must break my greater vow for the sake of our marriage," he continued. "I am an Esterici of the Secret Order of the Pythagorean Brotherhood. . . ."

Dr. Karls pointed to one of the monitors that displayed a live feed of the brightly lit corridor that housed the main injector, where the particle beam was inserted into the Tevatron accelerator. He said something about a recent modification.

Maria, though, was hearing once again her husband's incredible tale of a mathematical entity that had escaped from another universe, and whose existence Darby had proved, creating a disaster that was still unfolding. She couldn't believe it, yet she couldn't disbelieve it, either. With her mind in extreme dissonance, that morning she'd phoned an old colleague at Fermilab, asking if she could visit. She needed to get away to someplace where she could steady her thoughts.

The control room's operators slouched in their swivel chairs, their casual pose in contrast to their sharp-eyed vigilance.

They all simultaneously stiffened.

"God Almighty!" one shouted. "The beam's going faster than c!"

That got Maria's attention in an instant. Nothing could go faster than the speed of light. Alarms wailed. The monitor showed smoke billowing from the main injector. Dr. Karls raced for a phone.

So it was only Maria who saw the impossible.

For out of the smoke, a brown Beetle rolled into view along the main injector's wide access corridor. Even before the car came to a complete stop, its doors were opening. A pack of teenagers and children tumbled out.

She nearly fainted when she recognized two of them as Livey and Darby.

Then she was running as fast as she could out the door.

Maria raced her rental car down the service road and reached the emergency exit as it opened to a puff of smoke. The children emerged, coughing and hacking. Livey and a tall, black-haired boy had their arms around a badly burned boy, carrying him. Darby wore a knit cap tugged down over his ears. Behind him were a little pixie-haired girl and a bigger, paler girl.

"Livey!" Maria called out.

Her daughter showed no surprise upon seeing her. "Mom, Julian needs a doctor and we need a car, quick!"

Despite the emergency, Maria couldn't resist hugging Darby. There was an awful lot here she wasn't understanding, but she asked the most important question first. "Are you okay, sweetie?" He didn't relax, keeping his hands up to the knit cap on his head, and nodded stiffly. The little girl looked curiously at her.

Several Fermilab security cops roared up in their patrol cars. Maria told one to take the burned boy to a hospital.

"You get in my car," she told Livey.

"You coming, Roz?" Darby asked the big girl.

She shook her head. "I'll stay with Julian."

"Love," the little girl said in disgust.

Livey held out her hand. "Keys, Mom. Johnny will drive us."

"Absolutely not. I'll drive."

"Mothers," the little girl muttered.

Livey hesitated.

"We don't have time to argue," Darby snapped, opening the door to the backseat. Livey and the boy named Johnny followed.

The little girl got in front. "I don't think so," Maria said. "There's an airbag. You sit in the back. Livey, change places, would you?"

"God, Mom," Livey said. "Nothing's going to happen to Aether. Trust me."

Pick your battles, Maria told herself. "Where to?"

Darby glanced at a compass strapped to his wrist. "East. And step on it."

Maria zoomed onto the tollway, blasting through the tollgate without stopping to pay. She wanted to ask what the hell was going on, and wondered what it had to do with what Silas had told her. Truth to tell, though, she found herself much more interested in the way Livey was leaning up against the pale, dark-haired boy. She studied Johnny with surreptitious glances in the rearview mirror. There was something about the boy that she found disquieting. She'd have to have a careful, diplomatic talk with her daughter, make sure Livey wasn't getting into something that would hurt her. Johnny caught one of her glances. He seemed to know what she was thinking. Humor played across his face.

Those eyes . . .

Maria jerked her attention back to the road.

Despite her speeding, no patrol cars stopped her. The highway troopers were too busy at several accidents.

"I bet it's the GPS navigational systems," Darby said as they drove past a car that hadn't negotiated a gentle curve and had plowed off the road. "People better start learning how to drive again with their eyes instead of by computer." He leaned forward and turned on the rental's GPS system and studied the screen. "Yeah, like I thought. Out of whack, thanks to Bob changing the speed of light."

"But that's impossible," Maria exclaimed.

The little girl in front was swinging her legs. "Not to Bob."

"And who is Bob?"

"I think you're gonna meet him pretty soon."

Darby kept glancing down at his compass.

"What does that do?" Maria asked.

His only answer was a frown, almost a glower. It hurt her deeply, especially after yesterday, when he'd been chatty and friendly enough that she had dared hope for a reconciliation.

"It points to the Book," the girl said.

"Needle's pointing southeast," Darby said. "That means the next exit."

"That's Butterfield Road," Maria said.

"What do you know," Darby said. "Looks like we're getting closer to home."

Maria swung off the tollway and at the first set of traffic lights on Butterfield shot through a green. She didn't see the Honda Civic speeding through the red. The car cut in after her with squealing tires, straightened out, and picked up speed again. Maria finally spotted the Honda as it filled up her rearview mirror. She had only enough time to glimpse the odd license plate—ALGBRA—and the grimly determined face of the driver before the Honda smashed into the corner of her rear bumper. The wheel jerked in her hand as the rental began to fishtail. The Honda pulled alongside. Timing his move, the driver swung sharply to broadside the rental. The force of the blow added to the fishtailing. The rental began to flip. Time slowed down for Maria, allowing her to compose a prayer. *I don't care what happens to me, but please, God, don't let my children be harmed.*

Despite her seat belt, the side of her head hit the door. The blow was accompanied by a blinding flash, although the flash seemed to be more external than internal, as though the little girl sitting beside her had turned into light. The car rolled once, twice, windows shattering, and then came to a stop upright on the grassy shoulder.

A second passed, the only sound the ticking of the stalled engine. Maria gathered her wits and glanced around her. Darby, Livey, Johnny, and the girl were neat as pins in their places, as if they hadn't just tumbled around and around. Darby checked his knit cap, making sure it was still in place.

"Everybody okay?" she said.

"Can you get this car going again?" Darby said.

The little girl was humming. Maria stared at her for a second. Had she really seen the girl turn into . . . ? No, it had to have been the blow. She reached up and felt the bump on the side of her head. She would have a splitting headache later.

The girl pointed. "Uh-oh, he's coming back."

On the road's shoulder, the Honda Civic was pulling around in a U-turn. It stopped, facing the rental. The driver's door opened. The driver stepped out, a brown toupee flopping loose on his head. In his hand was a wooden board with silver-colored pegs arranged in a triangle.

"Is that Bob?" Maria asked. "He about killed us!"

"That's his disciple," Darby answered. He tried his door, which was jammed.

Another car shot past them and skidded to a halt on the shoulder, tearing up the grass. Three men in hooded olive robes blasted out the doors and surrounded the other man. One of the robed men seized the wooden board from the man and chucked it aside. Maria recognized him. "Silas?" she said.

In the back, Darby leaned forward. "What is *he* doing here?"

"Coming to our rescue, it seems," Maria said.

The man with the loose toupee backed away, screaming, "Bob! Help me!"

The men in the robes closed in. He knelt blubbering on the grass, his hands clasped together. "I only meant it for the best."

Silas motioned for Maria to get going.

To her surprise, the engine turned over and the gears still worked. She backed up and pulled onto the road, looking over her shoulder for oncoming traffic. She noticed Livey staring at Silas with a frown. Her daughter asked Johnny, "He's one of the *good* guys?"

Johnny nodded.

"You knew that and you still made me flip him off?"

"Just for fun," he said, looking sheepish.

Darby jabbed her with his elbow. "Let's save the chatter for later. We still have to find that proof and deal with Bob." He added, "And I bet I know exactly where we'll find both."

Ten minutes later, Maria was pulling up to 17 Beechwood. The compass on Darby's wrist was pointing straight at the house. The only car door that could open was Maria's. Darby squeezed by her like an eel before she could unbuckle her seat belt. She rushed after him, wanting to stop him and think things through. She sensed danger in the house.

"Darby, wait!" she yelled, and halted in astonishment as the front door opened and another Darby stepped out.

This Darby blinked in surprise and pushed his glasses up on his nose. "Mother?" he said. "What are you doing here?"

Maria stared in confusion at him, and then at the Darby with the knit cap. She closed her eyes and touched the bump on her head. When she looked again, both Darbys were still there.

"He's not really me, Mom," the Darby with the cap said. "He's Bob."

"That's right," Livey said, coming up behind them.

"Holy cow, there cannot be two of us, so how could this possibly be?" The second Darby jumped down from the porch and snatched the knit cap off the first Darby's head. "Observe, Mom."

The first Darby's ears were on backward. Maria stared at them with growing nausea. The second Darby grabbed his own earlobes and wriggled them. "Do these ears not look familiar to you? Who is the imposter here?"

"You liar," Livey said, taking a step with clenched fists toward him.

The second Darby, with the normal ears, ran to her side and clung to her arm. "Mother! I do not lie! I cannot lie! Please, holy cow, Mom!"

How much she had wanted this, her son needing her, loving her again. And surely the second Darby was the fake one, because ears just didn't flip around on one's head. Yet she had to be rational in this most irrational and bizarre situation. Taking the second Darby by the shoulder, she placed him next to the backward-eared Darby.

"I don't know what the heck is going on here," she said, looking at both of them, "but whichever one of you is my son, I want you to know I love you very much." She held out her arms. "A kiss?"

The Darby with the normal ears smiled hugely with delight and ran toward her. The other Darby scowled and folded his arms.

Maria swung her palm and slapped the smiling Darby across the cheek, and hard, too, sending him rocking back on his heels. "You fake."

That Darby put his hand to his cheek. "I have changed my opinion about you," he said coldly. "You do not have an elegant mind." He opened his mouth, which grew to an impossible size, filled with triangular teeth.

Johnny pointed a finger at this creature. A bolt of black lightning sizzled from his fingertip. Maria saw the bolt whirl around the creature without harming it and boomerang back to its source. Then the creature's mouth closed over her, and her world went dark.

45

WHEN DARBY SAW Bob swallow his mother, he didn't stick around. In that instant he no longer cared about saving the world. It was his mom he had to rescue, and he didn't have much time. As he sprinted into the house, out of the corner of his eye he saw Livey kneeling on the grass beside Johnny, who'd knocked himself out with his own lightning bolt.

He didn't need the compass anymore. His sixth sense told him where the Book was. He sprinted into the hallway, not taking the time to grab a chair to stand on, and jumped higher than he'd ever jumped in his life, grabbing hold of the handle to the attic stairs. They clattered open. He ran headlong up the steps.

Afternoon rays floated in from the dormer window and trailed across the attic's dusty floor. The light glinted off the brand-new combination padlock on Aunt Ludy's trunk.

Wiles appeared from nowhere and jumped up on the low rafter just above the trunk. He crouched, staring at the trunk like he would a mouse. There was something about the cat, something different, but Darby was too focused on the lock to pay full attention. Five wheels, not three. What would the combination be? A prime number sequence?

Aether stomped up the stairs and shoved him aside. She put her forefinger to the padlock's clasp.

"No, wait, not that way—"

Too late. Darby was nearly blinded by the flash. When his vision stabilized, the clasp had been melted. Sparks had fallen onto journals and a few loose newspaper pages, which were bursting into flame.

"—we don't want to burn down the house," he finished saying.

Aether chased the flaming paper, stamping them out. One glowing scrap fluttered into the corner by the *National Geographics*.

Darby flung open the trunk's lid.

In the center of the space within was a round blackness the size of an eyeball. The blackness was not itself a thing, it was the absence of everything, including light. It was a black hole, Bob's black hole. Since it was not eating up the planet, Bob must have somehow stabilized it within the trunk.

Lazily orbiting on its event horizon, almost touching the sides of the trunk, was the Book. Aether started to reach for it, but Darby grabbed her hand. "Don't. Just the slightest nudge, even the air pressure of your hand coming close, and it'll go into the black hole and be lost forever."

And his mom would be lost too.

The stairs slammed shut with such force that the telescoping rails twisted. The musty air quivered with triangles shiny in the gloom. Bob took his sweet time manifesting in his human form as the Vitruvian man, dressed in a custom-made suit. From the rafter, Wiles hissed, but Bob ignored him. He said pleasantly to Darby, "In game theory, this is called a win–lose situation. I win and you lose."

"Give me back my mom."

"But you hate her."

"I love her."

Bob *tsk*ed. "A shame you did not tell her that. Her last memory of you is you scowling at her."

Tears pricked his eyes. "Give her back!"

From below, Livey called out, "Darby, where are you?"

Bob put a finger to his lips. "This is between us. I propose a trade. I will return your mother if you agree to leave me alone. That is all I ask, to simply be left alone. No Q.E.D.s."

"No," Aether said at once.

Darby whirled on her. "She's my mom, not yours."

"Don't be so selfish. Bob's too dangerous. He'll start getting rid of crippled people and then sick people and then people who won't worship him."

Bob crossed his arms. "Then Darby's mother will unfortunately die in Hilbert space."

"So what," Aether said. "Darby will be with her again in heaven."

Darby couldn't believe she said that. "I want to be with her in this life, you stupid angel."

She began to glow. "Don't. You. Call. Me. An. Angel!"

Bob looked up at the cat, who was staring down at the notebook, tracking its slow orbit around the black hole. "Divide and conquer is a most excellent strategy, my dear Wiles," he said happily.

Livey called out again, this time from directly below. "Darby, are you up there?"

Wiles jumped from the rafter to the hinged lid of the trunk. He extended his leg toward the notebook.

His right front leg, the crippled one, which now looked whole and normal.

"No!" Darby shouted.

MONSTER'S PROOF

But the Book was not nudged into oblivion. There was something artificial about the leg that wasn't part of normal space-time, and so did not disturb the local environment. With extended claws, Wiles snagged the cover and fished the Book toward him, safely away from the black hole.

Darby and Bob both lunged for the notebook. With his left hand, Bob stiff-armed Darby, shoving him to the side. Darby lost his balance, his head banging on the corner of the trunk. He could feel the metal tearing his skin. The blow knocked his vision off-kilter. Still on his knees, he woozily saw Aether jumping up to grab Bob's hand, the one holding the notebook. She didn't use any of her powers. She used her teeth instead, sinking them into his fingers. He yowled with pain and let go of the Book.

The Book tumbled to the floor with a fluttering of pages. Darby snatched it and stuffed it down his shirt, wrapping his arms around it like he was a running back holding a football. Bob flung Aether off him, sending her flying into the corner, and grabbed Darby by the waistband of his trousers.

Darby loosened his arms and let the notebook slip down across his stomach, using his elbows to guide it to the side of his ribs. As Bob hoisted him into the air, Darby violently struggled, trying to bite Bob as Aether had done. But this was mostly to distract Bob, so that he wouldn't see Darby allowing the Book to fall to the floor, wouldn't see Darby kicking it, trying to get it to Aether.

Instead, the notebook skittered through a tendril of smoke and onto the twisted stairs, slipping out of view. Somebody was banging on the stairs, trying to release them. There was the acrid stink of something burning.

Bob deftly changed his grip so that he was holding on to Darby's ankles. He swung him over the trunk and held him above the black hole. "This should be interesting," he said.

Below, Darby heard Livey yell, "Johnny, help me get this down!" He grabbed at the sides of the trunk, trying to push himself away from the hole. Bob kicked one hand free, and then the other, smashing his fingers. Darby hardly felt the pain. He barely heard the stairs clunking down into place. The top of his head was above the black hole. He could feel the gravity tugging on his hair. The cut on his forehead was bleeding, and he watched a round, red drop of blood fall. He saw the hole pulling the drop into a thin red string before the blood faded from view forever. Just like what would happen to Darby when Bob let go.

Maybe he was going to see his mom in heaven after all.

46

LIVEY JUMPED AS high as she could, the tips of her fingers brushing the stair handle.

"Let me do that," Johnny said. He had staggered into the house after her. As he lifted his hands to the stairs, he collapsed again.

Livey ran and got a counter stool, which gave her enough height to grab the handle. The stair casing wouldn't budge. It was twisted and stuck. Banging with her fist didn't do anything. She jumped off the stool, still holding on to the handle and dangling over the carpet, trying to use her weight. The casing groaned and creaked, but didn't release. She wasn't heavy enough.

"Johnny, help me get this down!"

Johnny lurched forward on his knees and grabbed her legs, putting all his weight on them.

The casing gave way with a clatter, the stairs telescoping open with a screech of metal. Livey fell backward on top of Johnny's stomach. He *oof*ed. Something hit her on the head and fell to her side. It was

Darby's Shedd Aquarium notebook, splayed open on the carpet to page seventeen and the drawing of the house and its halo of triangles. As she picked it up, she realized now what Darby had meant by those triangles. Too bad she hadn't realized this earlier, but then again, how was she to have known? She could barely do that minus x times minus x equation that was below the picture, much less understand that it was part of a proof for some deranged mathematical monster.

From the attic came banging and scraping and shouting. With the notebook in hand, she charged up the stairs. In the attic, Bob was holding Darby upside down by his ankles, dangling him over Aunt Ludy's trunk. Darby was twisting madly around, this way and that, trying to grab the sides of the trunk. Bob kicked at his fingers. Wisps of smoke eddied around them.

"You are just in time, my dear Livey," he said.

"He's going to drop Darby into the black hole," Aether said. She had dust bunnies all over her hair. The smoke was thick behind her. Then she noticed the notebook in Livey's hand. Snatching it from her, she shouted "Q.E.D!"

Bob smiled. "I am right here."

She held up the Book, aiming it at him. "I order you to let him go. And give back their mom. And go back to where you came from."

Bob pursed his lips in thought for a moment. Then he smiled again. "My remarkable sense of duty to my worshippers and to this earth outweighs my need to obey. Indeed, I expect to be awarded the Nobel Peace Prize, which I will accept with humble pride on behalf of all Pythagoreans."

"Then I'll burn this up, right now!"

"Wait!" Livey cried. "Give it back to me." She grabbed it from Aether and blinked at the simple algebra equation under the drawing of the house. A minus x times a minus x equals a minus x squared?

"Regardless, it does not matter," Bob said. "I have made copies for all the Pythagorean Circles. They shall establish schools and institutions for the study of me."

As he spoke, his arms were slowly getting lower and lower.

"Arrgh!" Darby desperately bent up at the waist. Strands of his hair had elongated from his scalp. "Livey!"

"I would like to prolong this moment," Bob said, "but my muscles are wearying. I cannot hold on to you much longer, Darby. I regret the loss of your beautiful mind."

"What beautiful mind?" Livey shouted. "This proof is *wrong*. Darby, right here you have a minus times a minus and still got a minus!" She turned the notebook around and jabbed at the line. "See?"

Despite his predicament, Darby shook his head. "No way. No mistake."

"Yes, big way, genius. Look. You have minus x times minus x equals a minus x squared. It should a *positive* x squared. The proof is wrong."

Bob paled. He swung Darby away from the trunk just before his muscles finally gave way. Darby fell to the floor, landing on his shoulders with a grunt. "Fix the proof," Bob said.

Darby bounded up and took the notebook from Livey. "It can't be wrong."

Livey couldn't believe it. Just seconds ago he was in danger of his life because of the proof, and now he was saying it couldn't be wrong?

Darby studied the line, and then flipped a page back and forward again.

"Fix it," Bob shouted. Little triangles were popping up out of his face and the skin of his hand. Creases were appearing in his suit.

"I'm trying," Darby said. "Let's see, I took this derivative . . ."

"Darby!" Livey hissed.

"You don't understand, Livey. I worked so hard on this, it's so beautiful, and it comes to nothing because of some stupid little rule?"

She waved smoke away from her face and said in a low, hard voice,

"It is not a stupid little rule. A minus times a minus is a plus."

"But Mom! We have to keep Bob to rescue Mom!"

"Truth is truth, Darby, and what is true can't hurt Mom. It's the only way to save her."

"Oh man, oh man. I can't believe it. One tiny mistake. But she's right, Bob. The proof is wrong. It can't be fixed."

Bob grunted and winced, as though stabbed with sharp pain. "I shall find somebody else, somebody with a more elegant mind."

"Nobody can fix it, it's just flat wrong." Darby's eyes popped wide. "I know. In *your* universe, a minus times a minus is a minus. But not ever here."

Bob groaned, a ghastly sound. Triangles floated out of his mouth.

"Sorry," Darby said in a whisper.

Livey wanted to slap him. "Why on earth are you *sorry*?"

His face started to crumple. "Because all I wanted was a friend. Just one."

Bob seemed to gather himself for a moment, his expression both strained with the effort and also stern with warning. "Darby, I cannot depart with a lie ringing in my ears. My dear, dear boy, what you have truly wanted, all this time, is to forgive your mother. Then do so. Good-bye."

He sizzled away into triangles. His suit collapsed into a heap on the floor, and the triangles spiraled toward the trunk and into the black hole, which closed up with a loud *poof*.

There was silence, and then Aether said in a daze, "He's gone."

Darby looked frantically around him. "Mom! Mom!"

Their mother's voice rang out, "I'm right here." The stairs creaked under running feet. She appeared, holding her arms out to Darby.

She stopped and let her arms drop. Her face darkened with menace. "Where's my son?"

"Hunh?"

"The one with the backward ears."

Livey blinked. Darby's ears were back to normal, his glasses tilted on his face.

"Mom," she said, "that is Darby!"

Wiles limped into view from behind the trunk, his front leg back to its mangled self, and rubbed his head against Darby's ankle. He cocked his head and meowed at Maria.

She studied the cat for a moment, and then Darby. A smile rose to her face and shone in the tears of her eyes. She lifted her arms again. "Darby," she said.

He ran into them. She gathered her son into a hug.

He hugged her back, hard.

In a very small voice, Aether said, "Uh-oh, I think there's a fire back here."

47

THE FLASHING LIGHTS of the fire engines twinkled off the puddles of hydrant water. In the day's twilight, 17 Beechwood was a damp, black ruin. Radios snapped and crackled as the firemen began coiling their hoses. At the end of the block, the police held back the watching crowd, many still recording with their videos or their cells.

The fire had roared through the house with ravenous speed. As they dashed down the attic stairs, Wiles leading the way, Livey's mom was already calling 911 on her cell. Livey wanted to run into her room and gather up whatever she could, but Johnny grabbed her hand and pulled her out of the house.

In the middle of the street, Livey's parents were talking to the chief of police himself. Lurking in the background was Silas Djurek. The nickname Slimy Jerk flashed across Livey's mind, but she knew that things had changed, that she could no longer call him that. She would have to make some painful adjustments.

She was standing with Johnny on the lawn across the street. The streetlights came on. She shivered against the chill of the gathering night. Johnny put an arm around her. "I'm sorry," he whispered.

"We're all safe," she said, meaning more than just the fire, meaning Bob as well. "That's what counts. My stuff is just stuff."

Although it did hurt to lose all her photos and trophies and the little things of her childhood. Why deny that? It hurt, and hurt bad.

She took a deep breath and looked around. "Where's Aether?"

"Hiding," Darby said.

"Why?"

"She's afraid."

"But the fire's out."

"She started it, that's why." He cupped his hands to his mouth. "Aether, wherever you are, come here."

From high in the maple tree beside them came a brief glow. Aether jumped down. She didn't exactly fall, Livey noticed, but glided.

"Look at that," Darby said. "You're flying."

She landed and clenched one hand in the other, looking down at the grass by her feet. "Darby, I'm really, really sorry about the fire. I'm a dumb . . . a dumb angel."

He stepped toward her. "Don't you ever say that. You're a brave, smart, sentinel seraph."

She peeked up at him.

"Only you could have opened that lock in time. You saved the world."

Her instant smile glowed. Literally. "I have to go soon," she said. She cleared her throat. Her cheeks went pink, this color a normal glow, caught by the streetlight. "You can give me a hug, if you want."

Darby hesitated. Livey pinched him on his elbow. He shuffled toward Aether, raising his arms.

Aether held up a hand. "Wait. Not a long hug. I'm not your mom."

Darby gave her a short, stiff hug and then added a quick peck on her cheek. She winced.

"Don't wipe it off," he said. "You take it back to heaven."

"Heaven," she said. She turned to Johnny. "Do I really have to leave?"

"Our job's done, Aether."

"Can't you come with me?"

Sadness tinged his smile. "I wish I could."

She bit her lip. Tears welled in her eyes. She ran to him and buried her face in his shirt, her shoulders heaving. "It's so unfair," she sobbed. "We've been together all this time and now we can't be?"

Putting his hands on her shoulders, he gently pushed her away so he could kneel and look her in the eyes. "I have something to tell you," he said. "Something for you to hide in your heart and remember."

She sniffled, rubbing her eyes with her hand. "What?"

"I had a dream."

Her hand stopped rubbing. She lowered it. "But we never dream."

"I did. Listen: I saw hell, in a time to come. It was an abandoned house, shutters flapping in the lonely wind, the sound echoing through empty rooms."

She frowned. "Where did everybody go?"

"Back home."

Aether's elfin face remained blank for a second, and then a child's pure joy began to blossom.

From the west came a golden flare, as though the setting sun were spreading out a carpet.

"See you laters, alligators," Aether said and skipped toward the light.

The Ells' Montero Sport was a smoldering hulk, and the car Livey's mom had rented was being towed.

Livey wanted to go the clearing where they'd seen the moon-bow to say good-bye to Johnny, but without a car, they'd have to say good-bye in the shadowed privacy of Lincoln Park. She walked beside Johnny down the street, already telling herself that she wasn't going to cry, she'd be brave, she'd be happy that she had this time to be with him.

Beyond the lingering crowd, Johnny paused by a car that was parked illegally, a police business placard stuck on the visor. The chief's car. He peered through the side window. The door was unlocked, and keys dangled from the ignition.

He looked at Livey.

"Let's do it," she said.

A minute later they were cruising down Butterfield to the marsh. "I can't believe we just boosted the police chief's car," Livey said.

"You're going to have to drive it back."

Alone, Livey thought, a pang cutting through her heart. She forced the thought away, and raised a smile. "Easy, after driving a stick shift. Might even turn on the sirens. I'm a rebel at heart."

"That makes two of us," Johnny said, just as lightly. Then he grew serious. "Being a rebel sounds cool and courageous and all, but most of the time it's just a bad, stupid choice."

She was silent as the pavement sang under the tires. As he turned off onto the preserve's graveled road, she finally spoke. "What you told Aether, about your dream, is that really true? Is that really going to happen?"

"I don't know," he said quietly. "I haven't had any dreams before."

"I saw you when you were sleeping, you know. Your markings disappeared. You were so beautiful."

He took a hand off the wheel and pushed a cuff up his wrist. The tattoos were darker than ever.

◪ ◪ ◪

At the clearing they sat on the deadfall trunk. Autumn seemed to have accelerated in the last few days, with leaves fallen from the trees. Bare branches scratched the stars. Livey snuggled up to Johnny, his arm around her and keeping her warm.

They didn't talk. There was no need for words.

The moon eased into the sky, no longer full but still bright.

A moonbow appeared, a band of gray, barely touched by color.

Johnny changed, becoming his other self, the markings on his bare torso burning red and pulsing with heat. His scent grew bitter.

"It's time," he murmured.

Livey bit her lip. She was not going to cry, not her, not Godeliva Elizabeth Ell.

"I love you," she said, and that was all she was going to say, no weepy good-byes. So why was her voice all choked up, and what were these tears doing, scalding her cheeks? She wiped them away, but not before one tear fell on his wrist.

Johnny glanced down. "Look," he said, wonder in his voice. He lifted his wrist to her.

A marking's curve had been erased, the flesh filling in and becoming whole.

Johnny rose to his feet, a dark and terrible and lovely rebel angel. "Thank you, Livey." He bent to kiss her, a light brushing of his lips against hers.

Then, without fanfare or warning, he was gone.

Livey walked alone back to the car, the quiet darkness pressing in around her. Her heart was breaking, yet remained whole. Pain filled her bones, yet they hummed a slow and bittersweet melody.

When she reached the car, a sudden, sharp breeze shifted down through the sky, rustling the trees. The shutters of the abandoned house banged, the noise echoing through vacant rooms. It seemed to

Livey to be the emptiest and loneliest sound in the world.

A man stepped out on the porch, hugging his overcoat around him. "Hey, miss," he called out.

Livey stood still, her fingers on the door handle. Her breath misted on the air.

"Don't be afraid," he said. "But could you give me a ride?"

"Where to?" she said.

"Just somewhere out of here. Then I'll make my own way. Got family to visit." He jumped off the porch, his boots crunching on the gravel. The moonlight caught his face, his eyes bright and clear.

She opened the door. "Get in, I'll take you to the train stop."

He settled in the front passenger seat, hands folded in his lap. He smelled like old coffee grounds and fresh spearmint. He whistled a few bars of a child's campfire song softly and sweetly off-tune.

As she drove away, another gust of wind blew across the marsh. Again the shutters banged, louder this time, echoing through the empty rooms and out into the untold distance.

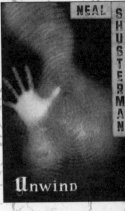